# No Easy Answers

# No Easy Answers

## Stort Stories About Teenagers
### Making Tough Choices

Edited by Donald R. Gallo

DELACORTE PRESS

Published by
Delacorte Press
Bantam Doubleday Dell Publishing Group, Inc.
1540 Broadway
New York, New York 10036

A portion of this book's royalties, earmarked for research in young adult literature, will go to the Assembly on Literature for Adolescents of the National Council of Teachers of English (ALAN).

**Library of Congress Cataloging-in-Publication Data**

No easy answers : short stories about teenagers making tough choices / edited by Donald R. Gallo.
    p.   cm.
    Summary: A collection of sixteen short stories, by Louise Plummer, M. E. Kerr, Jack Gantos, and others, about teenagers in situations that test their character.
    ISBN 0-385-32290-9
    1. Children's stories, American.  [1. Conduct of life—Fiction. 2. Short stories.]  I. Gallo, Donald R.
PZ5.N496   1997
[Fic]—dc21
97-1841
                                                                                                        CIP
                                                                                                        AC

The text of this book is set in 12/15-point Cremona.
Book design by Blake Logan

Manufactured in the United States of America

November 1997

10   9   8   7   6   5   4   3   2   1

This book is for all
the teachers and librarians who know that kids
will read if we introduce the right book to them
at the right time.

# Contents

# Contents

# Acknowledgments

Thanks are due to Bill Mollineaux and his students at Sedgwick Middle School in West Hartford, Connecticut, and to C. J. Bott and her tenth-grade classes at Shaker Heights (Ohio) High School, as well as to the students in my young adult literature class at Central Connecticut State University for helping us decide on the best title for this book.

Thanks also to those same Shaker Heights students and to Rick Valerio for their discerning judgments about some of the stories included in this collection.

This is also a good time to acknowledge the role that so many people have played in the production, marketing, and use of the books I have published during the past dozen years. These include

- the many superb writers who have submitted stories;
- the editors, copy editors, and production people who put the actual books together;
- the marketing people who advertise them;
- the classroom teachers, librarians, and college professors who have used my books and who have encouraged their students to use them;

# Acknowledgments

- the booksellers who have displayed them on their shelves and promoted them in their catalogs;
- the reviewers who have affirmed their quality;
- the friends and colleagues who have encouraged me;
- and most of all, the students who have read the books, enjoyed them, reported on them, written to me about them, and passed them along to their friends and family members.

Many thanks to all of you.

With a special thank-you to Katya.

# Introduction

*Teenagers have no moral standards!* Many adults, especially politicians, seem to believe that. An article in the August 25, 1995, issue of the *St. Louis Post-Dispatch* states: "Signs everywhere point to a society that's raising ethically illiterate children." William Kilpatrick, a professor of education at Boston University, has published a book titled *Why Johnny Can't Tell Right from Wrong*. And a number of national organizations have recently been formed to promote "character education" for young people, among them the Character Counts Coalition in California and the Character Education Partnership in Virginia.

Most teenagers, and anyone who deals honestly with teenagers on a daily basis, know that most kids do have ethical standards, do know right from wrong, and are very capable of judging the actions of their peers as well as the moral uprightness of the adults around them. Certainly there are teenagers whose behaviors—in gangs, on the streets, in social groups—are as corrupt as any negative behaviors of adults in similar situations.

The goal in this book is not to attack or defend the behaviors of contemporary teenagers or to explore the accuracy of the attacks against today's teens. Instead, we offer these sixteen stories about fictional teenagers who find themselves in situations that test the strength of their character. They are called upon to make moral choices, to face the consequences of their actions, to consider what it means to "do the right thing." They deal with computer blackmail, peer pressure, parental pressures, gang violence, drug use, sexual urges, unwanted pregnancy, retaliation, guilt, self-censorship, and atonement.

These new short stories, all written specifically for this collection by some of the best writers in the business, allow readers to judge for themselves the moral and ethical strength of the characters and to consider how they themselves might behave in such troublesome situations. These stories are by no means intended to serve as models of "proper" teenage behavior. In fact, the decisions that some of the characters make are clearly not admirable ones. But whether the outcome is positive or negative, these stories will cause readers to think about the alternatives and weigh the consequences of their own actions.

There are no easy answers.

# How Did I Get Myself into This?

As a talented photographer, Anthony has a
chance to get the shot of a lifetime. But then he
has to deal with the effects of his actions.

# The Photograph
## Will Weaver

"Naked?"

"Yes."

"Ms. Jenson? Our beloved phys ed teacher and girls' track coach?"

"Skinny-dipping. Absolutely. She was in the lake totally naked."

Lance Hickerson, our JV quarterback, stared hard at Bobby Johnson, one of our running backs, then turned away. "You wish," Lance muttered, peeling his sweaty football jersey over his head. It was a humid September afternoon in the locker room, and football gear began to clatter onto the floor as the other players voted with Lance. "As if . . . no way," the other guys jeered at Bobby. Me, I caught muddy footballs as best I could and bagged them; I'm Anthony Long, team manager, unofficial photographer, and self-appointed cliché—you know the type, too scrawny to make the team so hangs around athletes

any way he can. "Size may count in high school," my
mother says regularly, "but not in real life." The other
day I'd had it with that line, so I retorted, "Then why do
so many women have their breasts enlarged? And why
is there always an ad in the Sunday sports section for
male penile implants?" She was annoyed but as quick
as always on the reply. "Because some adults never
grow up."

Anyway, back to the locker room.

"It was Ms. Jenson," Bobby said, his voice muffled as
he shrugged on his jersey.

"She doesn't even date," Lance scoffed, "so I doubt
she'd be skinny-dipping."

"See it to believe it," someone else jeered.

"See them." Another guy yukked. There were hoots
and laughter.

"So ask my old man yourself!" Bobby shot back at
Lance.

Lance, sweat shiny in his dark hair, turned to Bobby
once more. Gave him a look. Bobby ignored him. "Okay,
start over," Lance commanded.

Bobby sighed. "I told you. My dad was fishing on Big
Reed Lake. He likes that lake 'cause it's quieter, not so
many boats, not so built up with cabins like some lakes
around here—"

"Yeah, yeah, I heard that part," Lance interrupted.

"So our fishing boat is painted camouflage 'cause we
go duck hunting a lot in October. My old man's too cheap
to get a decent fishing boat."

"Cut to the chase, idiot," Lance barked. He talks
to all of us like that; Lance has a great future as a

drill sergeant or a dog trainer. Sad thing is, we all take it from him.

"So it's about sundown when my dad came trolling around this reedy point, and close to shore. He was using the electric trolling motor, which is silent, and so she didn't hear him."

"At all? Ever?" a couple of knuckleheads ventured.

Bobby ignored them. "He said he didn't notice her swimming until she stood up and walked up onto shore. Naked. Totally naked."

"Ms. Jenson, wow . . . ," a deep voice murmured.

We turned.

Big Dave Amundson, our fullback, sat there with his jaw slacked, staring vacantly into the open square of his locker like it was a television showing the late-night cable film *Ms. Jenson, Wet.* Joe Schmitz, third-string fullback, whose Iowa Basic scores flatline in the twenties, leaned over for a look into Dave's locker.

"Gees, guys, don't get woodies!" Lance said. The players all cackled and jeered, and Joe grinned suddenly and stupidly. Dave just kept channeling on Ms. Jenson.

That was Andrea "Andy" Jenson, third-year teacher at Pine Crest High, Pine Crest (population 4,360), in northern Minnesota. She was a short, perky, athletic blonde from somewhere in Wisconsin and born to be a teacher: friendly, energetic, always asking questions about you—your life and how it was going. Everybody liked Andy Jenson, everybody except short, perky tenth-grade girls, who knew deep down they couldn't compete. Most sophomore boys, including me, would crawl naked through crushed glass for Ms. Jenson. I joined *The*

*Clarion,* our school newspaper, which meant endless meetings with geeky no-life girls, in large part because Andy Jenson was advisor. She encouraged my photography. "These are fine images, Anthony!" she would say, and the other girls always snickered as I blushed and melted down like a strawberry Sno-Kone (small) on the Fourth of July. Not pictures. Images. My job also allowed me to shoot team sports, including girls' track. Coach Jenson often practiced with her team and sometimes wore major Flo-Jo type spandex. I have one photo of her and some girls running the low hurdles; in the picture Ms. Jenson, legs outstretched, looks like a Baltimore oriole leading a flock of sparrows.

But Ms. Jenson naked? Some built-in censor wouldn't let my brain process that concept, so I tried to patch into Big Dave's channel: sundown, the last orange rays glinting; Ms. Jenson, back to the camera, standing at lakeside, water trickling down her spine bump by bump, disappearing into the towel that covered her middle. Why I put that towel there I'm not sure. Maybe at heart I'm a Republican—or just a wimp with women.

"So why would your old man tell you?" Lance asked Bobby skeptically.

"He didn't." Bobby sighed again. "I told you, I overheard him telling my uncle."

"I know where your old man and uncle are going fishing every night from now on," Keith Olson yukked.

Lance glanced at Keith with annoyance; Keith shrugged, then bent to pull off his shoulder pads. Lance returned his gaze to Bobby. He was thinking. And thinking took Lance a while. On the football field Lance didn't have to think—he was natural, he had radar like an air-traffic controller, always knew where his cornerbacks were, always knew when the blitz was on. However, in the classroom and in normal conversation, Lance sometimes went blank. Temporary power outage (TPO), we secretly called it. "Ms. Jenson gave me a friggin' D in ninth-grade phys ed," Lance muttered, sweat beginning to drip from his nose and sharp chin.

"Me too," Big Dave said evenly.

"Hey, Ant, throw me a towel," Lance barked, flicking away several bright beads.

"Just a sec, Lance." I was cinching the ball bag.

"Now! Ant."

"Of course, sire." Giving him my "I'm-not-worthy" body wave, I kowtowed into the towel room.

"And don't get cute about it," he said, not even glancing my way. When I tossed him the fresh towel, I kept my distance. I've gotten more than one major wedgie from Lance, and a cuff to the head that made my right ear whisper for two days, but luckily he was still thinking. He slowly toweled off his face, his back, his chest. Lance was the only tenth-grader who had to shave every day, plus he had hair on his chest. He looked like those stubble-chinned, sharp-jawed dudes in *GQ* and *Esquire* magazines who lounge around 1958 Porsches modeling baggy slacks and lime green sports coats that cost $1,200 apiece. Still thinking, Lance stripped down to his jockstrap, then sat there, his elbows on his knees and his eyes blank.

TPO.

Sometimes I wished I dared take photos in the

locker room. I'd snap one of Lance right now—except that he'd grind me into geek paste. Certain images catch my eye. When the players come in after practice and slump on the benches, heads down all in a row like tired birds on a wire, it's almost beautiful. Or when the guys are all in the shower, naked and white, standing under the spray and steam, vague, like ghosts, that really is beautiful. Don't get me wrong—it's not naked guys that jerk my cord—at least I'm pretty certain it's not. Rather, I think I might be an artist.

Once, after the players were all gone, there was a helmet left on the bench. A single, round, blue, battered helmet resting on pale wood. In the light the helmet looked lonely, sad, like some large bird's egg lost from its nest. I took a dozen photos of it from a dozen different angles. Ms. Jenson loved it. Even Lucinda Anderson, managing editor of *The Clarion* and future Wicked Witch of the West, begrudgingly ran the photo on page one of our fall "Sports Roundup."

Lance stood up, snapped off his jockstrap, and flung his sweaty towel neatly around my face.

"Gaa!" I said, momentarily mummified.

"Ant. You and Bobby hang after—we got to talk," Lance said as he headed into the shower.

"About what?" I said, unwrapping my face.

"About our friend Ms. Jenson," he said, and disappeared into the steam.

———

At eight o'clock that evening, wearing moldy-smelling duck-hunting suits and eye black across our cheeks, we lay in bushy green undergrowth about sixty yards from Ms. Jenson's lake cabin.

Stakeout.

Me, Bobby, and Lance.

I hugged my old Minolta, loaded with 400-ASA Tri-X and attached to a 300-millimeter lens, the kind as long as your arm. Bobby and Lance clutched binoculars. My duck-hunting suit, courtesy of Bobby, was oversize, rubbery, and already slippery inside with sweat. "For God's sakes, stop fidgeting," Lance hissed at me. He and Bobby peered across at her house, a new-style log cabin, really—but I stared up at the shiny green leaves alongside my face.

"Lance, I'm sure this is poison ivy," I said.

"It ain't poison ivy," Lance muttered, shifting his elbows, adjusting his focus.

"Shiny, three leaves, slightly oiled surface," I added.

"So what if it is? We just wash off afterward—after you get the photo, that is," Lance said. He grinned and waggled his dark eyebrows at me.

No doubt about it, the coolest thing to happen to me so far in tenth grade was Lance Hickerson driving up to my house tonight in his Pontiac Trans-Am and tooting the horn. "Got to go!" I had said to my mom, rushing off with my camera bag and tripod before she could interrogate me. On the other hand, I'd been lying here for an hour with mosquitoes torturing me like tiny, whining buzzards, with wood ticks certainly crawling up my pant legs—all to watch Ms. Jenson sit, fully clothed, reading a book on her porch.

"You having fun, Ant?" Lance whispered.

"Ah, sure, Lance."

"No pain, no gain, man," Lance said, poking me hard with his elbow.

My mother also once remarked that, in terms of clichés, Lance Hickerson was more of one than I was.

"She's standing up," Bobby hissed.

"Ant! Get ready," Lance said.

I raised up in time to see Ms. Jenson check her watch, look briefly toward her driveway, which wound through the pines, as if she might be expecting someone, then go inside.

"Shit," Bobby muttered.

"Just wait," Lance said. "The sun's going down. I got this feeling it's going to happen."

Just then something moved in the corner of my eye. Bobby whispered, "Get low; freeze!"

From the side of my eye I watched a boat come silently around the point. A camouflage-painted duck boat with two men fishing. Except that their poles were pointed in odd directions and the men crouched unnaturally low in their seats; both had binoculars.

"It's your father!" Lance said to Bobby.

"And Uncle Jack!" Bobby said.

Lance's long body began to shake with laughter so hard that the foliage (i.e., poison ivy) quivered wildly. Bobby followed suit, air hawking from his nose as he covered his mouth, but the two "fishermen" would not have noticed us if we had stood up and launched grenades their way. The two men craned their necks toward the shore, toward the cabin. But Ms. Jenson was nowhere to be seen. Bobby's father shrugged, Uncle Jack's shoulders slumped, and soon the boat trolled on, shrinking away down the lake.

"Man, have you got some leverage on your old man!" Lance chortled.

"Valley Fair, Mall of America, here I come," Bobby breathed.

"I'd hit him up for a damn car," Lance said.

Bobby lay back, smiling at the sky. "Camaro," he murmured.

I took the opportunity to set aside my camera and check for wood ticks crawling up my legs.

Just then I head a screen door slap.

"She's back!" Lance said. "Ant—get ready."

When I looked up, Ms. Jenson, wrapped in a chocolate brown towel, was halfway to the lake.

"Jesus," Bobby murmured, "here it comes."

I fumbled with my camera, set the tripod in position, but she was too quick for me. Just before I got her into the lens, her towel dropped and Ms. Jenson slipped into the water.

"Wow!" Bobby breathed.

"Ant—did you get that?" Lance whispered at me.

"I . . . think so," I lied.

"I didn't hear no click," Lance said, glaring at me.

"I guess it didn't go off; it sticks sometimes," I said lamely.

Lance grabbed me by the neck. "You don't get this photo, you're going to walk home, Ant—you got that?"

I choked, wheezed, and nodded yes. "Sure, Lance, no problem." I pretended to make an adjustment to the camera. Lance turned his field glasses back to the lake. I looked at the woods around; they were suddenly dark and deep and not at all lovely—and I'd have miles to go before I'd sleep: I had no idea how to get back to town.

"Did you see much?" Lance whispered to Bobby. "I mean, when she dropped the towel."

"Just a flash," Bobby said, disappointed.

"Me too," Lance said. "But hey—she's got to come out of the water sometime."

Sometime was a long time. Ms. Jenson swam for half an hour, all the way down to the point, keeping in the shadow of the shoreline, only her head and the short, steady flash of her hands visible. The sun was down now, the shore turning dusky and purple.

"Your old man had bad timing tonight," Lance said, watching Andy Jenson swim exactly where the boat had passed.

"But not us." Bobby grinned.

"Maybe, maybe not," Lance said, squinting. "It's going to be dark soon."

"I'm still good," I said quickly, pointing to my camera.

"You'd better be," Lance muttered.

Ms. Jenson crawled back into sight, passing within thirty yards of our stakeout, slowly moving to her dock. She had a sweet, rolling, rhythmic stroke. She swam the way she was at school, steady and stylish. I had liked her a lot as a teacher; she'd actually given me an A in ninth-grade phys ed, a class where tests mattered as much as throwing a softball a mile. Suddenly from behind her cabin came the thud of one car door; we swiveled our heads.

"Someone drove in," Lance whispered.

Duh, I thought.

Ms. Jenson kept swimming; she hadn't heard.

"Maybe her boyfriend," Bobby whispered.

"We'll finally get to see who's the lucky guy!" Lance murmured. Men in Ms. Jenson's life were a matter of great speculation around the school; so far, no one had discovered who she went out with.

"I bet it's Mr. Wood," Lance said. They're at the track together all the time."

"Mr. Wood is the assistant track coach," I said.

Lance's eyes went blank as he considered that fact. Definite TPO.

On the lawn, in the deepening shadows, a figure, medium height, short-haired, athletic, dressed in basic summer shorts and polo shirt, walked down to the dock. "Ahoy, sailorette!" came a strong voice. Ms. Jenson looked up suddenly and trod water; she waved and then quickened her pace toward the dock.

"Ant—get ready," Lance whispered.

I attached a cable release to the Minolta and looked through the viewfinder. At dock's end the figure knelt and waited for Ms. Jenson, who swam up, then back-paddled, coyly, just out of reach. There was murmured laughing; finally Ms. Jenson kicked closer and held up an arm as if to be pulled from the water. I held my breath.

"Now, Ant!" Lance breathed.

I squeezed—just as the person on the dock was jerked forward into the water. There was one startled whoop, a large splash, then coughing and laughter as Ms. Jenson swam away. I smiled. But the other swimmer was quick, and a good swimmer, and soon caught her; in a moment they were kissing, fooling around in the water. In another minute the other person's clothes began to fly up onto the dock with muffled *thwop!*s of wet cloth hitting wood.

"Keep shooting, Ant," Lance said.

"All I got are their heads," I said, but I snapped off a shot anyway.

"It's gonna happen soon," Bobby said urgently. The swimmers, murmuring, hugging, drifted closer and closer toward shore, toward shallow water where the last, violet light had penetrated the trees and lit the green grass and the bleached side of the dock.

And then it happened. The pair rose up in waist-deep water, arms wrapped about each other, and kissed deeply.

"Good God!" Bobby breathed.

"Her boyfriend is . . . is . . . is a friggin' woman," Lance murmured.

The light, the angles, the moment—it was perfect: I squeezed.

---

The next morning, with my ankles, wrists, and face beginning to itch like I was sunburned, bad, or else there was a fire smoldering under my skin, I biked to the school. I'd told Lance to meet me outside the darkroom at ten A.M. It was now nine A.M.; I wanted to see what I had on film before he showed up.

After I'd schmoozed with the janitor, Mr. Schlemke, who knew me to be a dependable sort and on the newspaper staff, he unlocked the darkroom for me. I let myself in. The odors of photographic chemicals bit at my nose—I made a mental note to remind Mr. Schlemke that the exhaust fan didn't work, then latched and locked the door behind me. I switched on the Do Not Enter light, which lit up red outside, then opened my camera. Unspooling the raw film, winding it in the stainless-steel can, pouring in the developer—I could do this in my sleep. Setting the timer, I began to agitate the can in a slow, steady motion. As my arm moved, I thought of Ms. Jenson, swimming, the way her arms came up and down, up and down.

When the timer went *ding!* I quickly poured in the stop bath, and twenty seconds later I dumped the stop bath and poured in the hypo. I flipped on the overhead light. Then I carefully removed the long strip of negative from the reel and rinsed it in water. I squeegeed the film, then held it up for a look. A few dorky photos of football, then Ms. Jenson's cabin, then one of Bobby's dad and uncle crouched in their boat. Next, one of the other woman being yanked from the dock into the water (a decent action photo), followed by a couple of head shots above the water. And then. Then the prizewinner.

Even in miniature it looked great. A side view of the two women holding each other tightly. Nothing really showed, nudewise. Just their arms, entwined, and a side-view hint of their breasts. Your eye went straight to their kiss. Balance, composition, light—it looked perfect. I thought of that famous World War II homecoming photo in which the sailor and the woman on the street are bent over like ballet dancers, kissing. My photo was nearly that good.

Except that Ms. Jenson was no anonymous woman on the street.

I stood back to think about that.

About what would happen, in a small town like Pine Crest, if her secret got out.

For long seconds I felt like Lance in a TPO. I tried to think it through. Really, what did it matter if her boyfriend was a girlfriend? What did it change? She was still a great teacher, great coach, great advisor—a great friend, even.

I swallowed and looked back at my negative. All I had to do was cut it up into tiny pieces. Sorry, Lance, the camera ate my film. It was the right thing to do. But before that, I had to see a print—a positive—just one real photo. From lying three hours in poison ivy I deserved that much.

At the enlarger, with the overhead light off again, I worked quickly; I wanted to be done and gone before Lance came around. Soon I was watching an eight-by-ten-inch image emerging in the developer. It grew into deep blacks, velvety shades of gray, and sparkling highlights on skin. The water just covered the two women's hips, their outside elbows were bent at perfectly symmetrical angles, their necks tilted forward equally (anyone could see it was Ms. Jenson). And from each woman's ear a droplet of water hung like a tiny diamond earring.

A quick dip into the stop bath and then into the fix and it was done. This was, by far, the best photo I had ever taken in my life. A grand-prize winner in any contest. I imagined it on the cover of *Popular Photography* or *Zoom*— or why not both? "Unnamed Women, Swimming," I would call it. This photo would get me a scholarship to art school, then a job with *The New York Times* covering Bosnia and Africa, but eventually I would become a freelance photographer like Robert Kincaid in *The Bridges of Madison County*, a squinty-eyed, deep-thinking loner whose camera told the truth about America, and who attracted women like flies. In the middle of such thoughts I heard footsteps outside. Instantly I flipped off the overhead light again, which lit up the Do Not Enter light outside.

"Ant," came a deep voice, followed by sharp rapping on the door. "You in there?"

Lance.

I froze.

"I know you're in there, Ant."

"Yeah—but don't come in, Lance—the light will ruin everything!"

There was a pause. "Well, hurry it up. I want to see what we've got."

"Sure, Lance, just give me a sec." Under the safelight, I looked frantically about the little room. In the garbage was a roll of old negatives, totally clear. I grabbed it and threw it into the fixer. The wet print of Ms. Jenson and her friend I fished out of the rinse and hastily stowed in the empty bottom drawer of the file cabinet.

The rapping came again.

"Okay, Lance, okay!" I said, and switched off the Do Not Enter light and unlocked the door.

Lance blinked, wrinkled his nose at the smells, and stepped in. "Well?"

I manufactured a crestfallen look. "Bad news, Lance," I said.

"What do you mean, 'bad news'?" he asked suspiciously.

I fished out the roll of negatives and held it up to the light. He peered at it. "I don't see nothing."

"That's just it. Something must have happened with the film."

"Like what?" he said angrily, grabbing my arm.

"I don't know, man, maybe bad film or something." I winced.

Lance swore, then pulled me up eyeball-to-eyeball. "You wouldn't be shittin' me, now, would you, Ant?"

He had me by the neck. I choked briefly. "No way, Lance!" I gurgled. He tossed me backward, then let his eyes—slowly—survey the room. His glance fell on the floor beside the file cabinet. From the bottom snaked a single tiny thread of rinse water. Damn.

Lance bent and jerked open the drawer, reached inside. "Well, well!" He grinned, holding up the photo. "Lookee what I found."

"Don't, Lance," I said. Don't what, I wasn't sure.

"Ant, if you weren't such a good photographer, I'd rap you upside the head for lying to me," Lance murmured, his eyes glued to the photo.

"It's my photo!" I said stupidly as he turned to leave. I grabbed at his arm, but he shrugged me off like an insect.

"Finders keepers, losers weepers, Ant," he said, and sauntered off down the hall.

———

Here's where lots of things start to happen real fast and where the story gets sad. First, that night my face, neck, and arms mutated into tiny watery boils; even my tongue swelled up. I hoped it might be only the gods punishing me, but it was worse: poison ivy. I got poison ivy so bad I had to go to the emergency room and get a shot, and a nurse smeared me with white cream that smelled like ammonia. Monday, I had to go to school looking like the Creature from the Black Lagoon. But by noon, no one gave me a second look: they had other things to giggle at.

My picture of Ms. Jenson and her friend, badly photocopied, appeared just before lunch. It was suddenly taped on lockers, pinned to bulletin boards, slipped under doors. Ms. Jenson was rumored to have been seen heading into the superintendent's office, where the door remained closed; slinking past her homeroom door, I saw our librarian, Mr. Davies, standing grimly at his podium. Between periods Lance winked at me in the hallway. "She's history." He smirked.

"Why'd you do it, Lance?" I asked. My voice broke; I was almost crying.

"I might not have—until that other broad showed up," Lance said.

"You would have anyway." My eyes were burning and spilling over.

His eyes went blank. "Get lost, Ant."

Worse, Lance didn't even get poison ivy.

Ms. Jenson was not in school the next day, nor the rest of the week, and on Monday her homeroom was cleaned out. Someone said they had seen her car, packed to the windows, leaving town. I doubted that, but it turned out to be true. She had resigned. Among the perky, bouncy, athletic senior-high girls, Lance, Bobby, and I (my poison ivy was the giveaway) were heroes. Among others, such as Mr. Wood, the assistant track coach, and Mr. Halgrimson, the principal, we were pond scum. Bobby and Lance got thrown off the JV football team (Lance simply moved up to varsity). Mr. Halgrimson sat me down for a long talk about "decision making" and "finding the right kind of friends" and "understanding people's rights to privacy." For a while I thought I might get off easy, but in the end he terminated me from *The Clarion* staff for "egregious misuse of school property," meaning the darkroom. The JV football coach also fired me as manager, but I would have quit anyway. I had spent too much of my life picking up after dorks like Lance Hickerson.

Thus, with no friends, no life, a walking pustule of poison ivy, I slunk from class to class feeling like some down-and-out character ("no prospects, no hope . . .") from a Charles Dickens novel. I considered quitting school but wasn't quite sixteen, plus just the idea was exhausting. Everything was exhausting. I began to skip classes, sneak home, and spend time in my room just vegging or sleeping. I didn't even carry my camera bag anymore.

As the days passed, so, slowly, did my poison ivy. Ms. Jenson's replacement settled in, and fall term wore on. But as everyone else seemed to forget Ms. Jenson, I didn't. I got increasingly edgy. Maybe it was the first signs of approaching winter, but I knew it was more than that: there was something I had to do.

Gradually I won back a slight nod, in hallway passing, from Mr. Wood, Andrea Jenson's friend. Abject despair works wonders with most teachers, and he was the one I focused on. One day I pumped up my spinal cord fluid and stopped by Mr. Wood's homeroom after school.

"Excuse me," I said, clearing my throat.

He turned from cleaning his chalkboard; his long eraser hung in the air.

"Well, if it isn't Mr. Long."

I got the feeling that he wanted to add, "the photographer."

I shuffled my feet. Cleared my throat again. "I wanted to . . . inquire about Ms. Jenson."

He stared at me. He's one of those very fit guys with slightly sunken cheeks that runners have, and razor-short hair. It suddenly occurred to me that he was not married, that he didn't ever seem to have girlfriend. My God—what if he? I twitched once—a large, spasmodic jerk (that's me)—then tried to cover my stupidity by coughing. He squinted closer at me, then turned to finish erasing his board.

"Why would Ms. Jenson interest you? I mean, beyond the obvious reasons," he said sarcastically.

"I just hoped that . . . things worked out for her. I mean, wherever she went."

Mr. Wood turned to stare at me again. "They have worked out," he said evenly. "She's living and teaching in Minneapolis now."

"Good," I said quickly, and turned toward the door.

"Anthony," Mr. Wood called.

"Yes?" I stopped.

"Ms. Jenson and I correspond. We're friends. We share some of the same interests," he said.

I swallowed, and nodded.

"I think she would want you to know that what happened, with your photo and all, was actually for the best. She's much happier in the city, which is where her partner lives."

I managed a quarter smile. I felt some huge weight begin to shift. Possibly even lift.

Mr. Wood smiled wryly. "And, if it helps any, you should know that Andy found your photo quite well done."

My eyes widened. "She did?"

He nodded. "As did I, I might add."

I smiled a bit more this time.

"She only wished she could have seen the real thing, not that ridiculous photocopy," Mr. Wood said with a brief look. He turned back to his desk.

My mind spun. "Mr. Wood?" I blurted. "What if I made her one? I mean, a really high-quality print, and sent it to her—along with a letter of apology—do you think she'd . . . ?"

"She'd like that," Mr. Wood said softly. "I know she would."

The very next day I worked with Mr. Wood himself in the darkroom. It was great to be back among the smells of fixer and developer, in the furry red light of this magic chamber.

As my print came alive in the developing tray, Mr. Wood murmured. "A truly fine photo," he said. "You're a very talented young man."

I shrugged.

He turned to me. "You have a future beyond Pine

Crest," he said. "I want you to know that. And I'm also going to speak to Mr. Halgrimson about reinstating your darkroom privileges."

I was glad the light was dim and red; so were my eyes right then.

When the print was dry, we went back to his office; I had already written my letter of apology, so we set about packaging the photo and getting it ready to mail.

"There's one more thing," I said, just before Mr. Wood sealed the big envelope.

He looked up.

I removed from my shirt pocket a sealed plastic sleeve. "This is the original negative," I said. "It really belongs to Ms. Jenson."

---

Only a few days later I received a letter postmarked from Minneapolis.

Dear Anthony,

Don't beat yourself up for what you did (though feel free to beat up Lance Hickerson—just joking). Mr. Wood says you went through some hard times, as did I, but I hope that they're over now, for both of us. If you ever come to the Twin Cities, don't be afraid to give me a call. We could visit places like the Minneapolis College of Art and Design, which I know you would like. Say "Hi" to Mr. Wood, too.

Your friend,

Andy Jenson

P.S. Also, I'm returning something to you that I know you'll use in good faith.

I looked deeper into the envelope. There, long and shiny, like a ticket to faraway places, was my negative.

# Will Weaver

Growing up on a farm in Minnesota, Will Weaver learned firsthand the joys and pains of the farm life he describes in his two young adult novels, *Striking Out* and *Farm Team*. In *Striking Out*, the hard life of Weaver's thirteen-year-old main character, Billy Baggs, changes when he starts playing baseball and discovers his skill as a pitcher. Billy's mother, at the same time, feeling that she needs to do more than be a farmwife, seeks work in town. Billy's taskmaster father is not happy with either decision.

In *Farm Team*, with his hotheaded father in jail, Billy must run the family farm. For recreation, he and his mother lay out a baseball diamond on their property and put together a ragtag team that challenges the organized team from town—with heartwarming results.

Both of those novels were named Best Books for Young Adults by the American Library Association. Interested readers can follow Billy into ninth grade, where he encounters star-crossed love and all kinds of trouble in Weaver's most recent novel, *Hard Ball*.

In addition to his books for teenagers, Will Weaver has written two novels for adults: *A Gravestone Made of*

*Wheat* and *Red Earth, White Earth,* which was made into a CBS television movie in 1989. For his fiction writing, Weaver has also been the recipient of prizes from the McKnight Foundation and the Bush Foundation.

Mr. Weaver lives in Bemidji, Minnesota, and teaches creative writing at Bemidji State University. He began the story of "The Photograph" after overhearing some eighth-grade boys gossiping about a young and attractive female teacher.

*If you set high standards and follow the rules, Bliss believes you can reach your goals. She's determined to let nothing stand in the way of her success.*

# Bliss at the Burger Bar
## Louise Plummer

Follow your bliss, Bliss. That's me. And my bliss is fast foods. I'm only eighteen, and I'm already night manager at Burger Bar in downtown Salt Lake City. The reason I'm successful is because I have goals. Right after graduating from Manti High School, which is about two hours south of here, I read Stephen R. Covey's *The Seven Habits of Highly Effective People.* And I thought, "Hey, I can be that." That was exactly one year ago this July. I didn't want to be like my older sister, Blythe, who has three kids under the age of four and has stretch marks that look like truck tires running up and down her stomach. Good-bye, bikinis.

Anyway, it was Blythe who drove me to Salt Lake when she had a Mary Kay Cosmetics convention up there in the Little America Hotel. I walked up Main Street toward the Crossroads Mall, and I passed Burger Bar with a Help Wanted sign in the window. And being the kind of "proactive" person that I am, I applied for and got the job that very day. In my future I visualize a Burger Bar franchise. Our Salivating Shake alone is better than anything McDonald's has. It's a real shake—not that soft ice-cream crap with a straw poked into it. Burger Bar is my bliss. It's the American way.

And America is still the best place to be, except when it comes to smoking. I've smoked since I was twelve, and I'm not stopping. It's relaxing and good for my mental health. I *believe* those Republicans who think that there's been a conspiracy in Congress against the tobacco industry. They're getting all these liberal Eastern doctors to say that smoking is bad for you. My grandma smoked three packs a day and lived to be ninety-two. I tell that to my mom, who thinks I should stop smoking. She's bought into all that health crap. And she says, "What about Grandpa? Grandpa died at sixty-five of lung cancer."

"Well, he didn't smoke, so you can't blame it on that," I say.

Then she says in this tone of voice that sounds like the high-and-mighty surgeon general herself, "He died of Grandma's *secondary smoke*. Grandma might just as well have killed him."

Secondary smoke. Puleeze. The conspiracy is mostly against women anyway. My mom's too busy making chicken-and-broccoli casseroles to see it. I walk down Main Street on my break sometimes, and there are women standing outside office buildings smoking, because they can't smoke inside. I never see men. As soon as women like something, men want to make it impossible for them. So women take up smoking, and suddenly it's a legislative issue. I'd blow smoke up most men's noses.

My fast-food managerial philosophy is to hire good people, train them thoroughly, and then let them do their work. Not as easy as you might think. Like tonight, this homeless guy, Old Faithful, appears. I saw him sleeping between two Dumpsters out in back one time. I don't know who gave him the name Old Faithful or even why, but that's what everyone calls him. He's wearing a plaid blazer with worn, dirty cuffs.

"You got a new coat," I say. I stand back from the counter to avoid smelling him. High School Hannah is making fries and I can tell from the way she blinks her eyes that she is trying to keep from making a face. The new boy, Dennis, stands behind the cash register. "Can I help you?" His Adam's apple races up and down while his nose shrinks into his face. I want to laugh.

I doubt Old Faithful even notices. He holds out his filthy, creased hand with a few coins in it. "An order of fries, please." His voice is asthmatic, and his watery eyes look over at Hannah and the tray of fries she's just salted.

Dennis looks at the money. "Fries are seventy-five cents an order," he says, businesslike, and then as if Old Faithful might not know, "You've only got thirty-two cents." Dennis rubs his index finger under his nose, hoping, I know, to keep Old Faithful's rotting smell out of his nostrils.

Old Faithful stares into his open palm, his head trembling slightly. "Could I buy thirty-two cents' worth of fries"—you can hear the phlegm in his voice—"please?"

It is seven in the evening, when most downtown

workers have gone home. Only one woman near the front of the place sits eating a ham and cheese and one of Burger Bar's Salivating Shakes.

Dennis turns to me with raised eyebrows. Can he sell thirty-two cents' worth of fries? Two girls walk in and, catching a whiff of Old Faithful, stand well back from him. I shake my head. No. The answer is no. Hannah stands poised and, still clutching the tray of new fries, stares into the old man's suffering gaze.

"Sorry, sir." Dennis's voice is efficient. "We can't do that." He looks over the old man's shoulder and addresses the two girls. "Welcome to Burger Bar. Can I help you?"

"Two Bravo Burgers, two orders of fries, and two Cokes." The two girls sidestep Old Faithful as he turns toward the door. He picks three uneaten fries off one of the tables that hasn't been bussed yet and thrusts them into his mouth. Then he takes the wrapper and licks the ketchup and mayonnaise half dried to the inside of the paper.

The two girls see it too and grimace. "Geez," one of them whispers. "Gross. They shouldn't let people like him in here." A couple of tiddlywinks.

Hannah has left the fries and is now squatting under the counter, digging around in her wallet for spare change. I place my hand on her shoulder and say in a low voice so no one else can hear, "We're not a homeless shelter or a soup kitchen. The customers would resent it if we gave food away to some people and made others pay full price. Do you understand?"

She nods at me, although I can tell she doesn't agree,

and she slips the coins back into her wallet. "What about the old burgers?" Hannah's talking about the burgers and fries that have been sitting longer than a half hour. We throw them out. It's the law. "They're still perfectly good and he could . . ." She looks eager.

"He can wait at the Dumpster," I say.

Hannah's face cracks like a fallen jar, and I want to tell her how you can't have opposing goals, how you can't be Mother Teresa and a successful Burger Bar manager at the same time. But I keep my mouth shut. There's nothing as pathetic as a whining fast-food manager.

That's when Hannah's boyfriend shows up in his Toyota 4Runner. It doesn't take looking out the window to see that he's arrived. The bass of his Bose stereo hurls Megadeth at us. The front windows tremble. He double-parks directly in front of the restaurant, gets out with his two clones, one female, and locks the car with the motor running and Megadeth booming into the street: "Mama! Mama!"

Hannah, half smiling, stretches her neck to catch a glimpse of him but then bites her lips when she sees he's not alone.

"Looks like he brought an entourage," I say. "That's good—more customers." I smile and nudge her because I want her to know there's no hard feelings about the Old Faithful incident.

The girl walks in first, wearing shorts and a halter. Hannah looks stifled inside her yellow-and-brown polyester Burger Bar suit; still she manages a pretty cheerful "Hi" when the three of them amble up to the yellow Formica counter.

I stand off to the back and wrap four Bravo Burgers. Dennis and Hannah can handle the high-school crowd.

"Welcome to Burger Bar! Can I help you?" This is Dennis. I look over and see him push those mammoth glasses of his up on his nose. He is genetically dweebed.

"What have you got to give me that I don't already have?" asks the one with the dimples. It's Hannah's boyfriend. His name is Milo, which sounds like a cheese, if you ask me.

"How about an Adam's apple?" This is his friend.

"I like your outfit," the girl teases Dennis. We're all wearing the same identical outfit, and I take her teasing personally.

Hannah takes over. "What do you want with your lard?" she asks. I have to smile inside. She's right to take the offensive with this group.

Milo smiles at her. He's handsome, I'll say that for him. "Can we just have lard, plain?"

"Yeah, but it costs extra."

"Fries and Cokes then." Milo turns to the other two. "Save me a seat," he says, and waves them off with his arm. They move together like cows toward the table.

Dennis goes to fill their order. I place the wrapped Bravo Burgers under the heat lamp.

Hannah leans across the counter and whispers, "I thought you were coming alone. I want to talk to you *alone*." Her voice pinches.

"I was coming alone, and then Fishbeck and Manderino show up." He shrugs. "What could I do?"

"Why have you left the car running?" Hannah's

voice is irritated. "I feel like you want to make a quick getaway."

I am making out the schedule for next week and look up briefly. Milo smiles at her and pushes a loose strand of Hannah's hair behind her ear. It would be a tender gesture if he wasn't so calculating, but it seems to relax her. "This downtown could use a little noise." His voice is lowered. "It's boring out there."

I don't like Milo. He's the kind of guy who would lay a doughnut if he wasn't afraid of getting frosting on his you-know-what. Hannah talks about him like he's some kind of transcended Ralph Waldo Emerson. Like their union is spiritual or something. The guy's just plain horny.

Hannah touches his finger, which plays with her earlobe. "I just worry," she says. "You could get a ticket."

He exaggerates a shudder. "Oh no, not a ticket! Oh gosh, oh golly. What will I do? A ticket! Oh no!" His teeth are perfect when he smiles. Judas Priest, what a brat.

Hannah grins.

Dennis has the order ready on a tray and rings it up. Milo pays with a twenty, picks up the tray, nods at Hannah, and says, "Come sit with us."

I look at my watch. I want to get a smoke in before Hannah goes on break. She must see this on my face, because she says to him, "I go on break in five minutes. I want to talk to you alone. Meet me out in back, okay?"

He nods and sits down with the other two cuties and tells some kind of joke that makes them all guffaw. They watch a cop walking around the 4Runner, looking down the street, scratching his head.

The guy, Fishbeck, pretends to speak as the cop: "Duh, what's this doing here? Duh."

The girl covers a snicker with her hand.

Milo jumps up and runs out the door. "Oh, Officer," he calls. When the door shuts, we can't hear him any longer. Hannah watches from the counter. I can tell that he is telling the cop a story; his hands dance in gesture, a smile plays on his lips. Judas, the guy is the devil himself. He charms the cop. They actually shake hands, and Milo gets into the 4Runner and moves it down the street.

"Can you believe it?" the girl says to Fishbeck. "Is he smooth or what?"

Smooth to his butt, I'll bet.

"He's so lucky." Fishbeck slurps through the ice for more Coke. "I would have been handcuffed and arrested by now."

When Milo struts back into the restaurant, they applaud him. Even the two girls who don't know him applaud him. He bows modestly with his head, grins, and, looking at Hannah, says, "I told you not to worry."

The guy pisses me off, so I find my cigarettes and go and sit out back in the alley on a plastic milk box, my back leaning against the cinder-block wall of the restaurant. I smoke and worry about Hannah. She's such an innocent. Sometimes she acts with real—what is that word—*bravado*—yeah; she acts with real bravado. Like when she tells me that her hobby is drying roses and that she steals all the roses from her neighbors' gardens. Like stealing roses is a felony or something.

"Have you ever stolen a car?" I asked her once.

"No!" She's really shocked, as if I asked her about venereal disease or something. "Have you?" she asks.

"Yeah," I say. "Down in Sanpete County, you're not a grown-up until you've stolen a car."

She gives me a careful look and then slugs me harmlessly across the shoulder. "You're kidding me."

"I'm not."

She lowers her voice for confession. "Sometimes I drive my mom's car when my folks aren't home, and I don't have a license."

Whoop-de-doo. The point is that Hannah, for all her talk—I should tell her about my breaking-and-entering experience—is Snow White.

But that Milo guy is no prince.

When I'm on my second cigarette, Hannah and Milo come out the back door. "Mind if I take my break?" she asks.

I blow smoke out my nose and nod.

"Let's walk down to the end of the alley," Hannah says. They pass the back side of the Tall Man's Shop, which is now closed, then Wong's House, a Chinese food place. The Wong brothers, who work in their father's restaurant, are also smoking, quietly speaking in Chinese to each other. Hannah leads Milo past the back side of the bookstore and the electronics store until they are at the end of the alley, a brick wall, lined with five Dumpsters, one for each business whose back side faces the alley. Each has a painted name on it identifying the owner: Burger Bar, Wong's House, and so on. The Dumpsters are overflowing with bulging plastic bags.

Milo's arms are around her, and he's feeling up

her backside. They're all kissy face. He's trying to get his tongue down her throat—the guy is greased with testosterone—but she pushes away slightly, as if she wants to talk. I can tell by the way she keeps turning her head from side to side, trying to avoid his body heat. Finally his open mouth covers hers. They don't seem to care about moderation and public space. They don't care where they are.

I am finished with my cigarette and go in. The Wong brothers stay to see the action. They grin like they've just discovered the adult channel on their parents' television. A couple of real dinks.

I don't think of Hannah again until about a half hour later when a big group of kids comes in and orders Bravo Burger meals, which means fries, drinks, and chocolate sundaes along with the hamburgers. It's one of our most popular items, because like the jingle says, "It's a Burger Bar Best Value." Anyway, Dennis and I are working our butts off trying to fill the order, and that's when I realize that Hannah hasn't come back. I'm pissed at first, but then I make a paradigm shift, which has become part of my managerial style, and I begin to think of Hannah as the valued employee that she is—Hannah is reliable to a fault—and as soon as we complete the orders, I go looking for her. Even before I reach the bathroom, I can hear her crying. It's a soft wail. It wrenches my guts. I open the door and see her bashed-up face reflected in the mirror. Tears and blood run together down her cheek and into the sink.

"Judas H. Priest," I say. Quick as anything, I wet some paper towels and begin wiping her face as gently as I can while she whimpers.

"Did Milo do this?" I already know the answer.

She answers by crying louder.

"I'll take you to the hospital," I say. I can tell she has a deep gash by her eye, which is already closing.

"No, no, no," she cries. "I can't go to the hospital." She weeps into the sink.

"You need stitches," I say.

"No! I can't go—" She clutches my arms. "Please, they'll find out—"

"You can't hide this." Her face looks like roadkill.

She shakes her head violently. "They'll find out I'm pregnant." Her face is pressed into my shoulder, which hardly muffles the convulsing cries. "I'm pregnant."

"Oh," I say. I stroke her hair. "Oh." I don't know what to do. Nothing in *The Seven Habits of Highly Effective People* has prepared me for this.

"He doesn't believe it's his." This sends her into a fresh wail.

"I believe you," I say, and I kiss her hair. I don't know what to do. And then, remembering that Hannah takes the bus to work, I say, "I'll drive you home."

She looks up at me and nods. "Thank you," she says, her voice shuddering.

I leave her long enough to give Dennis instructions on how to close up, because he's never done it before. His Adam's apple bobs up and down nervously, but he says, "I can do it." I hire good people. It's part of my managerial style.

In the car, I tell Hannah that she should call the police and have Milo arrested for assault, and she says— and this kills me—"He didn't mean to." Like he has a neurological disorder that makes him wham people with his fist. I try to talk her out of this, but she gets so upset with any of my suggestions that I decide I better cool it. "Put first things first." That's what Stephen R. Covey says. So instead I tell her I wish I could find a dozen more people like her to work for me because she's so dependable. "You really know how to work," I tell her.

Then we are at her house. I look up the slope of the lawn. The house is dark, and it looks like nobody's home. I say this to Hannah. I say, "Please let me take you to the hospital to get some stitches. Nobody's going to give you a pregnancy test. You don't look a bit pregnant. Please—"

"No." She's already opened the door. "It's almost stopped bleeding." She removes the wadded-up paper towel and shows me the cut, and it does look as if it's mostly stopped. It's dark now and I can't see much.

"Bye." Hannah waves at me. She stands on the sidewalk and waits for me to leave.

"Take a few days off," I call through the window. "I'll cover your shift." I accelerate slowly up the street. Is there something else I should do? In my rearview mirror, I can still see her standing there, a shadow under the streetlight. She continues waving as if to prove to me that she's fine. I think of turning back, but instead turn right at the end of the street and head downtown. You can't save someone who doesn't want saving. Any idiot knows that.

For the first time since I have come to Salt Lake, I feel lonely and wish I had a roommate. Rather than go home, I drive back to the Burger Bar. I'll calculate the receipts tonight. It'll get my mind off Hannah and the way she looked like she was eleven years old. Hannah's pregnant. Judas Priest. In the alley, the truck from the waste-disposal company that empties the Dumpsters passes me. One whiff of its wormy hamburger stench lifts me involuntarily off my seat. I park in my space and get out of the car.

There is a shuffling behind me. I turn quickly and see a dark figure just a few feet from me. In the middle of my shriek, I realize it is only Old Faithful. "Geez," I say, "you scared the crapola out of me."

He nods with wet, startled eyes as if I may have done the same for him. He has dropped something, and I lean over to pick it up. It's an old hamburger in an opened Styrofoam box. The lettuce is brown and slimy. He reaches for it with a crusty hand. Is he drunk? Sick? Stupid? Out of his mind? Does it matter? I realize that although I felt helpless with Hannah, I know what to do for this guy.

We're both holding on to the garbage burger now. "Hey," I say, "come inside with me and I'll fix you a fresh hamburger—a Burger Bar Special with all the trimmings—okay?"

He hangs on to the garbage burger like maybe he doesn't trust me.

I hold his arm and lead him to the back door, where I let go just long enough to get my key out. "Is that okay if I make you a burger?"

"Okay," he says, nodding his head.

"What's your name?" I push the door open and pull him inside.

He squints when I turn the lights on. "Harold." He hugs the old burger to his chest. "Harold Finlayson."

I think I just stare at him for a few seconds, I'm so surprised. Harold Finlayson is like—you know—a *real* person's name. I guess I was expecting something like Bud or Lou or Hey You.

"Well, Harold"—I recover myself—"follow me and we'll have dinner."

I'll bet there's a lot of stories behind a name like Harold Finlayson, and as we walk into the lighted Burger Bar kitchen, I decide to find out what some of them are.

# Louise Plummer

When she was five years old, Louise Plummer moved with her family to the United States from their home in the Netherlands. She now lives in Salt Lake City, Utah, with her husband, Tom, and the youngest of their four sons and teaches English at Brigham Young University.

Her first novel, *The Romantic Obsessions & Humiliations of Annie Sehlmeier,* is very popular in Salt Lake City, where it is set. Teenage readers easily recognize the high school and other landmarks that are described in the novel, and local librarians describe it as "the most stolen book in the library."

The pursuit of romance, obviously, is the main topic of that novel, as it is of Plummer's other novels, *My Name Is Sus5an Smith. The 5 Is Silent* and *The Unlikely Romance of Kate Bjorkman.* In *Sus5an Smith,* the protagonist leaves her boring hometown to pursue a career as an oil painter in Boston, where she becomes involved with a man twice her age who was once married to her aunt. That novel was named a Best Book for Young Adults by the American Library Association as well as by *School Library Journal.*

*School Library Journal* also named *The Unlikely*

*Romance of Kate Bjorkman* a Best Book of the Year. That novel's seventeen-year-old narrator, Kate, says she hates romance novels, but she uses *The Romance Writer's Phrase Book* to describe her own experiences with her older brother's handsome friend Richard, who visits during Christmas vacation.

In contrast to Plummer's novels, the events in "Bliss at the Burger Bar" aren't very romantic. They are based on a real experience that one of Plummer's college students described after she had told her boyfriend (in front of a Dumpster behind a McDonald's where he worked) that she was pregnant. Interested readers can find out more about Hannah's experiences in Plummer's next novel, *Hannah Ziebarth at Large.*

Combining their talents, Michael and his friends
create a clever computer game with an unusual
ending that will make them rich and famous.
Who could ever object?

# Moon over Missouri
## T. Ernesto Bethancourt

The way I see it, any kid born within a week of Christmas
gets the shaft from birth. You never get a birthday party—
too close to Christmas. You never get birthday presents.
You get *bothday* presents. My pal Jimmy's got it even
worse. His birthday is Christmas day. He never gets a
birthday of his own. That's because it's *God*'s birthday
and not his own. Talk about shafted.

I don't know what it's like for Jewish kids born
around that date. I only know three of them my age, and
none of them was born in December. I don't know anybody who's Muslim. That's easy to explain if you live in a
small town in the southwest corner of Missouri.

That wasn't my idea, either. My father got a chance
to teach in this burg. The university here got a huge private grant. They created a whole computer science
department, with Dad at its head. We moved here from
Los Angeles, where I was born.

So here I was, barely knowing anybody. To make it worse, when my birthday happens, it's bitter cold. Back home, sometimes, you can even go to the beach in December. Here, we had snow flurries on the twenty-third, which is my birthday. All this may not sound like too much to you, but I think it's all part of some kind of curse, tied to when you get born.

For instance, how could an eighteen-year-old high-school senior design the hottest CD-ROM adventure game program in the country, making a fortune along the way, and still end up not just broke but with half the world suing him, too? You've heard of *Ultimate Conquest*, I'm sure. It sold 300,000 copies. I wrote the thing, or let's say I put it together from my own ideas. Sure, there was input from Jimmy, Bradley, and Elza, but I made the choices of what went into the program.

I figure if anyone is to blame for all the lawsuits, it's my dad. He did the actual programming, including the microsubliminals. I didn't even know what microsubliminals were. Not back then, anyway. I sure know now. I'm in front of myself here. It all started a year and a half ago, when I first arrived in beautiful Wiltonsburg. The four of us met the first week of school and drifted into role-playing games. It was my idea to turn one of our games into something other people could play.

*In a flash of green fire and smoke, Zela the Sorceress appears. She is statuesque and gorgeous. She wears an iridescent, floor-length red gown. Her hair is arranged in classic mandarin style; her long fingernails match the flame-colored gown.*

*"I am Zela, Mistress of Illusion," she proclaims in a deep, throaty voice. "I will be your ally in Stage Two of* Ultimate Conquest!*"*

*She rapidly morphs from woman to Chinese lion to hunting falcon, then to a huge, fire-breathing dragon. . . .*

"Wait a minute," Bradley put in. "I thought it was supposed to be 'Zela, *Queen* of Illusion.' "

"Yeah, that's right," Jimmy said, checking his notes. "I got it right here. 'Queen of Illusion.' "

We all looked at Elza Hong. She gave us her shy, funny half smile and pushed her red-framed glasses up. She didn't look that queenly. Elza is five feet four with short-cropped hair, skinny, and has a slight case of acne. "Sorry, guys," she said in her high-pitched voice. "I thought 'Mistress of Illusion' sounded, well . . . more mysterious. Don't you think so?"

The three of them looked at me. As director, it was my call. "Okay with me," I said. "Just don't keep improvising, Elza. We've almost got the whole game down on hard drive." I looked over at Jimmy. "Change it in the script, will you?"

"Yeah, yeah," Jimmy grumbled. He leaned over the keyboard, working the Find/Replace function. "Not too bad," he pronounced. "Only three replacements in Zela's role. Two more in the Player's: first when he invokes her—second when he calls her off."

"Why do you keep calling the Player *he*?" Elza asked. "I thought we agreed that gender doesn't matter in *Conquest.*"

I sighed. "Honest, Elza," I said. "It doesn't matter. What do you want Jimmy to call the Player? He/She?"

Elza giggled. "Why not? Sounds almost Chinese: *Hi-Shi*."

"That does it for me," Bradley said. "We're getting silly now. What time is it?" he stood up and stretched his huge frame.

"Ten-fifteen, Central," said Jimmy, reading from his display. "Tomorrow comes early. I have a paper due for modern history."

"All right," I said. "We knock off till tomorrow night. Everyone clean up now. I got it from my dad about last week's mess."

The den looked like a battlefield. Empty soda pop cans, two giant pizza boxes, and a half-finished sack of barbecue chips were strewn around the room. Easily half the debris was from Bradley. It takes a lot of fuel to keep an engine like Brad's going. He's close to seven feet tall and plays guard on the basketball team. He hates it, but the scholarship he's got to the new university keeps him at it. In fact, I doubt if anyone on the team knows his real passions are music and poetry.

He gathered up his share of the stuff and headed for the door. "I'll drop this in the bin outside, Mike," he told me. "Don't know if I can make it on time tomorrow, though. Coach is still steamed about us almost losing last Friday. He's calling for more practice."

"Can you blame him?" Jimmy said. "It's the first winning team Sadler High has had in years. If you guys take district championship, he's golden. It won't hurt that scholarship of yours, either, Brad."

"Don't remind me," Bradley groaned. "Come on, Jimmy," he said. "I'll give you a lift. I got my dad's car tonight."

I walked the guys to my kitchen door and watched them get into the Olds Cutlass that Bradley's dad keeps in like-new shape. I had to smile at the picture they made together. Jimmy is five feet eight and chunky. He has red hair and is so fair-skinned, he doesn't tan in the summer. He just gets redder.

Jimmy and Bradley are the two locals in the Flaky Four. Elza is from San Francisco. Like me, she's here because of her dad's job. He was hired as the new department head of English. Both of us being new at Sadler and both from California brought us together. We had three classes together, first semester, including computer lab, where we met Jimmy.

He's a real genius at it. That naturally made him a total nerd to most of the Sadler students. They're either farm kids or their folks work at service jobs at the university. Bradley's a farm kid, like Jimmy. They live on adjoining farms and have been friends all their lives.

This alone tells you they both are outlaws and natural candidates for the Flaky Four. In this part of the country, a *white* farm kid and Bradley being best friends is rare. From what Jimmy tells me, they still get heat from both sides of the line. Bradley is too huge for them to mess with, and Jimmy is physically fearless to the point of being marginally nuts. Together, they are *not* messed with.

The Olds pulled away and out the driveway.

"Are you okay, Michael?"

I jumped. I hadn't heard Elza come into the kitchen. "You were standing there like a statue," she added.

"Just thinking about Brad and Jimmy."

Elza laughed. "Talk about Felix and Oscar. I think of

them as the *Odder* Couple." She dropped the soda pop cans into the recycling bin next to the sink.

"I would have taken care of that," I said. "Come on. I'll walk you home."

As we walked the two blocks to Elza's, there was a fresh, green scent of spring in the air. The moonlight was almost as bright as the puddles of light at the base of each streetlamp. The rows of neat, two-story homes, with identical manicured lawns and white fences, looked like a movie set of a small Midwest university town.

Although we were a block away from the Hong house, Eliza noticed that the porch light was still on. "Uh-oh," she said. "Grandma wants to talk to me. She's still up."

We stopped two houses before Elza's, and I collected my good-night kiss. The Dragon Lady—Elza's grandmother—doesn't like me one bit. Nothing personal, Elza keeps telling me. I'm just not Chinese. "What's on the D.L.'s mind now?" I asked.

"Same-old-same-old. My U.C. Berkeley application. I got my acceptance this week."

"What's wrong with Wiltonsburg? With all the upgrades they've done, their standing is just fine. And their English department has always been good. Just because *she* went to Berkeley doesn't mean *you* have to."

"Family tradition means a lot, Michael. I'd be third-generation. It means a lot. My brother's going to West Point really hurt her."

"Besides which, it gets you out of town and breaks us up. Who's kidding who here? You know what's on her mind."

"Nothing can break us up, Michael." She took my hand and gave it a private squeeze. "It's the Flaky Four that will be breaking up in June. Brad will be at the University of Missouri. And we don't know where Jimmy's going. He swore he'd never be a farmer."

"Don't write off the Four yet, hon," I said. "We have Stage Four of *Conquest* almost done. Jimmy says he can have it ready to give to my dad ten days after we write the Victory Ritual."

Elza looked anxiously over at her front porch. "I really have to run, Michael. See you . . ." She gave me a peck on the cheek and ran up the block. I watched until she went inside and the porch light went out.

As I walked back, I wasn't feeling too upbeat. I had been talking a good fight with the Flaky Four for months now. But there was little doubt in my mind that *Conquest* could solve all our problems. If it was a hit, the money would set us all free. Bradley could forget basketball and study music and literature. Jimmy could set up his own computer game business, with me doing the scriptwriting. Best of all, Elza and I could be together.

The idea was that Dad would do the programming and arrange for the sound and graphics for *Conquest*. Except he didn't know a damned thing about my plan— yet. There was also the last part of the game to be written. No sweat there. I had it all blocked out in my mind. I was sure it would play with the Four. Dad was something else. Then again, Dad has *always* been something else.

A week later, we had Stage Four done. Jimmy had it on hard drive and backup. That's when I sprang my idea for the Victory Ritual on the rest of the Four, at my house. Soon as Jimmy heard it, he let out a wild whoop.

"I love it!" he hollered. "I'm so sick of all that 'Now you rule the castle' crap!"

Bradley didn't say anything. He couldn't stop laughing. When I looked at Elza, she was smiling but not laughing. "I don't know, Michael," she said. "I think it's sort of well . . . embarrassing."

"Of course it is," said Bradley, still laughing. "It's more than that. It's outrageous! But Michael, can you get it past the censors?"

"What censors? This isn't going out on the airwaves. It's a program for private use. What's more, I think it's funny."

"Some people might think it's porn," Elza said thoughtfully. "There are lots of religious people who could stir up trouble. . . ."

The time of decision was on us. I stood up. "Am I the director and head writer or ain't I? I say we go with it."

Jimmy didn't hesitate a millisecond. "You got us this far. I'm with you, Mike."

"You got my vote," Bradley added. "I just can't wait to see the graphic."

"I thought we said the Player wasn't to be gender specific," Elza put in. "How do you get around *that*?"

"Easy enough. It's a *rear* view, isn't it? Besides, we have all the Allies do it, too. How's that for equality?"

"I like that even better!" Jimmy howled. "Give me a week—ten days on the outside. I'll have it ready."

We spent the rest of the session cracking up over my

idea. In between laughs, though, I kept thinking about what Dad would think. Most of all, what he'd *do* . . .

Spring break was coming up at the university. All I had to do was talk him into not dragging me off to Colorado for "quality time." Then I had to sell him on doing the master programming for *Conquest* and finding out about the graphics and music. There was also the matter of production costs for the pilot.

As to getting the pilot to a major software outfit, I didn't have a clue. One thing at a time, I figured. Sure, I should have told the rest of the Four. Fact was, at first it *had* been all talk on my part. It had sounded like a cool idea. Then everyone got so caught up in the game. Worse, they believed I could do what I said; I couldn't back off. Most of all, Elza believed in me.

I think too, a big part of it was I began to believe my own line of bull. What would I do if Dad turned me down? Go back to L.A.? Live with my sister, my mother, and her new husband? No! I had to deliver.

---

Jimmy put the materials in my hands early. It had taken him only a week. It felt funny that night, not meeting with the Four, but I knew Dad was free that night. He was sitting in the living room, going over some Colorado travel folders. "Dad," I said, "can you spare me a little time?"

He looked up and smiled. "Sure, Mike. That's what dads are for, aren't they?"

I sure hope so, I thought. I took a deep breath and started talking. . . .

Two days later, the Flaky Four assembled in our

51

living room. All of them had met Dad, in a way. More like "Dad, this is Elza, Bradley, and Jimmy," followed by a "Hi, guys" from Dad. That's why I was uneasy when Dad said he wanted to talk to all of us at once. He can be intimidating, I know. I grew up with it. Sometimes he can still get *me*.

Not that he's imposing, physically. He looks like what I might look like in another twenty years. He has the same skinny, six-foot build, dark eyes, and brown wavy hair. But years of teaching have given him a way of filling a room with his voice.

"I've read the material and played the disks," he began. "I have drawn some conclusions. I also have some questions.

"There's little doubt in my mind about the alter egos of Zela, Mistress of Illusion." He nodded at Elza and smiled. "And there's no doubt that Wheeler the Demon Driver is Mike. I've ridden with him driving. It's an experience.

"But which of you two is Abelard the Poet?" His eyebrows went up when Bradley raised his hand. I told you Dad gets teacher-type responses when he talks.

"And you wrote the words and all the incidental music, as well?" he asked. Bradley nodded. "Fine work. Was it also your idea that Abelard could charm the Fire Beast into sleeping?"

"Uh-uh. That was Mike's idea, Mr. . . . uh, Dr. Brandt."

"I see. And that means Jimmy is Jason the Perfect Warrior?"

"Right, Dad," I put in. "And Jimmy did all the basic

52

programming. He came up with the idea of the quick-flash action cues, too."

"Hold on, Mike," Jimmy said. "That was because you wanted them." He turned back to Dad. "See, Mike didn't want the game to have to come with a big instruction manual. And we didn't want to waste space on the disk with a long tutorial. You can just boot up *Conquest* and play it." He grinned. "You can't play it well, but you can play it. It's a tough one."

"I'm well aware of that. Interesting that what you call flash cues are close to something I've been working on. They are called microsubliminals. You don't need them to be visible at all, Jimmy. I must say, though, that working with what you had, you've done a remarkable job."

The two of them talked bytehead jargon for about five minutes. Finally Dad stopped and addressed us together. "Now, we come to the Victory Ritual, when the Player gets through Stage Four . . ." Here it comes, I thought: The Kiss of Death.

"I think it's hilarious and I love it!" Dad said. "What's more, it sets your game apart from every other I have seen. And I have seen them all, going back to Pac-Man in the 1970s. I worked on some of them, before I started teaching.

"Don't get too excited," Dad continued. "What you have here is very rough. It needs lots of work. I'm so impressed that I'm ready to help you. If it works out, I can even get the pilot to some people I know."

I think he might have talked even more. Dad will do that. But by then, we were all jumping around the room, hugging each other and laughing. When we got done and the room fell quiet, Jimmy said, "Well, what do we do now?"

"How about we send out for pizza?" Brad suggested.

———

Dad was better than his word. We had the pilot up and running in six weeks. Dad then took it to the computer convention in Las Vegas. He came back with a fat check and a contract for me to sign. MicroGiant, the biggest software outfit in the country, had bought *Conquest*. Then the reviews started coming in. *Computing Magazine* was the first:

## SWORD AND SORCERY SEND–UP A WINNER

MicroGiant's new interactive CD-ROM is fast, tough and what's more, funny! In *Ultimate Conquest* you will find no decapitations, no gore, but action enough to satisfy any adventure game addict. Picture the Player, beset by a field of venomous ambulatory plants. Player calls on the game character, Jason the Perfect Warrior. Jason arrives, not with sword, but a Weed Whacker.

That's just a sample. Any Player sharp and tough enough to win this challenging, fast-as-lightning game is in for one of the funniest game finales this reviewer has ever seen. We won't give away the ending. You must experience it for yourself. Ease of Play index is high. A novice can play immediately. Winning is another matter. Rating: $3^1/_2$ Stars.

That was just the beginning. Parents and teachers were all for *Conquest* because of the no blood and guts. Young people liked it for the speed and how tough it was to win, even though it was so easy to play. Most of all, everyone who managed to win cracked up at the Victory Ritual. They'd play it again and again.

When the Flaky Four graduated in June, we were celebrities. Bradley had the grades to get into Wiltonsburg U. Even better, he had the tuition money. He dropped off the team and enrolled as an English major, with a music minor.

Jimmy and I got a slew of hardware and started up our company, almost the way we had planned. The difference was, we were going to San Francisco. Jimmy was surprised when I suggested it one night when the Four were at my house.

"I don't know, Mike," Jimmy said. "I get nervous in Kansas City. Maybe it's my farmer background. Why San Francisco?"

"For one thing, it's close to Silicon Valley. Besides, Elza will be going to U.C. Berkeley. She has to. Family tradition. Her grandma went there."

Jimmy looked at Elza with surprise. "Your *grandma*? I thought she came from China."

Elza rolled her eyes. "You are a farmer at heart, aren't you? For your information, my family has been in the United States since the 1850s."

"Big deal," Bradley said. "My family's been here a lot longer than that. It just wasn't their idea to come." He turned to me. "I have to admit I'm going to miss you guys a lot."

"Don't think we're ditching you, Brad," I said. "We'll be back for holidays and probably the summers. Elza's folks are here and so's my dad. You can come out, too. It's not like you won't have the airfare."

Bradley grinned. "You know, I keep forgetting that? Sure, I can come and visit."

"Forget?" Jimmy hooted. "Doesn't a red Mustang convertible remind you? How about the new Olds Aurora you bought for your father?"

We all laughed, and soon we were making plans for the fall and the holidays. It was a sweet time, and things couldn't have been better. Then, two weeks later, it hit the fan, big-time. Maybe I should have listened to Elza about the Victory Ritual.

Dad was going over the mail when I got home from dropping Elza off. "Sit down, Michael," he said. "We have a problem."

"Are Mom and Ellie okay?"

"This isn't about family, son. It's a legal matter. It seems we are the lucky recipients of a class-action lawsuit."

"Who'd want to sue us?"

Dad held up a document in a blue folder. "This says that there are close to a hundred people. It's about *Ultimate Conquest.* Specifically, the Ritual."

"They're upset? What are they? Some religious group or something?"

"Not from the look of this. They seem to be good, solid folk. Some of them are in positions of high respect. That's the big problem. They claim that the subliminals in *Conquest* have carried over into their real lives. They

56

claim that anytime they win an argument or even another game, they have a compulsion to do the Victory Ritual."

I couldn't stop laughing at the idea. Dad waggled a finger at me. "Some of these complainants are lawyers and judges," he said.

I couldn't help it. I fell out of my chair, onto the floor, laughing like a crazed person. The picture of a judge dropping his pants and throwing a courtroom a full moon was too much!

"Are you quite through?" Dad asked coolly. I know that tone of voice. It straightened me up.

"This can't be for real, Dad. I know lots of kids and grown-ups who play the game. *They* aren't mooning people."

"That may be true. The difference, they claim, is that some people are highly susceptible to subliminal suggestions. Their lawyers say that the more the game is played, the stronger the suggestions get.

"They say there should have been a warning about the subliminals on the CD-ROM package and the disk itself."

"No big deal. We call MicroGiant and have them change the packaging. We have the addresses of all the buyers. They register for the warranty. We get out a mailing . . ." I trailed off. Dad was shaking his head.

"Come on, Michael. Use your head. For every registered buyer, how many other people use the disk? That doesn't even take into account any software pirate copies.

"I was on the phone with MicroGiant's lawyers an hour ago. Their sales figures indicate that with units already sold and others shipped, there's over a quarter million copies out there."

"Then I say that MicroGiant's got a big problem."

"They say it's *ours*." Dad held up a copy of the contract I had signed. "You forget that MicroGiant doesn't *own* the game. They only published it. There's something in this contract called a hold harmless clause. In it, we certify that the program is completely original and that any litigation is *our* responsibility."

"Sure. That's if we swiped the idea from someone, right?"

"There's more. Any suit about *content* is also covered. MicroGiant's lawyers say the lawsuits are based on program content."

"They're trying to weasel out, Dad. Their engineering staff knew exactly what was in the program when they okayed it."

"True enough. But their *legal* department is standing by the letter of the contract. We would have to sue MicroGiant to prove our point."

"Okay. We sue 'em."

"What will you pay a lawyer with? They've already frozen your royalty account. You can't sue an outfit that size on what you have left in the bank, Michael. And there's still the class-action suit."

"My gosh! I just thought of something. Are they going after the other kids, too?" In my mind I saw all the Four's dreams falling apart.

"No, Michael. Just you. You signed the contract as program creator. In theory, you didn't have to share the royalties with the others. You did that out of honesty and loyalty. On paper, you are responsible. They're in the clear."

"That's a relief." I shook my head in wonderment. "It's hard to believe all this. But I know we didn't mean to do anything wrong. We'll prove that, somehow. Things are bad, but they could be worse."

Which just shows you how wrong I can be. Two days later, the lawsuit was in the newspapers in the financial section. A week after that, I got a late-night call from Elza. "Did you see the Jay Leno show tonight?" she asked.

"No. I was sitting here, thinking."

"I was taping it for my grandmother. She goes to bed early. You've got to see this. I'll be right over."

I knew right then it was important. I waited on the porch so she wouldn't have to knock. Dad was asleep. She was at my place in five minutes. We went into the den and played the tape. It was in the opening monologue.

First Leno read the clipping from the paper. Then he did a half dozen moon gags. Then he turned to the band-leader and asked if Kevin had played *Conquest.* "Sure, Jay," he said. "The whole band is into it. Right, guys?"

The camera was holding on a long shot of the band, when suddenly the screen went blank for a second. When it came back on, the camera was on Jay. The audi-ence was hysterical. He looked toward the band and said, "I'd like to thank you for that point of view, guys." They said later, it was the longest recorded laugh in TV history.

I turned to Elza and said, "That's it, hon. I'm doomed!"

I can't say if the whole gag wasn't a setup. Maybe the

band didn't really do it. Only the studio audience knew. The next day, every news show on the air ran the clip. Overnight, there was an epidemic of mooning. And every single time, the mooner blamed it on *Conquest.* Also, for every ten moonings, there were twenty more lawsuits. We're still counting! I don't know what I would have done if it hadn't been for Bradley. He arranged an appointment with a cousin of his father's, one Lawrence P. Miller. He's a hotshot trial lawyer in Kansas City. We met in his office, downtown.

I knew right away he had to be a *distant* cousin. He was a dapper little man, with quick, almost birdlike movements. He had a rapid-fire way of speaking. Standing next to Bradley, he looked like a toy person. He wasted no time.

"I've told Bradley I will take your case, Michael," he said after introductions. "I truly believe ninety-nine percent of the suits are crap. Haven't *you* ever wanted to baffle your foes by throwing 'em a full moon?"

"I suppose . . ."

"Don't kid me. You know you have. But what stops you?"

"Lots of things," I replied. "Morality, my upbringing, background, and most of all, my picture of myself."

"Good for you, Michael," Miller said. "Now, what if somebody gave you an excuse for doing it? Allowed you to say, 'It wasn't my fault. The CD-ROM made me do it'? Would you then go around mooning the world?"

"I think not," I said. "I also think these people who are doing it really want to. They're just using *Conquest* and me as scapegoats. Is someone telling me a subliminal message reading 'Full Moon' and an image on the screen can make you do something? Give me a break!"

"Well put, Michael," Miller said. "I also think a lot of the lawsuits are predicated on greed. It's common knowledge there are millions involved. It's frivolous suits like this that clog our court calendars. This time, I think it will take a trial to settle this mess." He smiled. "And you're going to be the star witness for the defense."

"Wait a minute. Not me! What would I say?"

"Exactly what you just told me. You're a most articulate young man when you feel you're right. That's what good witnesses are made of."

"I don't have any money . . . ," I began.

"I knew that before I asked you here. Don't worry. We'll win this one. You'll get your back royalties. Then there's the money we'll get in settlement from Micro-Giant."

"What? How?"

"We sue them for hanging you out to dry, the way they did."

"More lawsuits?" I said. "I'm getting dizzy as it is."

Miller waved a hand airily. "Leave that part to me. I'm sure we can win."

I felt like a hundred-pound weight had been taken off my back. I stood up and put out my hand. "Mr. Miller," I said, "I can't thank you enough. When do we get started?"

Miller shook my hand firmly and warmly. "The trial, you mean? I'd say in about two years."

"*What?* Why that long?"

"I told you, the calendars are clogged."

"What do I do in the meantime?" I asked.

"Go home and get on with your life. Any more papers or phone calls you get, refer them to my office."

And here I sit, in Wiltonsburg. I'm working at the McDonald's for minimum wage and going to college here. Whenever we can, Bradley, Jimmy, and I get together and hang out. I sure miss Elza, though. She'll be home for Christmas in a month. Which is as close to a real birthday present as I'll probably ever get.

Maybe in time, all the mooning will stop. I hope so. No, I take that back. There *is* one I'd like to see. In a couple of more years, we'll have another presidential election. On election night, I want to see the winning candidate's victory speech!

# T. Ernesto Bethancourt

T. Ernesto Bethancourt, who grew up in Florida and New York City, began his writing career with an autobiographical novel that was later made into an NBC-TV movie titled *New York City Too Far from Tampa Blues.* But before becoming a writer, Mr. Bethancourt was a performer, playing blues guitar and singing in nightclubs and coffeehouses under the name Tom Paisley. He studied blues guitar under the famous Josh White and was highly influenced by black music that he heard in Brooklyn neighborhoods near where he lived. He now lives in Southern California, where he still sings and plays the guitar, most often for kids at the schools he visits.

Among his novels for young people are *T.H.U.M.B.B.,* a hilarious story about how two Puerto Rican boys attempt to add a little life to their high-school marching band, and *The Mortal Instruments,* a science fiction story in which a teenager with supernatural powers gains control over a weapon of mass destruction. Bethancourt is also the author of *The Tomorrow Connection, Where the Deer and the Cantaloupe Play,* and *The Me Inside of Me,* which explores the problems a seventeen-year-old Mexican American teenager encounters when he inherits a million dollars after his parents die in a plane crash. Several of Bethancourt's novels have been named Best Books for Young Adults, Notable Children's Books, and Young Adult Choices.

His most popular novels are the Doris Fein mysteries, the most recent of which is *Doris Fein: Legacy of Terror,* and *The Dog Days of Arthur Cane,* a clever look at life from a dog's perspective when a voodoo curse turns a teenage boy into a mutt. That story was made into a film for ABC television that is still shown on Nickelodeon.

Though the events in "Moon over Missouri" are fictional, Bethancourt notes that in reality video games contain warning labels that the flashing lights and quick cuts can trigger epileptic seizures. And as he was writing this story, Congress was debating limits for product liability lawsuits, while numerous lawsuits have backed up court calendars for years.

# It Seemed Like
# a Good Idea
# at the Time

Upset about his failing grade in Mrs. Whitman's
math class, Scott comes up with a clever
way to get revenge.

# I've Got Gloria
## M. E. Kerr

"Hello? Mrs. Whitman?"

"Yes?"

"I've got Gloria."

"Oh, thank heaven! Is she all right?"

"She's fine, Mrs. Whitman."

"Where is she?"

"She's here with me."

"Who are you?"

"You can call me Bud."

"Bud who?"

"Never mind that, Mrs. Whitman. I've got your little dog and she's anxious to get back home."

"Oh, I know she is. She must miss me terribly. Where are you? I'll come and get her right away."

"Not so fast, Mrs. Whitman. First, there's a little something you must do."

"Anything. Just tell me where to find you."

"*I'll* find *you,* Mrs. Whitman, *after* you do as I say."

"What do you mean, Bud?"

"I mean that I'll need some money before I get Gloria home safely to you."

"Money?"

"She's a very valuable dog."

"Not really. I got her from the pound."

"But she's valuable to you, isn't she?"

"She's everything to me."

"So you have to prove it, Mrs. Whitman."

"What is this?"

"A dognapping. I have your dog and you have to pay to have her returned safely to you."

There was a pause.

I could just imagine her face—that face I hated ever since she flunked me. That mean, freckled face, with the glasses over those hard little green eyes, the small, pursed lips, the mop of frizzy red hair topping it all. . . . Well, top this, Mrs. Whitman: I do not even have that nutsy little bulldog of yours. She *is* lost, just as your countless signs nailed up everywhere announce that she is. . . . All I have is this one chance to get revenge, and I'm grabbing it!

Now her voice came carefully. "How much do you want?"

"A thousand dollars, Mrs. Whitman. A thou, in one-hundred-dollar bills, and Gloria will be back drooling on your lap."

"A *thousand* dollars?"

Got to you, didn't I? Did your stomach turn over the way mine did when I saw that F in math?

"You heard me, Mrs. Whitman."

68

"Are you one of my students?"

"Oh, like I'm going to tell you if I am."

"You must be."

"I could be, couldn't I? You're not everyone's dream teacher, are you?"

"Please don't hurt my dog."

"I'm not cruel by nature."

I don't take after my old man. He said he was sorry that I flunked math because he knew how much I was counting on the hike through Yellowstone this summer. He said maybe the other guys would take some photographs so I could see what I was missing while I went to summer school to get a passing grade. "Gee, Scott," he said, "what a shame, and now you won't get an allowance, either, or have TV in your bedroom, or the use of the computer. But never mind, sonny boy," he said, "there'll be lots to do around the house. I'll leave lists for you every day of things to be done before I get home."

Mrs. Whitman whined, "I just don't have a thousand dollars. I don't know where I'll get so much money, either."

Sometimes I whined that way, and my mom would say, "Scotty, we wouldn't be so hard on you if you'd only take responsibility for your actions. We tell you to be in at eleven P.M. and you claim the bus was late. We ask you to take the tapes back to Videoland and you say we never said to do it. You always have an excuse for everything! You never blame yourself!"

"Mrs. Whitman? I don't mean to be hard on you but that's the deal, see. A thou in hundreds."

"Just don't hurt Gloria."

69

"Gee, what a shame that you have to worry about such a thing. She's a sweet little dog, and I know she misses you because she's not eating."

"She doesn't eat dog food, Bud. I cook for her."

"That's why she doesn't eat, hmm? I don't know how to cook."

"You could just put a frozen dinner in the microwave. A turkey dinner, or a Swanson's pot roast. I'll pay you for it."

"A thousand dollars plus ten for frozen dinners? Is that what you're suggesting?"

"Let me think. Please. I have to think how I can get the money."

"Of course you do. I'll call you back, Mrs. Whitman, and meanwhile I'll go to the store and get some Swanson's frozen dinners."

"When will you—"

I hung up.

I could hear Dad coming up the stairs.

"Scott?"

"Yes, sir?"

"I'm going to take the Saturn in for an oil change. I want you to come with me."

"I have some homework, sir."

"I want you to come with me. *Now.*"

———

In the car, he said, "We need to talk."

"About what?" I said.

There was one of her Lost Dog signs tacked to the telephone pole at the end of our street.

"We need to talk about this summer," he said.

"What about it?"

"You *have* to make up the math grade. That you *have* to do. I'm sorry you can't go to Yellowstone."

"Yeah."

"There's no other way if you want to get into any kind of college. Your other grades are fine. But you need math. . . . What's so hard about math, Scott?"

"I hate it!"

"I did, too, but I learned it. You have to study."

"Mrs. Whitman doesn't like me."

"Why doesn't she like you?"

"She doesn't like anyone but that bulldog."

"Who's lost, apparently."

"Yeah."

"The signs are everywhere."

"Yeah."

"But she wouldn't deliberately flunk you, would she?"

"Who knows?"

"Do you really think a teacher would flunk you because she doesn't like you?"

"Who knows?"

"Scott, you've got to admit when you're wrong. I'll give you an example. I was wrong when I said you couldn't have an allowance or TV or use of the computer, et cetera. I was angry and I just blew! That was wrong. It wouldn't have made it any easier for you while you're trying to get a passing grade in math. So I was wrong! I apologize and I take it back."

"How come?"

"How come? Because I'm sorry. I thought about it and it bothered me. I'm a hothead, and I don't like that about myself. Okay?"

"Yeah."

"Maybe that's what's wrong here."

"What's wrong where?"

"Between us."

"Is something wrong between us?"

"Scotty, I'm trying to talk with you. About us. I want to work things out so we get along better."

"Yeah."

"Sometimes I do or say rash things."

"Yeah."

"I always feel lousy after."

"Oh, yeah?"

"Do you understand? I shouldn't take things out on you. That's petty. Life is hard enough. We don't have to be mean and spiteful with each other. Agreed?"

"Yeah." I was thinking about the time our dog didn't come home one night. I couldn't sleep. I even prayed. When he got back all muddy the next morning, I broke into tears and told him, "Now you're making me blubber like a baby!"

Dad was still on my case.

"Scott, I want you to think about why Mrs. Whitman flunked you."

"I just told you: she doesn't like me."

"Are you really convinced that you're good at math but the reason you failed was because she doesn't like you?"

"Maybe."

"Is she a good teacher?"

"She never smiles. She's got these tight little lips and these ugly freckles."

"So she's not a good teacher?"

"I can't learn from her."

"Did you study hard?"

"I studied. Sure. I studied."

"How many others flunked math?"

"What?"

"How many others flunked math?"

"No one."

"Speak up."

"I said, I'm the only one."

"So others learn from her despite her tight little lips and ugly freckles?"

"I guess."

"Scott, who's to blame for your flunking math?"

"Okay," I said. "Okay."

"Who is to blame?"

"Me. Okay? I didn't study that hard."

He sighed and said, "There. Good. You've accepted the blame. . . . How do you feel?"

"I feel okay." I really didn't, though. I was thinking about that dumb bulldog running loose somewhere, and about Mrs. Whitman worried sick now that she thought Gloria'd been dognapped.

Dad said, "I think we both feel a lot better."

————————

We sat around in the waiting room at Saturn.

Dad read *Sports Illustrated,* but I couldn't concentrate on the magazines there or the ballgame on TV. I was down. I knew what Dad meant when he'd told me he felt bad after he "blew" and that he didn't like himself for it.

I kept glancing toward the pay phone. I stuck my hands in my pants pockets. I had a few quarters.

"I'm going to call Al and see what he's doing tonight," I said.

Dad said, "Wait until you get home. We'll be leaving here very shortly."

"I'm going to look around," I said.

I didn't know Mrs. Whitman's number. I'd copied it down from one of the Lost Dog signs and ripped it up after I'd called her. I hadn't planned to follow up the call, get money from her: nothing like that. I just wanted to give her a good scare.

I went over to the phone book and looked her up.

Then I ducked inside the phone booth, fed the slot a quarter, and dialed.

"Hello?"

"Mrs. Whitman? I don't have your dog. I was playing a joke."

"I know you don't have my dog. Gloria's home. The dog warden found her and brought her back right after you hung up on me."

I was relieved. At least she wouldn't have to go all night worrying about getting Gloria back.

"I was wrong," I said. "It was petty. I'm sorry."

"Do you know what you put me through, Scott Perkins?"

I just hung up.

I stood there with my face flaming.

"Scott?" My father was looking all over for me,

calling me and calling me. "Scott! Are you here? The car's ready!"

———

All the way home he lectured me on how contrary I was. Why couldn't I have waited to phone Al? What was it about me that made me just go ahead and do something I was expressly told I shouldn't do? "Just when I think we've gotten someplace," he said, "you turn around and go against my wishes.

*"Why?"* he shouted.

I said, "What?" I hadn't been concentrating on all that he was saying. I was thinking that now she knew my name—don't ask me how—and now what was she going to do about it?

"I asked you *why* you go against my wishes," Dad said. "Nothing I say seems to register with you."

"It registers with me," I said. "I just seem to screw up sometimes."

"I can hardly believe my ears." He was smiling. "You actually said sometimes you screw up. That's a new one."

"Yeah," I said. "That's a new one."

Then we both laughed, but I was still shaking, remembering Mrs. Whitman saying my name that way.

When we got in the house, Mom said, "The funniest thing happened while you were gone. The phone rang and this woman asked what number this was. I told her, and she asked whom she was speaking to. I told her and she said, 'Perkins . . . Perkins. Do you have a boy named Scott?' I said that we did, and she said, 'This is Martha

Whitman. Tell him I'll see him this summer. I'm teaching remedial math.' "

I figured that right after I'd hung up from calling her about Gloria, she'd dialed *69. I'd heard you could do that. The phone would ring whoever called you last. That was why she'd asked my mother what number it was and who was speaking.

Dad said, "You see, Scott, Mrs. Whitman doesn't dislike you, or she wouldn't have called here to tell you she'd see you this summer."

"I was wrong," I said. "Wrong again."

Oh, was I ever!

# M. E. Kerr

M. E. Kerr is one of several pen names belonging to Marijane Meaker, one of the foremost authors of books for teenage readers since the publication of her first young adult novel, *Dinky Hocker Shoots Smack!,* twenty-five years ago. In 1993 the American Library Association recognized her lifetime accomplishments by giving her the Margaret A. Edwards Award. She is also the recipient of the National Council of Teachers of English ALAN Award for outstanding contributions to young adult literature.

Among her earlier novels are *The Son of Someone Famous; If I Love You, Am I Trapped Forever?; Is That You, Miss Blue?; What I Really Think of You;* Him *She Loves?;* and *Little Little.* She is also the author of three teenage mystery-detective novels starring John Fell: *Fell, Fell Back,* and *Fell Down.* In addition, Kerr writes books for younger readers under the name Mary James; *Shoebag* and *Shoebag Returns* are two popular titles.

Kerr's *Gentlehands* and *Night Kites,* both American Library Association Best Books for Young Adults, remain two of her most notable publications, with *Gentlehands* being listed by the ALA as one of the 100 Best of the

Best Books for Young Adults published between 1967 and 1992.

More recently, Kerr's *Deliver Us from Evie* has gained a great deal of attention from readers as well as critics because of its sensitive and uncompromising examination of what happens to a farming family in Missouri when a flood threatens the family's security and word circulates about their daughter Evie's romance with a girl in town.

M. E. Kerr's most recent young adult novel is *Hello, I Lied,* a story about a famous rock star, a summer in the Hamptons (where Marijane Meaker lives), and a boy-girl romance.

Betsy knows very well what her boyfriend, Winston, wants. But she's not willing to give in. Maybe Patsy can help.

# Duet
## Ron Koertge

"Betsy, you've got to sleep with me. I'm going crazy."

There was this long silence at the other end of the line. Then she said, "Okay."

I couldn't believe my ears. "You mean it?"

"Right now. This instant. Drop everything and get over here."

I looked out my bedroom door, as if I could see down the hall, down the stairs to the dining room.

"But Mom's got dinner on the table."

"Well, then I guess you've missed your chance, haven't you?"

"Can't you wait until tonight?"

"And play second fiddle to a pork chop? No way."

We both just held the phones, my black one, her cream-colored one. Then I said, "You weren't really going to, were you?"

Another long silence. Finally, "No. And I'm sorry. I shouldn't tease you. I just get tired of being so serious about it all the time. And it's always the same: you want to, I don't."

"But why don't you? It's natural."

"I wish I could explain exactly why I won't have sex with you, but it's hard to put into words."

"Try."

Betsy was quiet for a little while. Finally she said, "I just like being intact. Maybe that's all there is to it."

"Are you ever going to want to?"

"I want to now. I just won't."

"But when? I'm eighteen. I'm at my sexual peak."

"I've never understood 'sexual peak.' It sounds like a tourist attraction: Don't Miss Sexual Peak, Turnoff Three Miles."

"It means I'm the sexiest I'll ever be. It's all downhill from here."

"That doesn't sound so bad. You can coast."

I switched the phone from one hand to the other. "Why am I so much in love with you, Betsy Lowell? You drive me crazy."

Betsy's voice dropped an octave. "I'm in love with you, too, Winston Miranda."

I knew she meant it, I knew she wasn't kidding me anymore. Or indulging me. Or parrying my advances. Or humoring me.

I said that I was sorry to be such a pain about sex and everything. "You're so much more mature than I am."

"It's the beard." She waited for me to laugh, and I

did. "Plus," she added, "girls are just different from boys. My mom says teenage boys can't help themselves."

I stood up. "You told your mom I wanted to sleep with you?"

"I didn't say it that way, not 'Winston Miranda wants to sleep with me.' I said that a friend of mine has this boyfriend named Dunston Banana who wants to sleep with her. Wasn't that clever?"

"What did you really say?"

"Nothing specific. Mom and I just talk sometimes. About all kinds of things. Sex, too."

"My dad asked me if I was in love with you. When I said yes, he gave me some condoms."

"Is that why you want to sleep with me, because you're in love?"

"Sure. But partly, you're just, you know, desirable."

"Gee, what a nice word."

"God, everywhere we go guys check you out. Married guys, too."

"I like it that you don't get jealous. A lot of boys go ballistic when other guys look at their girlfriends."

"Well, at least I do something right."

Betsy sounded thoughtful when she asked, "Winston, could you make love to a desirable girl you weren't in love with?"

"At the moment I could probably make love to a pork chop, the one you wouldn't play second fiddle to."

"I'm serious."

She was, too. I could tell by her voice. Most people's voices tell a lot, but Betsy was a singer, so her voice was extra sensitive.

"Winston?"

"I'm here, I'm here. You want to know if I could make love to a desirable girl I wasn't in love with."

"Right."

"Is this one of those trick questions?"

"No. Just tell the truth."

I took a deep breath. "Probably. Okay, probably."

"And you wouldn't fall in love with her while you were doing it?"

"I don't think it works that way."

"It's just physical, right? Like sneezing."

"Except that I'm pretty sure you don't say 'God bless you' afterwards."

"I just mean that it's a physical release, don't you think? Not necessarily emotional."

"Probably, yeah."

"So you could do it."

"How did we get on this subject?"

"Well, I was just thinking that what you want is perfectly normal, and it's a shame that you can't have it."

"So?"

"So why don't we find somebody for you to do it with?"

"Did I dial one of those 900 numbers by mistake? What are you talking about?"

"Winston, it makes sense. Not everybody is like me. There's lots of girls who do it."

"Lots? What high school have I been going to?"

"Some. A few. You know who they are."

"I don't either."

"Oh, you do too. All boys know. Marcia DeMonbrey, right?"

"How do you know about Marcia DeMonbrey?"

"What do you think girls talk about?"

"Homework, where to go college next year, graduation . . ."

"And which girls do it. But I don't want you to sleep with Marcia. She's careless."

"She is?"

"Trust me. Name somebody else."

"No way."

"Are you afraid you'll hurt my feelings?"

"Maybe, yeah. Wouldn't you think that I wanted her as much as I want you?"

"But you don't love her. You just want her. It's transitory, right? Lust is transitory."

"I guess."

"So name somebody else."

I looked around my room. There were just enough kid things to make me feel weird. My model cars seemed to frown at me.

"Winston?"

"Rose McQueen," I blurted. "Okay?"

Betsy sounded disappointed. "Oh, Winston. Rose McQueen copied from me once."

"So? You're smart."

"We were filling out applications. She copied my weight. Try somebody else."

"No."

"Please. Just one more."

"Loraine Wilson."

'No, she smells her fingers."

"What? What does that mean?"

"I don't know, but it's not a good sign. Let me think."

I could hear her fingernails tap on the plastic receiver. "Could you do it with Patsy?"

"Patsy Soto? She's your best friend."

"Could you?"

"Patsy's rich and popular. Patsy could get any guy she wants. Why would she bother with me?"

"So the answer is yes?"

"No. I mean, yes. I mean I don't know."

"I'll bet Patsy would sleep with you if I asked her. Like a favor, you know?"

"A favor is when you borrow her car, not lend her your boyfriend. Don't ask her anything."

"You ask her then."

"Are you kidding? Patsy intimidates me."

"But she's interested in sex, too. Like you are."

"Forget it. Forget we ever had this conversation. It's too stupid. I'm sorry I started this. I'll never talk about sex again, okay? I promise. I have to go now. I have to eat dinner."

"Say hello to the pork chop—my rival."

———

Two nights later I walked toward Patsy Soto's front door. Her house—her parents' house—was huge, with a wide curving driveway covered with gravel so white it looked as if somebody washed it.

I stood on the front porch and looked around. I couldn't believe this was happening. Not to me, anyway. Not in Bradleyville, Missouri. I half expected a bunch of kids to come piling out of the bushes and throw cold water on me. A big joke, right? A prank.

Just then the door opened, and I jumped.

"Hi," said Patsy. "I thought I heard somebody. What are you standing out here for?" She grinned at me. "We're not going to do it on the welcome mat, are we?"

"I was just thinking."

She stepped aside; I went in. "What were you thinking about?" she asked. "My luscious body?"

I blushed. "God, Patsy."

She darted ahead, vaulted a low couch, then surfaced slowly, like a seal. I saw her close-cropped black hair first, then her green eyes. "Come into my parlor."

"I'm not a fly."

"But you've got a fly."

I didn't know where to look. "Everything you say makes me blush."

"I'll stop." She sat up straight. "I'm nervous, too."

"Really?"

"Sure. I don't do this all the time." She looked over one shoulder. "You know that, don't you? I don't do this all the time."

"I never said you did."

"Want something to drink?" She pointed to a little cart on wheels, right beside the spotless fireplace. "My dad's got every kind of booze in the world."

"Uh, no thanks. I've got my dad's car."

She fiddled with a heavy glass and some clumsy-looking silver ice tongs. A cube got away and arced onto the carpet, so she leaned to retrieve it. Her jeans were really tight. She was barefoot. I took a deep breath.

Down went the glass with a thump. She popped opened a can of Diet Coke. "Did Ricky say I slept with him?" she demanded.

"Huh? No, Ricky didn't say anything to me. I'm not exactly in that cliquey jock—"

"But you heard he said I did?"

I looked down at my shoes. "Yeah."

"That's a lie."

"Okay."

She took a step toward me. "Winston, I didn't."

"Okay, okay. It doesn't matter."

"It does to me. I don't like boys who brag. You'd never tell anybody."

"About this? No. Never."

Patsy relaxed a little. She pushed up the sleeves of her white blouse. "You look nice."

"You too."

"Did you get dressed up?"

"Sort of. These are the pants I wear to church."

"I'm flattered."

"I hope they don't catch on fire next Sunday."

Patsy laughed. "Betsy's right. You are sweet."

"I wonder. If I'm so sweet, what am I doing . . ."

She finished for me. "Here with me?"

"I didn't mean it like that."

"Sweet people have sex, Winston."

"I know, I know."

"And anyway, we're not doing anything."

"Maybe not, but I'm thinking things."

"Honest?"

"Are you kidding? Yeah. You're really good-looking."

She clapped her hands. "Well, all right." She patted the cushion beside her. "Come and sit down."

I slipped in beside her and stared at the giant fireplace. It was made of huge slabs of slate laid on top of each other like a rich kid's science project, a kid who'd just gone out and bought some geology.

She smiled and tucked one foot under her. Her toes were unbelievably pink and clean.

"We don't have to do anything, Winston, but it looks like we're very compatible."

"It does?"

"Sure. We both want to do what we want to do."

"Why do you want to?" I blurted.

Her right hand floated off the back of the couch and landed on my shoulder. "I don't have low self-esteem, okay? And I'm not some hands-on activity center for every libido with a driver's license.

"But probably when I go to college and for sure when I get my own place, I want to make love to whomever I want as often as I want." She reached for my chin and pulled my face toward hers. "Does that shock you?"

"Not as much as your using *whomever* correctly. Nobody does that."

Patsy laughed out loud. "See, you're the kind of man I want to be with. You're not going to bore me to death afterwards. You're not going to spill pathos on me or call some song 'ours.' I mean, I want to spend a lot of time by myself, but when I want sex I want it to be with interesting men like you." She licked her lips. "My motto's going to be Passion and Solitude."

I sat back. "Wow."

"What?"

"I just never heard a girl talk like this before, that's all."

She reached for my hand. "Remember in English class when we read *A Room of One's Own*?"

"Yeah, but I don't think Virginia Woolf had so many guys in her room."

" 'Of one's own,' " she said deliberately. "Where one can do what one wants. And if that includes interesting men from time to time, so be it."

"I don't feel all that interesting. You've always been way out of my league. You've got a convertible, for God's sake. You're going to Berkeley."

"Winston, you're interesting now because you're honest and because you're nervous and not afraid to admit it. You're interesting when you're witty. And you like Betsy; that automatically makes you interesting."

"I don't just like Betsy, I love her."

She scooted closer. "I know you do. That's why you're perfect. That's why *we're* perfect: you just want sex, I just want sex."

"Is that all you want? Really?"

She flashed me a really wicked grin. "Specifically, yes. But in general I want to disturb the peace. If you know what I mean."

I rubbed my face with both hands, like I'd just dived into the deep end. "You're really something."

She scooted closer. "You know how on *Oprah* they'll have these gays or lesbians on, and they'll always say, 'I knew who I was since I was eleven'? Well, I know who I am, too. And I don't want to deny it, either."

"You're a lesbian?"

She laughed and showed me her perfect teeth. "No, I'm an iconoclast. I don't feel like the other people; I don't believe in what they believe in. Maybe what they want isn't bad, but for me it's not remarkable enough." Patsy opened her arms to me, to the room, to everything. "And God knows I want to be remarkable. And that includes in bed."

"But aren't you afraid of, you know, catching something from somebody?"

She shook her head. "So far they've all been virgins. Like you."

"All?"

She held up two fingers. "And we used latex condoms. Just like we're going to use latex condoms."

"But how about later, when you're older and professionally remarkable and stuff?"

She frowned. "I know about AIDS and STDs and all that. And I know things are risky. But if you're careful and if you know whom to ask and then once their pants are down if you know what to look for . . ."

"What to look for?" I sat up straight. "Are you serious?"

"Hey, I went into St. Louis to the Free Clinic and talked to a nurse. She showed me some photographs."

How romantic. I tried to imagine Cathy checking out Heathcliff in the heather. I tried to imagine Juliet:

*Romeo, dear, let's leave nothing to chance.*
*I need to take just a peek in your pants.*

"You don't have to wait until you're older to be remarkable," I said. "In my book, you're already there."

"So is that like a proposal? Do you want to go in the bedroom? My folks are at the opera in Forest Park. Everything's cool."

I almost stood up, then asked instead, "Why do you think Betsy arranged this?"

"You don't know?" She took a sip of her Coke. "She's afraid of losing you, Winston. She's afraid you'll find another girl."

"I don't want another girl."

"Good. 'Cause if you start running around with Marcia or Rose, I'll personally break your kneecaps with a baseball bat."

I looked over at her. She seemed like she meant it. "Were you, like, jealous or mad or anything when Betsy and I started to go together? 'Cause I knew you guys were tight and I told Betsy that we could double-date or just the three of us could go somewhere, but . . ."

Patsy toyed with the top button of her blouse until it came undone. "I was mad for a while. We never let boys mean all that much to us. Ever. Then we got together again and all she talked about was you, and I was glad for her, you know?"

"Yeah. Well, I know this isn't some revenge thing."

"Like what? I pick you up at the ARCO station, bring you back here, make love to you, then tell her? No way. Since Betsy set this up, I'd file it under Irony." She fooled with my hair. She leaned closer. A lot closer. "Let's kiss, okay? I'm kind of a connoisseur of kisses."

I swallowed hard. "Okay."

Patsy took my hands out of my lap and put them on her shoulders. "C'mon, you know how to do this."

Patsy put the tip of her tongue in my mouth.

"Oh, man," she said. "You've got such soft lips. Betsy said you were this ace kisser."

"She told you that?"

"Talk later, kiss now."

This time it lasted longer, and it was wetter. Patsy, still locked to me, crawled onto my lap, straddled me. She held my hair like reins.

We just did that for a while. A lot of that. But just that. Finally Patsy dismounted and tugged at me. "C'mon."

"Patsy," I panted. "I can't."

"You could've fooled me."

"I mean *I* can't. I don't feel like I did before."

"You don't feel sexy?"

"We talked too much. About Betsy. I thought it was just going to be . . . I don't know what I thought it was just going to be. I sure didn't think it would matter. But it does matter, doesn't it? To me, anyway."

"Winston, it's just pleasure. It's two consenting adults in the dark. . . ."

"I'm sorry, Patsy. Honest."

She dropped onto the couch. She said, *"Whoosh,"* and ran both hands through her hair. "I can't believe it," she said. "I can't remember the last time a guy turned me down for anything."

"I didn't turn you down, Patsy. I turned *it* down."

We both just sat there for a minute or two, though *sat* sounds too prim. Sprawled is more like it. Like we'd been tossed ashore after a storm at sea. Wreckage.

All of a sudden she sat up and buttoned her blouse. "Are you going to go by Betsy's now?" She sounded cool and professional.

"I guess."

"You should. She's probably waiting for you." She got to her feet and angled toward the door. "C'mon."

I fell in beside her. "I don't blame you for being mad."

"I'm not mad," she snapped. "I'm just testing my reliance, okay?" Betsy stopped, rolled down the sleeves of her white blouse, and buttoned the cuffs. "I'm just going to think of this as a learning experience. It's probably going to happen to me when I've got that room of my own, right?"

"Probably not. No guy in his right mind would turn you down."

She opened the heavy door. "What are you going to tell Betsy?"

"The truth."

"Yeah, but . . . I mean—all of it?" She cocked her head. "Even how nice the kissing was?"

"Is she going to ask that?"

"You can tell her you didn't like it if you want to. I'll back you up."

I shook my head. "I don't want to lie to Betsy."

"And I don't want her to be hurt. Kissing's important to girls. It's all we do for, like, years."

I looked toward the driveway, curved like a lucky horseshoe.

"I'd better go," I said. "Thanks for everything."

"Hey, this wasn't a study group; we can't start shaking hands now. Kiss me again."

I liked kissing Patsy, I admit it. But it felt funny. Or I felt funny about it. When she didn't end it, I did. I pulled back. Like girls do. *That* felt funny.

I drove toward Betsy's house, then just sat in the car for a few minutes. It was barely ten o'clock on Friday. I wondered if she'd watched *X-Files* without me.

A lot of lights were on, but her parents' Taurus

wasn't in the driveway. When I got out of the car, some man walking his dog kept glancing at me: Neighborhood Watch, probably. Well, I wasn't guilty, okay?

When I got to the door, I could hear she was working on some music. It was probably Bach; Betsy was into that serious stuff. So I waited until she finished. Then I knocked.

"Who is it?"

"Winston."

I heard the dead bolt slide free. She stood in the open door; the light behind her lit up her hair. She wiped her hands on her pants.

"You don't look different," she said.

"I'm not. Nothing happened."

"Really?"

"Not what we, you know, planned."

"Was Patsy . . ."

"Patsy's fine. I just . . . We just . . . Nothing happened."

"So you're still . . ."

"Intact, yeah."

"Didn't you want to?"

"Sure, but I didn't."

She glanced down at her gray sweats. "I didn't know if you'd come over afterwards. I didn't know how long it'd take. So I didn't . . . So I don't look . . ."

"You look great."

Betsy leaned toward me. "You smell like Patsy."

"We sat beside each other on the couch."

"Is that all?"

"No. It wasn't a discussion, you know. So we kissed."

Betsy stepped back. "You kissed her?"

"What was I supposed to do, just rush in there and—"

"Was she a good kisser? Did you like it?" Both her hands flew up. "Don't tell me. I don't want to know."

"Look, can I come in?"

"Sure. Sorry." She stepped back, sort of flattening herself against the door like I was carrying something big.

I knew the inside of her house as well as I knew my own: her mother's Southwestern paintings on the walls, a barrel cactus in a red pot, the couch with its worn arms, the dining room table always covered with escrow papers and letters from banks and her father's real estate stuff.

"Did you like it?" she blurted. "Kissing her, I mean?"

I looked down, too. We both studied the carpet.

"Sure," I said, sounding edgy.

"Well, don't get mad. You're not the one who should be mad here, you know."

"Well, God, Betsy. I thought you'd be glad that Patsy and I didn't have sex. I thought you'd be relieved or happy or flattered or something. Instead, I get the third degree. What would you have done if I'd nailed her?"

She grimaced. "I hate that phrase."

"This was your idea, remember?"

Her lower lip started to quiver. "I wanted you to be . . . I don't know—happy, I guess. Not so discontented. I thought I had the answer. Obviously, I didn't. All I knew was that for all the things we have in common, what we do with our bodies isn't one of them."

I walked over to the piano, the one her parents had saved for, then surprised her with two years ago. I ran my hands over its smooth surface. I straightened some sheet music.

"We're not that different," I said finally. "Neither one of us is willing to take that one big step yet. Not with each other, not with other people."

"Why didn't you with Patsy?"

I shook my head. "It wasn't like it was going to be a sin or anything. I just couldn't stop thinking about you, so it seemed, I don't know, inconsiderate. Anyway, it sure wasn't as easy as I thought it was going to be."

"Because of Patsy?"

"No, she was fine. It was me."

"And was Patsy okay with that?"

I nodded. "Patsy's deep. I never met anybody who thought like her before."

"And even though she was deep and interesting and has bigger boobs than me and is a great kisser you still didn't do anything?"

"Right."

She grinned for the first time since I'd got there. "You aren't supposed to say 'Right.' You're supposed to say 'Oh, she wasn't all that interesting.' "

"Okay: Patsy's kind of dull and she wears a Wonder Bra and she'd be a better kisser if she wasn't addicted to those garlic pizzas."

Betsy put her arms around me. "Winston, I was so worried."

"It's okay now."

"I thought you might love it. Not even her, just it. And you'd want to keep doing it and doing it."

"Only stopping long enough to send out for Chinese food and condoms?"

"Oh, I don't know. It was a stupid idea. I was stupid."

"I was stupid, too. And you know what that means, don't you? Now we can't get married because our children will have embarrassingly low SATs." I put my arms around her tighter.

"I'm afraid to kiss you. I'm afraid I won't be as good as Patsy."

"Let's try."

It was great. Naturally. Like it always was. But different, too. Sweeter, maybe. Deeper somehow.

Betsy put her forehead against mine. "I'm as sexy as Patsy," she said. "Just wait and see."

"I'll wait as long as you want."

"Good." Then she put her mouth next to my ear. On my ear. "While you're waiting, do you want some juice?"

"Man, if Patsy had asked me like that, I'd still be over there."

While she was in the kitchen, I looked at some music on the piano. I could see her standing at the counter. "What are you working on?" I asked.

"It's a piece for the concert just before graduation. A duet." Betsy stopped in the kitchen door. "And I like duets." She smiled and held out the apple juice. "Just me and one other person."

# Ron Koertge

Ron Koertge is known for humorous, lively novels that explore the problems with sexuality and identity of usually insecure teenage boys, much like Winston in "Duet." In high school, Koertge says, "I knew a very aggressive girl—which was pretty rare in the fifties, by the way. She was very bright and independent, and she scared me." That experience, coupled with his belief that if you are writing about teenagers, "writing about sex seems inevitable," resulted in this amusing and realistic story.

Five of Koertge's first six novels for young adults were named Best Books for Young Adults by the American Library Association; *The Arizona Kid* was identified as one of the 100 Best of the Best Books for Young Adults published between 1967 and 1992. In that novel, sixteen-year-old Billy Kennedy spends the summer with his gay uncle in Tucson, Arizona, working at a racetrack, where he meets and falls painfully in love with ornery and exciting Cara Mae.

Romance and insecurity also play crucial roles in *Where the Kissing Never Stops* and *The Boy in the Moon*. *Mariposa Blues,* like *The Arizona Kid,* involves a racetrack but concerns a thirteen-year-old boy's confrontational relationship with his father. And *The Harmony Arms* examines a fourteen-year-old boy's relationship with a number of oddball characters in Los Angeles, including a ninety-year-old nudist vegetarian and a girl the boy's age with a camcorder for keeping a record of her life as it happens.

*Tiger, Tiger Burning Bright* is Koertge's most highly praised novel; it has earned a number of awards, including being honored as an ALA Best Book for Young Adults, a *Bulletin of the Center for Children's Books* Blue Ribbon Book, a Bank Street Child Study Children's Book Committee Children's Book of the Year, and a Judy Lopez Memorial Award Honor Book. Koertge's most recent novel for teenagers, called *Confess-O-Rama,* deals with the alternative-art scene in Los Angeles and features the spunkiest girl Ron Koertge says he has ever invented.

Jim and his buddies are tired of watching the gangs in their neighborhood get away with their violent behavior. It's time they did something about it.

# Confession
## Gloria D. Miklowitz

*POLICE REPORT:* THE FOLLOWING IS THE STATEMENT OF THIRTEEN-YEAR-OLD JIM JAMES, KNOWN AS JJ, IN THE SHOOTING OF SAMBOY PARKS AT FIFTH AND ELM, SAN GABRIEL, APRIL 10. JAMES AND THREE OTHER MEMBERS OF THE PROTECTORS GANG HAVE BEEN REMANDED TO JUVENILE HALL TO AWAIT HEARING ON APRIL 17.

---

Why'd we form the Protectors? You gotta ask? I mean, what about the graffiti? What about the gangs? What about the drugs in school and nobody cares shit about it? Christ, you can't go to the john without risking your life! You gotta ask?

Danny started the club last year when we began seventh grade. Just after his sister got raped right in their building. They never caught the guys who did it, either, though we had our suspicions. That was when I made up my mind. Nobody gonna do that to Lacey, my kid sister. Not if I could help it.

Danny got us together. That's me—JJ, Carlos, and Bruno. We been friends since second grade. Danny says, "What we gonna do about the hood? Stand around and let the gangs take over?"

"What *can* we do?" Bruno asked. "We're just four kids. They got guns. They got big numbers."

"Yeah," Carlos added. "They got *power,* man!"

Danny's been itching for revenge ever since what happened to his sister. I couldn't blame him. I knew he had something in mind and if I waited, he'd come out with it. And he did. "I say we fight back. We form our own gang. But not like theirs. We be the Protectors!" he said.

"Cool!" Carlos agreed right off. I think he was dreaming of a fancy club jacket in red and gold, something to make him look big and important.

"Way to go!" Bruno added, always ready to agree with whatever Danny said.

"JJ?"

"I don't know," I said. "Yeah, we need protection, but what about the cops? That's their job."

"Like much good *they* do!"

"What'd we do? Carry chains and knives and guns? We gonna be the law?"

"You chicken?"

"Hell, no!" My face got hot when the guys glared at me like I didn't belong.

"So what's your problem?"

"Guns," I said. "I don't like them. How we gonna fight back when all the gangs use them? Besides, the hood's got enough guns without us."

"Did I say we'd use guns?" Danny tapped his forehead. "We gonna use the gray stuff. We gonna *persuade* and *negotiate*. That's how we gonna deal with our problems."

Didn't make sense to me. I thought about the kids dealing drugs at school. About the locker thieves and the risks you took going to the toilet alone. *Persuade* and *negotiate* with guys like that? Come *on*!

"We won't use weapons," Danny promised. "We'll use other methods. Satisfied?"

Bruno and Carlos waited for me to answer. "Yeah, I guess," I said, shrugging. "But no guns!"

————————

"Where you going?" Lacey asked, running after me to the door. I'd come home from school just long enough to check that she was safe. And long enough to bag the paper and matches Danny asked us to bring.

"Out. And you can't come. Lock up behind me."

"I'm coming!" Lacey grabbed my arm and her eyes got big with hope. She spends a lot of time alone, watching TV after school. Going out's a treat. Suddenly she noticed the bag.

"What're you hiding?" She danced around, trying to grab the bag from behind my back. "JJ! You selling dope? I'm gonna tell!" she cried.

"I'm not dealing dope!"

"So, what's in the bag?"

"Nothing!"

"You're lying!"

Feeling cocky about what I was about to do and

mad that she thought I could be a dealer, I said, "All *right!*" and told her about the Protectors. It was dumb because it was boasting and I knew it. If it ever got out who the Protectors were, we'd be in bad trouble. Not just with the cops, either.

I took Lacey by the shoulders and squinted at her real mean. "Now listen good! What I just said is a secret, hear? You can't tell a soul, not a soul!"

Lacey stared at me like I was God. "I wouldn't, JJ. You know I wouldn't tell!" she promised. "Cross my heart."

———

The first job we planned was against Rolf Steiner and his Eastside gang druggies at school. I met Danny and the guys at the back door to the gym. Bruno had a key. He didn't say how he got it.

We slid into the building and headed for the lockers. I could hear the band practicing in the auditorium and my heart flipped in my throat. I felt like a SWAT team guy must feel just before doing something dangerous.

Halfway to the lockers we heard the security guard coming. Danny motioned and we ducked into the rest room. We each took a stall and crouched on the toilet lid so our legs wouldn't show. The guard came in, whistling. I could hear him pee in the stall next to mine and jammed a hand over my mouth to hold back the giggles.

We'd agreed in advance on the targets—three lockers. The lockers belonged to guys in the Eastside gang, guys you didn't mess with. They came to school mostly to do business. And their business was selling drugs. Sometimes you'd see one or another in class, sitting in back with arms folded over long-sleeved khaki shirts no matter what the weather. He'd be half-stoned and chewing gum and no one, not even the teacher, called him on it. Not since Mr. Hyde got beat up on his way home from school and not since Mrs. Ramos went to the hospital when five guys cornered her and did things she wouldn't talk about for fear of worse.

It made sense, going after thugs like that. We saw ourselves as vigilantes. We weren't out for blood. We just wanted to persuade the Eastsiders to move their business elsewhere. Out of our school, at least. That's how we thought.

Danny stood watch and each of us took a locker, one we knew belonged to a gang member. I laid my bag on the ground and drew out the paper. I slid sheets into the cracks under and around the locker so the door looked like it wore a ruffle. Down from me I saw Bruno and Carlos struggling to slide their papers in place, too. Then I pulled out the matches. I could imagine all the stuff inside the locker, the smelly sneakers and gym clothes, the battered books, candy wrappers, bags of rock cocaine, the pills, the grass. And I felt good.

Danny came to my side. "Ready?"

"Yeah!"

"Go!"

He pulled a lighter from a pocket and lit one sheet of paper, then moved to Carlos's locker, then Bruno's. "Symbolic," he said. "This way I'm responsible, too." As he went down the line I lit the rest of the pages around my locker. The white sheets crisped into dark brown smoking curls real fast and the fire spread inside. Pretty soon you smelled burning trash and chemicals.

"Way to go!" Carlos whispered, raising a fist in triumph.

"Should we maybe leave a message?" Bruno asked.

"JJ?"

"Hell, no. I think we should get the F outta here, fast!" I said. "Don't leave anything to tie this to us." I grabbed my empty sack and tossed it.

"He's right, guys, let's go!" Danny said.

We turned around and raced down the halls to the back door. I was proud. We hadn't used weapons. Score one for *persuasion.*

––––––––

It was all over school next day. Rolf and his gang put out word that whoever torched their lockers was dead meat. The cops came and asked questions. Mr. Adler, the principal, held the usual meeting in the auditorium. "I will not tolerate vandalism in this school!" he shouted. Like always.

"But he'll tolerate drugs," Danny whispered.

"Yeah," Bruno echoed.

"If anyone knows who's responsible for this latest crime, come forward. Your identity will be protected!" Adler said.

"Maybe we should start a rumor that it was the Pitbulls who did it," I whispered. The Pitbulls got their kicks from spray-painting walls, setting fires in wastebaskets. Like that. They were our next target. It tickled me to think we could maybe sic one gang on the other. Let them wipe each other out.

"Yeah," Danny said, but he knew I was kidding.

We laid low for a week, acting innocent and listening to the rumors. Drug sales were off, probably because the supply burned. Rolf and the Eastsiders were pretty desperate. (Their suppliers were pressing for payback.) They suspected every kid who looked their way. They pressured those who owed them and rumors spread.

For a while I worried. What if Lacey bragged to a friend about me? And the friend told another friend and so on until it got back to Rolf? But as the week passed and nothing happened I relaxed and we started plans for our next action.

We decided to hit the Pitbulls. Give them a little of their own medicine so they'd know how it feels when their own property got trashed.

I liked the idea. We'd go after their wheels, what they valued most. In a way it was less dangerous than the locker raid. No matches, knives, chains, or guns. The only stuff we'd need was screwdrivers and spray paint.

We planned it for a Saturday night. That's when the Bulls partied at one of their girls' houses. We could find out which house and do our job while they were partying, after midnight.

"This is going to be *so* easy!" Carlos chirped. He rubbed his hands together and his round face beamed.

"They'll be *so* smashed, they'll never know what hit them," Bruno said. "Not till they head home!"

"What about the cops?" I asked. "They patrol pretty heavy that part of town."

"Always worrying about the cops," Danny said, frowning. "Tell you what. We'll time them and do our stuff *after* they pass, okay?"

"Okay," I agreed.

Since the locker fire Lacey knew everything that was going on. "What if the Eastsiders think the Pitbulls did their lockers?" she asked when I told her our new plans. She watched me closely, expecting I'd put her down.

"Why would they think that?"

"The Pitbulls might want to take over their business?"

She had a point. If the Eastsiders didn't trust the Bulls, what better place to get them all than at one of their Saturday-night parties?

"What about that?" I asked Danny, not admitting Lacey came up with the idea. "What if we run into the Eastsiders Saturday night?"

Danny thought a moment, then said, "Not to worry. We'll scout the place first. If it checks out, shouldn't take more than a few minutes and we're gone." He patted his jeans pocket like he forgot something.

I got a tingling down my arms and legs. "No weapons, *right*?" I eyed his pocket.

"If you say so," Danny smiled, innocent-like. "But it's dumb not to be prepared."

I knew all along that Danny's plan to negotiate and persuade would mean action, not words. But as long as it didn't involve weapons, as long as no one got hurt, I could go with it. What we were doing wasn't right, sure, but we meant good. And our crimes were not bad like the things the gangs did.

The end justifies the means, doesn't it?

Saturday night I slipped out of the house after Mom and Pop were asleep. I wore a dark T-shirt and jeans. I had to go to the bathroom a half dozen times before leaving. Danny had "borrowed" his dad's Chevy, which was falling apart and as old as he was, thirteen. He was wearing an open flannel shirt, which he kept pulling down over a green T, like he was trying to hide his belly.

"Scared?" he asked when I climbed in. He handed me a ski mask and we drove off to pick up the guys.

"Yeah, I'm scared. You?"

"A little. Bring your paint and screwdriver?"

I held up the can. "Mine's red. What's yours?"

"Green. Merry Christmas!"

"Where is it?" I asked, pulling the mask over my head.

He nodded at the floor near my feet. "In that."

I pushed a paper bag with my shoe. It hardly moved. Sweat ran down my neck suddenly. "What's in it? Rocks?" I tried to sound lighthearted.

"The spray can and a couple *extra* things." Danny slowed at a corner and Carlos and Bruno jumped in. They started nervously babbling, both at once.

"*What* extra things?" I asked.

"Don't worry."

"I worry. Like what? A gun?"

"Yeah, a gun, but I'm not gonna use it; you know that. It's not even loaded. It's just to scare them, in case we're cornered."

"Stop the car. I'm getting out."

The talk in back stopped. "You can't quit now!" Carlos said.

"He's not leaving," Danny said. We were approaching the street where the party was going on. "Calm down, JJ. You know me. I just brought it to persuade."

"You promised," I said, voice squeaking. "You *promised*!" Cars were parked bumper-to-bumper in front of the brightly lit house. I saw shadows through the curtains in the living room, kids moving around, dancing.

"Now we park, kill the lights, and wait, right, Danny?" Bruno asked. "Until the squad car goes by?"

I opened the door to get out, ready to walk home the three miles, when Carlos gripped my shoulder. "Don't chicken out on us, JJ," he said. "We're in this together. We need you."

"I swear to God I won't use the gun!" Danny grabbed my arm. "See?" He bent and pulled the gun from the bag, opened the glove compartment, and shoved it in. "See? Satisfied? Okay?"

It wasn't okay. I didn't like what I'd got into but couldn't back out or I'd lose my best friends. I sat back in my seat, arms crossed over my chest, and stared out the window at the bungalow houses and garbage cans lined up for Monday pickup. I got more and more anxious with each minute. Finally, a patrol car came down the street, moving slow. It stopped in front of the party house, then drove on.

"Let's go!" Danny opened the driver's side door and leaped out. The rest of us followed. "We work together. I know the cars. Let's get at it!"

I felt a huge rush, even more than when we burned the lockers. Maybe because so much could go wrong. Someone could come out of the house and catch us. The Eastsiders could show up and figure things out. The cops could swing by sooner than we expected.

We worked fast, hardly talking. Every now and then I could hear music coming from the house, or loud voices. We spray-painted the motorcycles and six cars and punctured their tires. On back of the last car I wrote, "Clean up the hood or we'll be back."

"Now, wasn't that easy?" Danny asked as we hurried back to his dad's car. "And we did it all peaceful. No knives, chains, or guns, just like you wanted, JJ."

"Hey!" someone suddenly shouted from near the house. Two guys ran down the street toward us. "Hey! What're you guys up to?"

My mouth went dry and my heart nearly stopped as I yanked the car door open.

"Oh, man!" Carlos cried. "Samboy!"

Danny swung into the driver's seat, locked his door, and fumbled with the ignition key. Before he could start the car Samboy and his gang surrounded us. One guy jumped on the roof and peered in at us through the windshield. Another pounded the door with a metal rod until the glass cracked.

The noise brought a lot of the kids out of the house and lights went on all over the block.

"Get out!" Samboy ordered, peering in at us, though he really couldn't tell who we were with the masks on.

"Hey, Samboy!" someone called. "They totaled your wheels!"

Samboy swung around and grabbed a crowbar from someone. "We're gonna whup the shit outta you scumbags! Out!"

Carlos started to cry.

Bruno sounded like he was having an asthma attack.

I was so scared I nearly wet my pants. I prayed the patrol car would come by. Right now!

"Open up, shithead!" Samboy pounded on the car window with a fist, then raised the crowbar like he was ready to strike.

Danny kept trying to start the car. I gritted my teeth. If only we could get going, the guy on the roof would fall off and we'd be outta there, safe. Until school, anyway. But Danny couldn't get in gear and we kept stalling.

Samboy swung at the window. It cracked into a thousand pieces.

"Shit!" Danny screamed. From his waistband under his flannel shirt he pulled something dark. I froze.

"No!" I screamed, and tried to grab the gun away from him.

Danny stabbed me with an elbow. "Shut up! Get the other one. In the glove compartment!"

"No!" I scrunched down in my seat like I could disappear. *He promised! I believed him! I should have known! I must have known!*

Danny rolled his window down and pointed the gun with both hands at Samboy. "Back off!" he screamed. "Back off or I'll shoot!" His hands shook and his voice went shrill.

Samboy laughed. "You ain't got the guts!"

"Danny, don't do it! Don't!" I cried, trying to grab his arm.

"Back off, or I'll shoot!" he screamed again, nudging me away. He made a strangled cry.

"I dare you!" Samboy said.

That's when the gun went off. I heard this awful roar. Danny sobbed. Carlos screamed. Bruno choked. Blood splattered all over me. All over my face and shirt!

And that's it. There's no more to say. That's the whole story. We didn't mean to hurt anyone, honest. We just wanted to make the hood better, safer.

Honest. I'm sorry.

# Gloria D. Miklowitz

Gloria D. Miklowitz has dealt with serious problems of teenagers in most of the more than two dozen published books she has written for young adults. She examines the effects of divorce in *A Time to Hurt, a Time to Heal,* teenage pregnancy in *Unwed Mother,* life on the streets in *Runaway,* rape in *Did You Hear What Happened to Andrea?,* steroid use in *Anything to Win,* suicide in *Close to the Edge,* religious cults in *The Love Bombers,* child abuse in *Secrets Not Meant to Be Kept,* racial discrimination in *The War Between the Classes,* AIDS in *Goodbye Tomorrow,* teenage marriage in *The Day the Senior Class Got Married,* vigilantism in *The Emerson High Vigilantes,* murder in *The Killing Boy,* and nuclear devastation in *After the Bomb* and *After the Bomb—Week One.* She has received a number of awards for her work, including the Western Australia Young Readers' Award for *Did You Hear What Happened to Andrea?,* the British Bucks Herald Publisher's Award for Top Teen Fiction for *Secrets Not Meant to Be Kept,* and the Wyoming Soaring Eagle Award for *Desperate Pursuit.* Three of her books have also been made into award-winning after-school television specials.

Miklowitz's extensively researched stories have led her on a number of adventures, including a trip to the Amazon with forty seventh-graders from Michigan, during which she showered with river water, slept on a floor mattress with netting overhead, and climbed by rope into the rain forest canopy. Newspaper stories about gang violence prompted her to write "Confession." "I've always been curious about taking the law into one's own hands," she says. "Is it ever justified? Can it backfire?"

Her most recent novels are *Past Forgiving,* a story about a fifteen-year-old girl whose boyfriend verbally abuses her, then hits her, and ultimately rapes her, and *Camouflage,* a timely story about a fourteen-year-old boy whose father is involved with an antigovernment militia group that blows up a federal building.

# What Do I Do Now?

Martha has always been a supporter of
sentimental causes, especially the rights
of defenseless animals. But now she has a
really serious cause in her own town.

# Simon Says
## Monica Hughes

He appeared in our Grade Ten class halfway through the
fall term. Simon Brett. Tall, with brown wavy hair and
hazel eyes. Cool, like he didn't care that all the girls in
class were sizing him up one way and all the guys
another. He wasn't pushy; he didn't put up his hand
when Mrs. Mackintosh threw out a question, but if she
asked him anything outright he always had the answer.

*Too good to be true,* I told myself. *So you can just
forget about him, Martha Heprin. 'Cause you haven't got a
hope in hell of him ever noticing you.*

But forgetting's not that easy, is it? And Simon Brett
kept sneaking into my thoughts and even into my secret
diary. I felt kind of stupid writing about him. *But heck,* I
told myself, *a girl's entitled to dream, isn't she?* So I went
ahead, imagining him noticing me instead of Alison or
Colleen or Melissa.

In fact he didn't pay attention to any of us. He sat at

his desk, looking a bit bored, like he was doing Mrs. Mackintosh a favor just being there, though he was always polite and got straight As on his work. Pat Conor, our phys ed teacher, found Simon could run like a hare and got him on the school track-and-field team and then began grooming him like he was Vernon High's new hope against the county. So he earned the respect of the guys and settled in as Mr. Anonymous.

Soon there was something new to talk about: a grand-looking building going up on the highway just outside Vernon. Very classy, a sprawling one-story complex finished in white stone, with the name Neobiotek in brass inset in a boulder that was part of the landscaping of mugho pines and juniper. Landscaping yet! In Vernon we've mostly got dusty bushes and sidewalk.

Everyone in town had his or her own idea of what was going to be there. The Cash and Carry cashier, Susan White, said she'd heard that they'd be testing secret toxins for the military.

"How come she knows that if it's so secret?" Mom asked when I passed this particular rumor on. Mom's very logical. She works part-time in the town library and keeps the books for Dad's small animals veterinary clinic.

Colleen said she'd heard they'd be testing cosmetics and household chemicals. "That's why they need all that space," she went on vaguely. "To keep the rabbits and things."

"Rabbits?" I repeated. "You mean like dropping perfume and cleaners in their eyes to test how irritating they are?"

"I thought that was banned," Melissa put in.

I shook my head. "Not completely. Not yet. That's why I only use cosmetics that aren't tested on animals."

"Oh, you . . . ," Melissa said, but not really putting me down. Everyone in Vernon knows I'm nuts about animals. I'm always getting involved in collecting for Save the Whales or Don't Net Dolphins, stuff like that. Dad says I'm a sucker for a sentimental sell, though he's hardly one to talk. When he treats some little kid's budgie or puppy he never charges more than the kid's allowance will bear. He *says* he makes up the difference by overcharging rich old ladies with fat Pekes. But since there aren't any rich old ladies around Vernon, we don't come out ahead, not enough for trips to Hawaii or Mexico, for instance. More like a week's camping in the mountains. But that's okay. And I respect Dad for his attitude.

Anyway, at the end of this conversation about Neobiotek someone said, "We should get up a petition. What about it, Martha?" And everyone laughed.

"Sure," I said. "But I'm going to have to find out some more about it first. Maybe Dad's got the inside scoop."

You might wonder why this particular incident should stick in my head, so I could replay the conversation about Neobiotek word for word. Well, it was that very afternoon that Simon Brett walked me home from school, so of course every moment of the day that led up to that momentous event was extra valuable and went into my diary that night—no longer make-believe.

It wasn't a long walk, unfortunately, since we live in an apartment above the clinic on the edge of town, no more than ten minutes from the high school, which is on the highway, with kids bused in from the country as well as town.

"So you figure your dad will know what they're doing at NBT?" he asked.

"Huh?"

"At Neobiotek. Will he be working for them?"

"Goodness, no. He's just got the local practice. I don't suppose he *will* know, but I can't think of anyone else who might."

"Maybe *I* can help."

I stopped and stared at him, noticing for the first time that his eyes weren't actually hazel, but kind of green. Spooky-looking. And his eyelids were no longer drooping, giving him that bored, half-asleep look, but wide open. His eyes sparkled, like there was a whole lot going on inside, more than I could guess.

"C-Can you?" I managed to stammer. My heart was pounding like mad, but at the same time my brain was saying, *Cool it, Martha Heprin. Why would he be interested in you?* I swallowed and told myself firmly, *It's the animals he cares about, and that should be enough.*

"I've got contacts back in the city," he went on. "I think I can find out some stuff in the next couple of days if that'll help."

"That'd be great," I said.

"I really respect your attitude," he went on. "You're different from the others." We reached the clinic and stood for a minute on the sidewalk, kind of sizing each other up. Then I ran upstairs to the apartment with my head in a whirl and my heart thumping like crazy, to write the memorable day down in my diary.

So it was a bit of a letdown when he didn't say a

word to me in school the next day. *You see, it's the animals he cares about, stupid,* I told myself briskly. And I tried to believe that it didn't matter. After all, he *respected* me. Respect is okay, but I sure wished I was as glamorous as Isobel, for instance, so he'd fall for me as well as respecting me.

A couple of days later, when I'd given up all hope, he caught up with me after school. "Let's go for a walk. Somewhere where we can talk without being overheard."

"The park's okay," I suggested, so we walked among the fallen leaves, past the swings and the teeter-totter. I took deep breaths of the bitter fall air and told my heart to stop pounding and my brain to pay attention to what Simon was saying.

"They're going to be doing a bunch of really nasty stuff," he told me. "Work on the brain and the nervous system."

"Like . . . ?"

"Exposing animals' brains and seeing what responses they get to pain. Stuff like that." He spoke quite casually, his eyes half closed, like it didn't matter.

I shuddered, remembering a book I'd read about animal testing—*Plague Dogs,* it was called. "That's horrible," I gasped. "We've got to stop them. I'll run off a poster on my computer tonight. We can go around town on the weekend, getting people to put it in their store windows. Then, once everyone's aware of what's going on, we can circulate a petition—"

"Whoa!" He looked directly at me then, his green eyes wide and sparkling. "Hold on with that 'we,' girl. I can't get involved."

"But you started this . . ."

"I can't compromise my sources," he said grandly. "I'll feed you material as I find it out, but I've got to stay undercover."

"I see." I didn't, not really, but I was impressed. Impressed enough to design a flyer on the family computer:

```
              Citizens of Vernon:
           Do We Want A Facility Engaged in
                 Torturing Animals?

                Close Down Neobiotek
      or We Will Have the Blood of Innocent
                 Animals on Our Hands

            Animals Have Rights TOO!
```

It looked pretty good. I ran off fifty copies and took them to all the stores in town. Boy, what a depressing way to spend a Saturday! Not even the health-food store or Natural Beauty would put it up.

"Neobiotek's the first decent industry coming this way in years," everyone said. "And they'll be shopping in Vernon if we make them welcome."

"Not for your cosmetics, they won't," I told Amy, who owns Natural Beauty.

"You'd be surprised," she said. "And you don't know what they're testing there anyway, do you?" I couldn't tell her I knew, because I'd promised not to involve Simon.

I finished up back at the clinic with my whole pile of flyers. "At least you'll let me pin up a few here, Dad, won't you?"

He read it through. "No way! This is just hysteria. Where are your facts, girl?"

"Everyone s-s-says . . . ," I stammered, wishing I could bring Simon into it.

"Hearsay. I'm surprised at you. What about research? Where would you go if this were a school project?"

"The library, I guess." I looked at the pile of flyers and groaned. "Should have checked first, shouldn't I?"

The library isn't my top favorite place on a sunny fall Saturday, but Mom was working and I thought she'd give me a hand. But all she did was point me to the subject catalog and the periodical index, as if I didn't know.

"There'll be so much," I whined. "It'll take me forever."

"Use the new computer search," she said. "And check two things," she added briskly. "The date. You don't want to use outdated material, stuff that's already been legislated out. And the sources. The opinions may be biased or from some other country with fewer regulations." She patted my shoulder and went off to help some kid with his dinosaur research.

I sighed and looked longingly out the window at the people walking by and wondered what Simon was doing right then. But soon I got down to work. There was nothing at all on Neobiotek itself. Not a word. Scads of stuff on rabbits and cosmetics, rabbits and nicotine addiction, rabbits and . . . really depressing stuff. Nothing new, except from a group called Free Animals on a Friendly Planet that sounded truly flaky.

I went home and looked up *Brett* in the phone book. Luckily there was only one, Lucy Brett, who must be Simon's grandmother, I worked out. I phoned and asked for Simon.

"It's hopeless." I told him about my horribly frustrating day.

Silence. "Simon, are you there?"

"Yeah. Look, Martha, can you meet me for a burger at that place on High Street?"

"You mean Joey's Grill," I said automatically. Then it clicked in my brain. Simon Brett was asking *me* out for a hamburger on Saturday night. I gulped and pulled myself together. "Sure. You bet. What time?"

"Six okay?"

My mind ran through the list of essentials: shower, dry hair, change into fresh jeans, and press that top Mom gave me for my birthday. "Sure," I said without missing a beat. "See you there."

---

I thought he'd pick one of the booths, but when I got to Joey's, Simon was already sitting at a table for two near the window, away from the crowd, but visually conspicuous. He didn't say anything but "Hi. I'm glad you could make it." Then the waitress came by and we ordered.

"It may be a while," she warned. "We're real busy tonight."

"That's okay. No hurry," Simon said, which made me feel great, like he wanted to spend time with me.

"So what's the problem?" he asked as soon as the waitress left.

I told him again about the hopeless morning and the equally futile afternoon I'd wasted at the library. "There just aren't any hard facts. It's all rumor. I can't get people to protest when they don't know exactly what they're protesting against. And what you said about animals' brains . . . Simon, I've got to have proof."

"It's not like you to give up, Martha." He flipped a finger against the buttons on my jean jacket, Save the Whales and Protect the Northwest from Clear-cutting.

"These are different. They're established. They've got newsletters and stuff."

"But they all had to start somewhere, didn't they? With a single person caring enough to step out of line." His sparkling green eyes met mine and my stomach did a flip.

Luckily our burgers and fries arrived at that moment, so I pulled my eyes away from his and concentrated on the food. After a bit I said cautiously, "Just what did you mean, step out of line?"

"Take risks." His voice was casual, but it sent warning goose bumps down my back.

I swallowed. "What kind of risks?"

He put his hand over mine. "We'll talk about it later." His hand was warm and reassuring. Just at that moment I saw Alison and Melissa walk past the window, their eyes just about popping out of their heads at the sight of the two of us. I couldn't help feeling smug. Me, Martha Heprin . . .

"Don't worry about it now," he went on. "I'm sorry you had such a rotten day. Say, how about a movie? If you're free, that is."

"Sure," I managed to say. "The show starts at seven-thirty. They're running *Dead Man Walking.* You'll have seen it already, I guess. Vernon's always weeks behind . . ."

I'd have gone on babbling forever, but he squeezed my hand, said, "That'll be great," and got up to pay.

The movie was awfully grim and so realistic it gave me the shivers. I don't think I'd have enjoyed it at all without Simon sitting next to me, his shoulder reassuringly warm against mine, my hand in his.

"What do you think?" he asked as we came out.

"I like the way it leaves it up to you to decide. I mean movies usually go one way or the other, don't they? In this one you get to appreciate everyone's point of view, even if you've got strong ideas of your own."

"And you're a person with strong ideas, aren't you? Not just about the death penalty." He smiled down at me and swung my arm gently to and fro.

"Sure. Once my mind's made up about something I'll go for it all the way. Mom says that's a definition of *plain obstinate.* Maybe she's right."

"I think it's just great." He looked down at me, his eyes sparkling, and then went on: "Look, I notice people in Vernon keep early hours, but let's just walk along the highway a piece."

"Sure. You must find it really boring after the big city and all that. I mean, living with your grandmother." I was dying to find out more about Simon's life, and I hoped he'd open up.

"Yeah," he said. "It is that." His face was suddenly sullen, like a light had gone out inside.

"And what does the future hold?" I prompted. "Will you go on living with her? Your parents . . . ?"

He laughed. It was amazing how quickly his face

could change. Like night into day. "Curious, aren't you?" He swung my arm again.

"Sure." I wanted to tell him that when you care about someone the way I did about him you want to know all about him. But of course I didn't. "Sure," I said again.

"My father's planning to move either to Chester or Vernon. He hasn't made up his mind yet; but the house is sold and I'm boarding with Gramma."

"Where'd you rather live, Vernon or Chester?"

"D'you really need to ask?"

He stopped and I thought, Here comes the big moment. And I wondered if I was ready for it. Only he wasn't looking at me, but across the road, and I realized that we'd walked as far as the new Neobiotek facility.

"All those animals," he said softly. "Trapped in cages. Being tortured."

"I just wish there was something we could *do*, but it's hopeless."

He turned and caught hold of my hand. When he stared into my eyes, my heart flipped and I found it hard to breathe normally.

"We *can* do something. Really give them a jolt."

"Like how?"

"Break in. Release the animals. Maybe throw a bit of paint around."

"Simon, you *can't*!"

"Not by myself. But with your help. We'd drive here in Gramma's car. Then you could distract the guard— some excuse like the car won't start. While he's helping you, I'll slip in and do it."

"But it's wrong. It's illegal."

"So's torturing animals. I thought you'd got principles, Martha."

"I have." I was almost in tears. "But . . ."

"But your principles only go as far as selling Save the Whales buttons. Pretty safe."

"You're not being fair, Simon." I dug out a tissue and blew my nose.

"You're not being honest with yourself, Martha."

Wasn't I? Where does a person draw the line? I sniffed back tears and shook my head dumbly.

"Come on," he said. "I'd better walk you home."

He didn't say a word the whole way. But at the door to our apartment he turned me to face him again. "Hey!" He ran a finger across my wet cheeks. "It's okay. Just think about it, all right?" He slipped off his class ring and put it on the middle finger of my right hand. "Just a reminder that we're in this together. Does it fit okay?"

"You bet. Thank you." Actually it was a bit loose, but I figured I could wind yarn around it or something. "I should give you something. . . ."

"You don't have to."

"Sure I do." I unpinned my Save the Whales button and fastened it onto his jacket.

"I'll wear it proudly," he said, and kissed me. Not a real kiss, but lightly brushing my lips with his. Then he walked away, leaving me standing there with electric shocks running up and down my body.

I spent that night in a wakeful muddle. Was Simon right? Or was I? I couldn't even write it in my diary. It was too serious. And I didn't have the right words.

When I walked into class on Monday, the whole

atmosphere was different, like I was a star. Alison said, "Hi, Martha," and Melissa asked if I had any more whale buttons for sale. I'd been trying to sell them for months with little success, but by the end of recess I'd got another thirty dollars for the fund. It was amazing how a hamburger and a movie, and Simon wearing one of my buttons on his jean jacket, had suddenly turned me into an important person. I should have felt great, but I didn't. I felt rotten. I guess it was the sleepless night.

Simon didn't talk to me at recess. I felt a bit flat but also relieved that I wasn't going to have to put on some kind of flirty show, the way Colleen does with her boyfriends, for instance. That's just not my style.

Right after lunch he caught up with me and said, "I want to ask you something important."

"Sure."

He looked around. "Somewhere private." He took my hand and pulled me around to the side of the school away from the entrance. "Does your dad have kennels or hutches, places to keep animals?"

It was so different from what I'd expected that I just stared with my mouth open. Then I pulled myself together. "Of course. He has facilities at the back of the clinic for animals that are under observation or recuperating after surgery."

"I mean outside. Where they mightn't be noticed for a couple of days."

I shook my head. Then I remembered. "There's an old hutch at the back of the yard. I used to keep rabbits when I was a kid. Why?"

"I'll tell you later. Last night I was talking about

taking risks. Well, I'm going to. You'll see. Next time it'll be the two of us. Could you meet me back of your place after dark?"

"I guess so. Sure."

"Ten o'clock should do. Don't let me down, Martha." And he was gone, leaving me standing bewildered, till the bell woke me up and I had to run to class. "Next time it'll be the two of us," he'd said.

———

I cleaned out the old hutch, put in fresh bedding, water, and rabbit food right after school. At a quarter to ten I slipped out of the house and into the yard. The moon was full and the late daisies shone with ghostly light. Mom and Dad and I were all too busy to pay much attention to the garden except for throwing in a few seeds, and it usually looked a mess. But by moonlight it was really romantic-looking. The right place for an assignation.

A car stopped a couple of houses down. Then the side gate squeaked and I saw the shadowy figure of Simon. He was carrying what looked like a potato sack.

"Where's the hutch?" he whispered right off, paying no heed to the romantic evening.

"Over here. What *is* that? And why all the secrecy?"

He reached into the sack and pulled out two brown-and-white rabbits, the kind they sell at the local pet store.

I stared. "What on earth? If you want to keep rabbits, Simon, there's no law against it."

"I didn't *buy* these, Martha. I liberated them."

"Liberated?" I still didn't get it.

"From Neobiotek."

"You mean you actually broke in and *stole* them!" I stared at his face. It was like a mask in the moonlight, pale, the eyes glinting. "You did it? I thought you were joking. Oh, Simon!"

"You wanted proof of what they're doing there. Here's your proof." He had a penlight with him and he turned its tiny beam onto the rabbits' faces. Their eyes were red and swollen, with scummy tear and mucus tracks matting the fur of their cheeks.

I swallowed. "We've got to take them to Dad. He'll irrigate their poor eyes, reduce the irritation."

"You can't do that." Simon grabbed my arm. "He'll want to know how I got hold of them."

"He'll understand. He'll sympathize, honestly."

"No. You've got to swear not to tell anybody."

"Okay, Simon, I swear. But we can't leave them like this. You hold on to them and I'll go find something to wash out their eyes." I pulled my arm from his grasp and ran toward the house. Luckily the house key also fitted the door to the clinic. I slipped in and looked along the shelves. There was the eye lotion. My hand was trembling so much I nearly knocked it off the shelf. Swabs.

I made Simon hold the rabbits still while I painstakingly dripped drop after drop of saline solution into their poor eyes and mopped them clear with the swabs.

"There, that should do it," I whispered at last. "You can put them in the hutch now."

Simon hadn't said a word all this time. Now he just

pushed the rabbits into my arms and said, "I've got to go. I've got Gramma's car and I told her I'd be right back." And he was off.

As I replaced the eye lotion I noticed Dad's Polaroid camera. He uses it to supplement his case notes and to illustrate the article he occasionally writes for a veterinary journal.

*Brilliant,* I thought, and took a couple of pictures of the rabbits, which by now were contentedly nibbling lettuce leaves. I put everything away and slipped back into the apartment without anyone noticing. Dad was watching a game on TV and Mom was doing the books. In my diary that night I wrote:

> *I'm determined to do whatever it takes to help Simon.*
> *Treating defenseless animals this way is the worst kind*
> *of cruelty. No holds barred now!*

Next day he didn't even ask me how Flopsy and Mopsy were doing, but I caught him after school and told him anyway. "And I took photographs and I'm going to design a new poster that'll show people in Vernon just exactly what's going on at Neobiotek. Then they'll have to pay attention."

His expression was like a bucket of water in my face. "W-What's the matter?" I stammered. "What'd I say? I thought—"

"Photographs?"

"Polaroid. They came up great. They'll make a terrific impression on a poster, Simon."

He seemed to be making up his mind about something. He shrugged and gave me a quick smile. "Sure. Why not? But remember, you promised not to say where you got the rabbits."

"Of course. I'll just say the rabbits were obtained from Neobiotek in the condition shown in the photographs. This poster's going to work, Simon."

"I hope so. But it's not enough. I talked about risks, remember? What I want . . . what I *really* want is to liberate all the animals."

"Of course. That's why we'll circulate a petition after the poster. This is only the warm-up."

He shook his head. "Like I said, we've got to break into Neobiotek and let the animals go."

"But I couldn't—"

"You're not going to let me down now, are you, Martha? Now I've got the proof you wanted."

"Of course not. You know I . . . But . . ." I stopped, the enormity of what he was suggesting overwhelming me. "Look," I went on urgently, "if the posters have an effect and if I can get enough signatures on a petition, we won't *have* to do anything . . . anything so drastic."

He stared at me silently and then loped over to where the track team was assembling. I walked home feeling like I had a hole where my heart ought to be. I pushed the feeling out of the way by working on the poster. Then I went over to the library to run off copies. It cost a fortune in quarters, but the photographs came up great.

First thing Saturday morning I delivered them. That old saying about a picture being worth a thousand words is for real. Every store let me put up a poster in the window or next to the cash register. I went home knowing I was making a real difference, not just selling buttons for worthy causes. Simon would be proud of me, and he'd give up this harebrained scheme for breaking into Neobiotek.

The good feeling lasted right through Sunday lunchtime, when the doorbell rang. Dad went, expecting it to be an emergency call. A man in a dark suit stood there, with a dark expression on his face and one of my posters in his right hand. In his other hand was a briefcase.

"Dr. Heprin," he said. "My name is Paul Dover, of Prewitt, Prewitt, and Dover, representing Neobiotek."

I jumped to my feet. "Then it's me you want to talk to," I said. He had piercing gray eyes, and when they bored into me I felt like St. Joan must have before being burned at the stake. I swallowed and promised myself—and Simon—that I wouldn't say a word to incriminate him.

"What's all this about?" Dad asked, and Mr. Dover handed him the poster. "Where'd you get this picture, Martha?" he asked.

"I took it myself with your Polaroid. It's the poor rabbits that Neobiotek is torturing." I glared at Mr. Dover, though my stomach was doing flips.

"Where are the rabbits now?"

I thought of refusing to answer, but there didn't seem much point. "In the old hutch at the back of the yard."

"This I have to see," said Mr. Dover, not as angrily as before. So I led the way out to where Flopsy and

Mopsy were contentedly munching on fresh carrots I'd put out for them. Mr. Dover reached into the hutch and lifted out Flopsy. "Nothing much wrong with this rabbit's eyes."

"Of course not. D'you really think I'd let them go on suffering? I washed them out just as soon as—" I stopped. *Watch your mouth, Martha,* I warned myself. "As soon as I got them," I finished lamely.

Mr. Dover looked at me intently. "Well, well," he said, and put Flopsy gently back into the hutch.

Somehow this made me madder than if he'd raged. "Is that all you have to say?" I stormed.

"Oh, no. For a start I can assure you that Neobiotek is not using any rabbits at this facility. Nor do we do any research on cosmetics. I don't know where you got your information, but this poster is sufficient provocation for Neobiotek to bring a libel suit against you. Or, since you are a minor, against Dr. Heprin here," he went on casually.

"Against *Dad*? But you can't. He's got nothing to do with it. It was just me and . . . just me. And the rabbits *did* come from your lab."

"How do you know, Martha?" Dad asked. "Did you verify your source?"

That was when the bottom fell out of my world. How *did* I know? Because Simon said so. How did I know he was telling the truth? Because he *had* to be, because he was Simon. Because I trusted him.

*Because you're in love with him, stupid,* said a cold voice inside my head.

"I think we'd better all go in and sit down," Dad said,

while I stood there with my mouth open and my thoughts banging around in my head like hornets trying to get out. "Mr. Dover?"

When we were back in the living room, Mr. Dover reached into his briefcase. "If you are prepared to sign this disclaimer and name your source, Neobiotek might be persuaded to forget this whole unfortunate incident." He held out a piece of paper.

"But I *saw* them. Their eyes . . . Dad, it was awful."

"Martha, stop being obstinate. Mr. Dover has explained that there *are* no rabbits at the lab and—"

"People lie," I interrupted. "How am I to know he's not just protecting his client?" At the expression of outrage on the lawyer's face I could feel my cheeks flaming, but I was determined not to give in. All great enterprises have their martyrs. I stuck my chin up, trying to feel strong and powerful. Then I remembered that Dad would be the martyr, not me. In spite of myself my eyes filled with tears. "Oh, darn!"

Dad handed me a tissue. Mr. Dover was still staring at me, his gray eyes cold, like pebbles. Suddenly he got to his feet. "Perhaps there is a way out of this impasse. Dr. Heprin, will you and your daughter accompany me on a tour of Neobiotek?"

Before I had time to do more than mop my eyes and blow my nose, we were driving along the highway to the new complex. There was only one car in the lot, the security guard's, I supposed, and I wondered how Simon had managed to break in. And why, if he'd done it once, he needed my help. Mr. Dover unlocked the main door and ushered us into a spacious lobby.

"The central wing is primarily administration," he explained to Dad. "The east wing is devoted to ongoing research, fulfilling FDA requirements for new drugs and so on." He spoke to Dad all the time, and I just trailed along behind, like a naughty child. It was humiliating, but I soon forgot about myself in the interest of seeing what was behind those secret walls.

There were rows and rows of shiny clean cages, each containing a white rat. I had to admit they looked contented with their lot. Dad asked scientific questions and Mr. Dover answered him willingly. Or so it *seemed.* Then we returned to the foyer.

"The west wing is where our experimental work is going on. Obviously I can't go into details of exactly what, but you can certainly inspect the subject animals."

I steeled myself for the expected horror, but all I saw were more clean cages and white rats. By the time we got back to the entrance my head was spinning. It didn't make sense. I stared blankly at the slab of marble on the wall engraved with the list of directors and so on. And there it was, staring me in the face:

Neobiotek Project Manager: Thomas Brett.

I must have gasped, because both men stopped their conversation and looked at me. "Are you all right, Martha?" Dad asked.

"Sure," I managed to say. I pointed at the name. "He's the one in charge?"

"Yes." Mr. Dover turned back to Dad. "He would have got in touch with you personally, Dr. Heprin, but he's away at the moment. On his honeymoon, in fact."

*Not Simon's father,* I thought with relief. "He's young

to be in charge of all this," I said casually, and Mr. Dover blinked at me.

"Not particularly. About your father's age. Why would you think . . . ?"

"Being on his honeymoon and all."

"Ah. It is, in fact, a second marriage. He has a son who must be about your age . . ." He stopped in midsentence and gave me his gimlet glare again.

I covered my face with my hands, but it was too late.

"Well, well." His voice was almost kind. "I suppose I should have guessed. So, you *are* going to sign this retraction, aren't you, Martha?"

He smoothed the piece of paper on top of the reception desk and I meekly signed it.

"What do you intend to do with it?" Dad asked.

"A copy to your local newspaper. And in every store where your daughter left a poster."

I cringed. How was I ever going to show my face anywhere in Vernon? I could just die!

"And the name of her collaborator?" Dad asked. I held my breath.

"I don't believe we need to pursue that any further," Mr. Dover said.

"Thank you," I managed to whisper. I crawled after them back to the car and we drove into Vernon.

"Would you let me out here, please?" I asked Mr. Dover, a block from Simon's grandmother's house. Simon was in the yard raking leaves. I stamped over to him.

"So where did you really get the rabbits?"

"I told you . . . ," he began. Then he laughed. "At a pet shop in Chester."

"A *pet shop*?" It didn't make sense. "But their poor eyes." He laughed again, and I realized that I didn't know him at all. "Well, Simon?"

"It was just a drop of detergent. Nothing serious."

"You're sick, Simon Brett." I turned away.

He grabbed my arm. "I had to do it."

"*Had* to? Let go my arm."

"Not till you listen. Till you hear my side of it. Dad just dumped me on Gramma and went off with that blond bimbo. My new mom—that's a laugh. I was going to get back at him, that's all. If only you'd cooperated, it'd have been easy. All I was going to do was mess the place up a bit, spray-paint, stuff like that. Dad's new toy! But you had to go on about *proof*. So I got you proof, that's all."

"That is so gross." I pulled my arm free and ran down to the sidewalk. "And don't ever talk to me again, Simon Brett. You *used* me, the way you used the rabbits."

———

For the next two weeks I could hardly bear him sitting behind me in class. It was worse even than the reaction to that paper I had to sign. Life was just about at its lowest ebb. But then Simon's father came home from his honeymoon and decided to live in Chester, rather than Vernon. Simon vanished from our school, and there was just his empty desk to remind me for the rest of the term.

I gave Flopsy and Mopsy to the kindergarten petting zoo, and I guess they'll live happily ever after, or for as long as rabbits do. Sometimes the little kids play with them outside. When I see the rabbits' floppy ears and twitching noses I have to go run around the track just as hard as I can. Trying to leave my memory of Simon behind.

# Monica Hughes

Born in Liverpool, England, Monica Hughes spent part of her childhood in Egypt before returning to be educated in England and Scotland. She worked in Zimbabwe (then called Southern Rhodesia) before moving to Canada in 1952, where she married and raised four children. Since she began writing for young people, she has published thirty novels, about two-thirds of which are science fiction.

Among her best-known science fiction works are *Keeper of the Isis Light* and its two sequels, *The Guardian of Isis* and *The Isis Pedlar.* That series begins with the story of sixteen-year-old Olwen, who has been living on a distant planet with the help of a humanlike robot after her parents' death. *The Keeper of the Isis Light* was an American Library Association Best Book for Young Adults as well as an International Board on Books for Young People Honor Book, and *Guardian of Isis* won the Canada Council Prize for Children's Literature.

The most awards have gone to Hughes's *Hunter in the Dark,* a painful novel about a contemporary teenage boy who discovers he has a fatal illness, despite his parents' efforts to protect him from the news. The reader is then taken on a wilderness survival journey as Mike tries to come to terms with his approaching death. For that book, Monica Hughes received the Bay's Beaver Award, the Alberta Culture Juvenile Novel Award, the Canada Council Prize for Children's Literature, an ALA Best Book for Young Adults, the Silver Feather Award from Germany, the Writer's Guild of Alberta R. Ross Annett Award, and a Boeken Leeuw award from Belgium.

Among her more recent books are *Invitation to the Game*, a novel about virtual-reality experiences that turn into reality for a group of teenagers in a futuristic England; *The Seven Magpies*, a mystery-adventure set in a castle in western Scotland in 1939; and *Where Have You Been, Billy Boy?*, which follows the adventures of a boy from 1908 who time-travels to 1993 Colorado via a magic carousel and is trapped there when he finds the carousel in ruins.

Haunted by his past, Cory wonders if he
can ever pay for his earlier mistakes.

# The Un-numbing of Cory Willhouse

Virginia Euwer Wolff

Cory Willhouse's eyelids flipped open before his thoughts had a chance to come to the surface in the predawn dark. The voice on the radio had gone by too fast to convey actual sense, but the words "Kim's Market and Grocery" and "fire" rang in his ears.

In the jolt from deep sleep to daily life, Cory knew something terrible was going on. What kind of terrible, the where, the when, were only vague fragments of sound.

"In this morning's commute, you'll want to take it slow coming onto the Thirty-sixth and Two-seventeen connection. There's a traffic signal malfunction there, and the rain isn't making it any easier.

"And again: Broad Street is closed between Sixth and Seventh so firefighters can clean up after a blaze destroyed Kim's Market and Grocery early this morning. Looks like rain all day, and here's a tune to get you through the next four minutes." The music began.

The where and the when suddenly became too clear.

In Cory's memory the backs of Paul's legs pounded up and down, running ahead of him in the late afternoon, and his own feet followed, thudding. His hands clutched little plastic packages, and his brain kept giving orders to his legs, "Run faster, faster, faster!"

They had been nine years old. It was Halloween.

The rush of the air as Davy, Chipper, and Paul raced at top speed around the corner, with Cory running last—the feel of poofing air as he and Paul had collided and nearly lost their balance—the packet of plum candy falling out of a pocket and Paul's hand reaching out and catching it in midair . . . Six years later, it was as real as ever.

By the time they had caught their breath, divided up the stolen packages, concealed them awkwardly in their shirts and socks, and separated to go home so their mothers could take them out trick-or-treating, Cory's stomach had ached so gnawingly that he spent the evening hiding behind his pirate mask and trying not to say anything. He'd been afraid that if he opened his mouth, the facts would leak out. He hid the dried cuttlefish snack, the *goguma* crackers, and the melon-flavor candy under his pillow. He left his trick-or-treat bag full of candy bars, licorice ropes, and M&M's on the kitchen table. By nightfall he'd decided he never wanted to think about food again.

He had lain in his bed thinking, *I hurt in my guts.*

Not a Halloween to remember.

Except that he couldn't forget.

The *saki ika,* the *dasimaodeng* noodles, the little bag of dried lotus root—all the things they had grabbed from the shelves of Kim's Market and Grocery—had turned out to taste peculiar, even icky. Every single thing except the melon candy. The half-opened packages stayed in Cory's bedroom, stuck in drawers, propped behind books and games, teetering on the edge of his closet shelf, reminding him. He had taken the *kal bi,* Korean barbecue seasoning mix, to the kitchen and inserted it between two other packages in the cupboard. Over and over again, he had heard his parents trying to figure it out: "Did you buy this?" "No, I thought you bought it." "Well, I didn't." "I didn't, either." "You must have." "No, I didn't." "Well, Korean barbecue mixes don't walk into people's kitchens."

Eventually his mother had used the *kal bi,* and his parents said short ribs had never tasted so good. Cory had tried to eat it, but made an excuse to leave the table before dinner was over.

Cory, Davy, Chipper, and Paul were and were not a club. They had never made up a name for themselves, and they hadn't had a formal meeting place, but they had a few basic, unwritten rules.

Each escapade had to be a little more daring than the preceding one. Emptying a classmate's crayons into the geranium pots on the classroom windowsill had led to emptying all the toilet paper containers in the boys' bathroom onto the floor.

Part of the dangerous allure was in the moment of nearly getting caught. It was in the frightening thrill of his heart pumping in his throat as a teacher rounded a corner, stepped through a door, and almost but not quite caught his eye.

Cory had practiced being two people, one who was on the level and one who sneaked. Almost as if he could change his shape. That, too, was one of their unwritten rules.

The rules had seemed to emerge, not in any individual voice. In fact, looking back on his fourth-grade year, Cory couldn't remember any particular individuality at all.

New secret words became code: from the time Chipper put a strip of five exploding caps at the fulcrum of the seesaw and frightened several second-graders, they had gotten "Did you see what I saw?" "No, I saw what you see." The four boys had found it hilarious. From the Halloween afternoon chase, they had "You're off your Kim," "He's off his Kim," meaning someone was being loony. Davy, Paul, Chipper, and Cory had roared with laughter when they found the opportunity to say these words, weighted with private, clubby meanings.

Now, lying in his bed early on this rainy morning of his sophomore year, Cory heard the name Kim's Market and Grocery and wished he couldn't remember any of it.

He got out of bed, made his way to the bathroom, and tried to figure out a way not to know what he knew.

He had never gone near Kim's Market and Grocery after that incident. At first, out of fear. Later, out of guilt. Still later, out of an effort to erase the event.

Cory stood brushing his teeth.

Mr. Kim had chased them but not far. He must have had to turn back from the sidewalk chase because there was nobody left minding the store. His wife was nowhere to be seen; she was probably in their apartment behind the store, taking care of their little kid, who was maybe three or four years old.

Cory looked at himself in the bathroom mirror.

He wanted to trade places with someone. Anyone.

He rinsed his mouth. Green minty foam bubbled out and swirled around and around the sink before gurgling down the drain.

Well, not just anyone.

He wanted to trade places with someone who had no guilty memories.

He turned off the water, and a song ended on the radio. "The commute this morning is messy," the radio went on, "and avoid Broad between Sixth and Seventh, where firefighters have gotten an early-morning blaze under control. Get ready for a signal malfunction at Thirty-sixth and Two-seventeen. And this just in, a three-car accident on the Interstate near Exit Thirty-four. How about a little music to take our minds off all that?" The music began again.

Cory turned on the shower and waited for the water to warm up. Mr. Kim's face wouldn't leave his mind.

The friendship of Davy, Paul, Chipper, and Cory had loosened over the years. They had, in their different ways, outgrown their close confederation of schemes, strategies, and narrow escapes. Now Cory had no classes with Paul; Davy's family had moved fifteen blocks farther away; and Chipper spent all his energy on soccer. The four boys lived at the edges of one another's lives. Close enough to say hello to, too detached to use the code words.

Seeing them—any of the three of them—reminded him too clearly of the immature kid he had been. In Chipper's face he had to remember the day they had pilfered a dollar from the coat closet, getting a unique joy from the fact that they had absolutely no clue about whose dollar it had been. Davy had been the one who couldn't stop saying, "Did you see what I saw?" And it was Paul's nine-year-old legs Cory kept remembering, running ahead of him around the corner from Kim's Market and Grocery on Halloween.

In the shower, Cory couldn't help hearing over again, ". . . so firefighters can clean up after a blaze destroyed Kim's Market and Grocery early this morning." Shampooing his hair, he tried to focus on his biology homework. Not a thing appeared in his mind.

A decision took shape in Cory long before he sensed it. Later, he would look back and remember seeing shampoo lather going down the drain as separate pieces of thought came together.

"I'll do something," he said as he grabbed a towel.

What it was he didn't know yet.

By the time he had gone through four morning classes without hearing much of what was being said in any of them, he was ready to skip lunch, catch a number 9 bus, and look at Kim's Market and Grocery.

Yellow police tape stretched across what remained of the building. Leaning across the tape, Cory peered through partial walls and jagged glass at the remains.

Heaps of sopping wet ashes covered everything; metal frames of display cases stood skeletal with prongs of steel poking up. Blackened, bubbled wall fragments leaned unsteadily. A clock face dangled; its innards hung in the smoky air, the hands standing at 3:07.

On a ladder at the edge of the burned-out store was Mr. Kim, looking older than Cory remembered him, pulling fragments of board and paper from a partial wall.

Returning to school on the bus, Cory decided to skip track practice after school and go back to Kim's Market and Grocery. Exactly what he would do, he didn't know. There had to be something. There couldn't not be something.

Less than three hours later he said hello to a little boy, a child who looked like maybe a third-grader, who was piling burned metal fragments in a box and humming to himself.

"We had a fire," the boy said in clear, unaccented English.

"I know. I heard on the radio. Can I help?" said Cory.

"Sure. There's another box over there." The boy pointed to a pile of cardboard cartons teetering near a jumble of burned boards.

Cory took a carton from the pile and looked around. Where to begin? Maybe separating big pieces of glass from other debris. He needed gloves.

"Tomorrow I'll bring gloves," he said. He was surprised to hear himself say it out loud or say it at all. He went on, in a squat, picking out glass from piles of unidentifiable remains.

"Yeah, you can get cut if you don't have gloves on," said the little boy.

They worked side by side on the floor for a while. The boy hummed and then asked, "What's your name?"

"Cory. What's yours?"

"Joey."

"Hi, Joey."

Through a torn doorway came Mr. Kim, looking surprised and vaguely alarmed to see Cory. Cory couldn't see whether or not there was any light of recognition in his face, any beam that registered, "This is one of the four nine-year-old boys who stole from me six years ago." Cory kept his head turned partly sideways, to be on the safe side. He pretended to be surveying the damage.

"This is Cory," Joey said to his father. Then something in Korean. Mr. Kim said something back and Joey turned back to Cory. "He wants to know what you're doing here."

"I just want to help," Cory said, his head still turned sideways.

Joey and his father had another short conversation and Mr. Kim walked away. Cory and Joey went on picking up debris. Joey hummed.

––––––––

Cory set his alarm for 5:30 A.M. He had to speak to his track coach before school. It was not going to be easy. He would have to steel himself so the coach wouldn't succeed in talking him out of his resolute plan. He put a pair of leather work gloves and a sweatshirt in his pack for the afternoon at Kim's.

"You *what*?" said Mr. Shields. He was indignant, disappointed, and suspicious. "First you miss practice, you don't explain, now here you are, all bright and chipper, and you say you have to miss practice *again—*"

"Maybe I'd better quit the team," Cory said, focusing on keeping his voice and eyes steady.

Mr. Shields softened. "We can talk this over, Cory. We can talk anything over. If you're having problems . . ."

"I'm not having problems, Coach. I'm really not. I just have something else I have to do after school for a while."

"For a while? What do you mean, for a *while*? Have you thought about the eight hundred meters? Have you given *any thought* to the eight hundred?"

"I know. I don't know. Days. Weeks. I don't know. Yeah, I've thought about the eight hundred. I've got next year. Look, maybe I'd better quit the team."

Mr. Shields's hand was on his shoulder. "Cory, are you in trouble?"

"No. No, I'm not. I'm just going to be busy, that's all."

Mr. Shields took his hand away and cocked his head to one side. "I don't know what's going on with you," he said. "But I do know this: it's darned hard to pull any commitment out of sophomore boys. That's a fact."

They looked at each other for several seconds. Then Cory said, "See you, Coach," and moved away from the stare.

It had taken three minutes. Less. Cory knew he was right. But it was nothing he could explain. Not to anybody.

Concentrating on his classes suddenly became easier.

He'd made up his mind. The decision filled him with energy. He knew what he was doing.

By the second afternoon that Cory appeared at what used to be Kim's Market and Grocery, Mr. Kim and two other people were on ladders, stretching measuring tape across sections of the store.

"Hi, Cory," Joey said from a stepladder. He pulled off a piece of seared, brittle wall, tossed it on the floor, and said, "They're going to start with the floor. It's too burned to hold the weight."

*Sympathy always sounds so useless,* Cory thought as he said, "That's really too bad, Joey. Can I help?" It sounds useless *unless you put something constructive with it.*

"Sure," said Joey, and then spoke to his father in Korean. They had a conversation with head-shaking, and Joey reported to Cory, "My dad says you can't help. He can't pay you. There's no money to pay you."

Cory didn't even have to think. "That's okay. He doesn't have to pay me."

Joey translated for his father. Kim looked down from his ladder, considered Cory with his eyes, and shook his head.

"Joey, tell him I really mean it. I can come after school. I'm serious."

Joey did. Mr. Kim looked doubtful and pointed to a heap of blackened, crumbling wood fragments and a broom.

Cory did mean it. Gradually, over a period of days, weeks, it came to him that that was what he had meant in the shower that early morning.

He settled into a daily routine of school and Mr. Kim, school and Mr. Kim. And Mr. Kim on weekends.

Joey, a fourth-grader, worked beside him or near him, humming. He was the hummingest little kid Cory had ever known.

Cory swept up enough debris to fill the three garbage cans dozens of times. He laid and hammered floor underlayment. He helped frame the new market and apartment behind. One of the men lent him a carpenter's apron with pockets for tools. He wore it every afternoon and got comfortably used to the weight around his hips. He guessed his job title was carpenter's assistant if anyone had asked.

The only person who came close to asking was his mother. She tried. That Cory would quit the track team to help rebuild a store destroyed by fire was something the Willhouse family had never imagined. They were thrilled and confused. Between praising his generosity and scratching their heads about why, Cory's parents began to see that he wasn't going to answer their questions in any detail, and they settled into a distant friendliness toward their son.

That was just what he wanted. He didn't want anyone to look at him too carefully.

Mr. Kim clearly had no idea who Cory really was. Maybe he had long ago given up on identifying the four nine-year-old boys, as he'd given up on the chase that afternoon. Cory advanced closer to him.

"Mr. Kim, you had no fire insurance?" he asked one day.

Mr. Kim looked up from the boards he was bracing. "No. Piano lessons. Joey," he answered. "Good on piano. Before."

The upright piano Cory had helped carry out of

the Kims' burned-out apartment was ruined: dried, bubbled varnish covered what remained of the charred front and sides; steam damage had done the rest. Most of the keys had popped off. "So you play the piano?" Cory asked Joey.

"Well, yeah. I took lessons."

One of the carpenters spoke up. "Not just that. Joey won two competitions. Of the whole city. First prize both times. He was the youngest."

"Hey, Joey, good job. Where do you practice now?" Cory asked him.

"I don't," said Joey. "At my uncle's they don't have one. A piano."

Cory looked around. Somebody had to do something about the piano.

After many afternoons of sawing, hammering, lifting, carrying, measuring, watching, listening, learning, and sweeping up, Cory had two blood blisters, a shallow gash in his left arm, and the kind of nightly physical exhaustion that brought with it an exhilarating pleasure. The store and apartment were taking shape. They even had windows. Cory and Joey had maneuvered dozens of boards into place by balancing the weight between them and had become an odd partnership. Cory was the one with height and vertical reach; Joey was the one with two languages. And his mental calculations were often as quick as Cory's. Humming all the way.

Joey's mother worked with them, diligent and silent. The crew consisted of Mr. Cho and Mr. Park, who were actual carpenters; Joey's parents; Joey; Cory; and some uncles and aunts on weekends. Cory felt a bit like an impostor. His Korean hello, *Ahn-yung-ha-sae-yo,* didn't have anything like the right feel to it, but the Kim family accepted it in good spirits.

He kept measuring his motives.

On the morning of the eleventh day of work with the Kim family, Cory woke with a surprising phrase in his head: *the un-numbing of Cory Willhouse.* He lay still, listening to it. During all those years since the Halloween in fourth grade, he had made a consistent effort to erase the robbery of Kim's Market and Grocery from his life. Now, in waking up this morning, his thought process had slowed down so that he could watch it, and what he saw there astonished him. He noticed that he'd used Kim's Market and Grocery as a model, teaching himself how to be numb about other things he didn't want to know. The bombing in Oklahoma City. The shooting in Scotland. The starving in Africa. The killing in Bosnia. *Don't think about it. Thinking about it feels terrible. Put it out of your mind. Look for things that make sense.*

And, strangely, it had sort of worked.

*You can't do anything about those horrors anyway.*

Cory had gotten so good at detouring around the horrible that he'd become a very comfortable person to have around. Kids, kids' parents, teachers liked him. They liked being with someone who was so reasonable, so cheerful.

He'd found out how not to think about bad things. Not thinking about them had become the easiest way to get along. And gradually it had become the only way to get along.

It made feelings easier. Slighter. Of a shorter attention span. A narrow range of manageable feelings. That was it.

But now: he was feeling more for the Kim family than he could remember feeling for anyone, anything—in years. Since when? He couldn't remember the last time he'd felt so much for the events of other people's lives.

And what he was feeling felt good. He couldn't get enough of it. Going to the Kim family's worksite every afternoon was energizing him, making him bigger. The tiredness at the end of the day was rewarding.

————

"You just can't get enough of that construction work, can you?" Cory didn't have to look to know who it was. He hadn't seen Paul in weeks. Now here he was, in the hallway between classes, hand on Cory's shoulder and voice in Cory's ear, just loud enough to be understood.

Cory shrugged. He'd known that Paul, Davy, and Chipper would say something, sometime. He just hadn't known what, or when. And he didn't know what he would say back to them.

"Yeah, I guess so," he said. That wasn't right. That wasn't what he meant.

"Well, you know what you're doing," Paul said, and moved away into the congested hallway. As usual, Cory saw Paul as both a fifteen-year-old and a nine-year-old running ahead of him on Halloween.

That afternoon the insulation arrived, and Cory and Joey became an insulation installation team. And they watched carefully as the electrician wired the ceiling and put in wall outlets. Joey and Cory asked, guessed, and explained to each other the jumble of wires that made up the circuitry.

Cory saw Chipper coming during lunch the day after he and Joey had finished insulating the third wall. Chipper sat down next to him in the cafeteria, leaned sideways toward him, and said, "Are you off your Kim, Willhouse?"

"Hey, it's been a long time, Chip. What's up?"

"That's what I want to know. You're helping rebuild that store, aren't you?"

"Oh, you know," Cory began. "Just something to—I don't know. They've got a nice little kid. Joey. I just got into the habit. I don't know, I went there and looked, it was all ashes . . . I don't know."

"Well, good for you," Chipper said, and got up to go. "I mean, good for you. See you." And he walked away.

Did Chipper mean it? Or was he being sarcastic? Was he being sarcastic the first time, but then he meant it the second time?

And had Cory himself meant what he said? "I just got into the habit." That wasn't it. What he'd meant was, *Chipper, do you have any idea how good it feels? You can't imagine: That weight—lifted off me. I mean it—I feel fabulous. You should try it.*

The Willhouse family continued to be mystified and proud.

Cory helped install Sheetrock and couldn't remember ever feeling better. The store was coming back to life.

In placing an ad in the school newspaper asking for donations to help the Kim family replace their piano for "a prizewinning ten-year-old pianist, winner of citywide competitions, whose piano was destroyed by fire," Cory thought he was taking a simple step. In thinking that way, he was wrong.

A reporter from the school paper wanted to interview him. What was Cory's relationship with the young pianist? Was Cory a musician himself? What was his reason for wanting to help the ten-year-old fire victim? Why was he helping rebuild the store and apartment? Did he have hopes for a career in construction? Had he been a regular customer at the market? Was he studying the Korean language?

Cory's answers were as uninformative as they had been to his parents, to his coach, and to Chipper and Paul. He didn't want to tell anybody anything. A student photographer took pictures of Cory and Joey painting a wall at Kim's Market and Grocery and published it with a short feature: "Sophomore Helps Save Family, Ease Pain."

Cory had painted himself into a corner. He wanted to hide in it until everyone went away.

His math teacher told him that now she understood why he'd seemed preoccupied in class and that reading about him had warmed her heart: "Sometimes we get very discouraged about teaching. It's kids like you that make us want to get up in the morning and keep going."

Coach Shields cornered him. "Cory, I didn't know. I'm proud of you. And I want you back in the fall for cross-country. I just didn't know."

Davy knew.

It was in the boys' bathroom, and it was during lunch, and it was just Cory and Davy, and Cory's stomach sank.

"You're a hero, Willhouse," said Davy, his voice echoing off the tile walls. Cory remembered the way they had been as children, with high voices and little bikes, with trust in each other's nervy presence, and an agitated sense of new mischief around every turn.

"No, I'm not."

"Yeah. You are. Everybody thinks you're a hero." Davy sat on a washbasin.

"Well, everybody's wrong."

"I know that, and you know that."

"Look, Davy, I just—I don't know, it's not—I just—" *I felt so ashamed of being such a rotten kid I had to do something. I only meant to help.*

"You just got wonderful. That's what."

"No. I mean no. That wasn't—Davy, listen."

The two looked at each other and Cory went mute.

"Willhouse, you're a phony." Davy got off the washbasin and walked out.

That word.

Davy was right. Every afternoon, Cory smilingly lifted boards, installed insulation, helpfully painted, soaked paint rollers and brushes, good-naturedly moved ladders, passed tools to Mr. Kim and the others. He'd learned to call a hammer *mang chi,* to say *pen chi* for pliers. He ate the *bahn-chahn* that Mrs. Kim's sister brought in from time to time. He learned to say *Kam sa ham ni da* (Thank you) and *Chun man ae yo* (You're welcome). He listened contentedly to Joey's humming. He'd even raised eighty-two dollars to help replace the piano.

And it was an act.

He was a hypocrite.

Why hadn't he thought of it that way before?

The next morning Cory woke knowing it was going to be really bad. It was going to be really, really bad, and he was going to do it anyway. He was going to own up to Mr. Kim.

Mr. Kim, who had lived vaguely in Cory's mind for years as the face of a store owner looking startled and angry, and then becoming a set of heavy footsteps behind him, terrifying him, and then stopping. Letting Cory get away. And now, a builder, rebuilder, Cory's boss, who fed him, thanked him, praised his work in Korean, whose praise had to be translated by his ten-year-old son.

The schoolday was endless, and yet it went too fast. Cory wanted to hurry through it and he wanted it to last forever. He wanted to stand in front of Mr. Kim and tell him the truth, and he wanted to evaporate.

"Mr. Kim, I have to talk to you."

"Hi, Cory." Mr. Kim smiled at him.

"Mr. Kim, I have to tell you something."

"Painting way over there," Mr. Kim said logically, pointing to where Joey and Cory had left off the day before.

"Where's Joey?" Cory asked.

"Here I am, Cory." Joey came running in. Voices had an extra layer of sound in the new construction; every word echoed.

"I need you to translate," Cory said.

"Okay, what?"

"Well, I have to talk to your father. It's complicated."

"Okay." Joey spoke to his father in Korean. Mr. Kim walked over to them both and stood still. Joey stood between Cory and Mr. Kim, waiting to begin.

*This little kid shouldn't have to hear such a bad thing. This is wrong. I should put it in writing. I shouldn't say it at all.*

"Mr. Kim, there's a reason why I wanted to help you when the fire ruined your store. It goes back to—Well, the reason is—I mean, it's not what it looks like." *I have to do it now. If I wait one second more, I won't do it at all.* "Mr. Kim, I'm not a nice person."

Joey looked at Cory in bewilderment. "Oh, you are. Cory, you're a real nice—"

Taking his eyes off Mr. Kim's waiting face would feel like a reprieve. But looking down at Joey would be even worse. He stayed on Mr. Kim. "Joey, tell your father I stole from him once. Uh—Mr. Kim—Mr. Kim—When I was nine years old, I stole some food from your market and I ran out. You—" *Starting out was the hardest part. Going on won't be as bad. That's so strange, isn't it? No—going on is much worse. Starting to say it was easy. Going on is impossible.* "You ran after my friends and me. Then you stopped."

Joey stared at Cory. Mr. Kim waited.

*I'll keep looking at Mr. Kim. For a couple of seconds he still doesn't know yet.* "Go on, Joey. Tell him exactly what I said."

"I don't want to."

"Joey, tell him."

And then Cory looked down at Joey.

161

"Are you sure?" Joey asked.

*I wish I weren't.* "Yeah. I'm sure."

What happened to Joey's face was the worst of all. Mr. Kim could have done anything he wanted to Cory, and it wouldn't have mattered if only Joey hadn't looked that way. If only he hadn't had that slowly collapsing look of brand-new grief. He translated for his father.

Every motion in the room stopped.

Mr. Kim's eyelids lowered by just a breath. Surprise, hurt, insult, disappointment, anger. The same face Cory had seen in a flash behind the counter as he'd begun to run out of the store clutching bags of food that would end up not tasting sweet enough.

Mr. Kim held Cory in his unblinking gaze. Cory's mind tried to wander toward harmless things: a piece of molding not trimmed yet. Electrical outlet covers lined up on a bench, ready to be screwed into walls. *Mang chi,* hammer. The moment crept past. Nobody flinched. Cory wanted to disappear. He kept his eyes on Mr. Kim. *This moment can't last for the rest of my life. It will be over sometime.*

Finally, Mr. Kim spoke. No rage, no forgiveness. Just that stare. What he said didn't take very long.

Joey translated: "My dad says you already have your punishment." There was another silence. Then Joey went on: "He says you'll figure out what it is."

———

Cory lay on his bed, shaking his head back and forth at the ceiling. How simpleminded he'd been. To think he could make up for his fourth-grade crime by helping rebuild the store. And then to think he could admit the crime and make everything be all right again.

*It's not all right. It'll never be all right.*

He told himself what a jerk he had been and in how many different ways. It was more exhausting than the weeks of construction.

His big plan, his high hopes, his firm resolve. The results were zero. Or nearly zero.

What kept coming back was the detail that had gone through his mind as he stood on the new floor of Kim's Market and Grocery, looking at Mr. Kim's face. *This moment can't last for the rest of my life. It will be over sometime.* What he knew now was that it wouldn't be over sometime. It would go into his memory, along with the sight of himself grabbing a few plastic packages of food from the store and running away in panic.

He could pile a whole life full of events on top of that Halloween afternoon, and it would still be there. That was the truth.

But the next truth, the new one, was this: now he *knew* it couldn't just get forgotten.

Cory turned off the light. He had an early day tomorrow. Although he had no idea how he would face Joey every day, he was determined to keep on working at Mr. Kim's. Until what? Until the store reopened? Until Joey began humming again? Cory Willhouse closed his eyes.

# Virginia Euwer Wolff

Virginia Euwer Wolff recalls that when she was in fifth grade, "I went with another girl my age on what began as an escapade and ended up with her writing really terrible words on a public wall. I was so bug-eyed in awe of the nerve it took to do such a thing that I didn't try very hard to stop her. I did tell her to stop a couple of times, but then I just stared as she continued." Wolff's concern for "how we feel long after doing something shameful" resulted in this story about Cory Willhouse.

Wolff is best known for her novel *Make Lemonade,* the story of a poor teenage mother and the determined girl who baby-sits for her two children. That novel was named a Best Book for Young Adults and a Notable Book by the American Library Association, was *Booklist*'s Top of the List winner for 1993, and won the Golden Kite Award from the Society of Children's Book Writers and Illustrators, the Oregon Book Award for Young Readers, and the Bank Street Child Study Book Award.

Wolff is also the author of the award-winning *The Mozart Season,* the story of one summer in the life of a twelve-year-old violinist preparing to play in competition, and *Probably Still Nick Swansen,* a tender story about a special-education student who must deal with repeated rejections as well as his guilt over the death of his sister. The American Library Association voted *Probably Still Nick Swansen* one of the 100 Best of the Best Books for Young Adults published between 1967 and 1992.

Virginia Euwer Wolff lived in Connecticut, Massachusetts, New York, Ohio, Pennsylvania, and Washington, D.C., before returning to her native Oregon and settling in Oregon City. Besides writing, swimming, and playing the violin, she teaches English at Mt. Hood Academy, a high school on the slopes of Mt. Hood for skiers who are aiming toward the Olympics. She has a grown son, Tony, who is a professional jazz guitarist; a daughter, Juliet, who is a psychotherapist; and two grandchildren, Max and Sarah.

What can you do when your closest friend takes
advantage of your generosity again and again?

# Eva and the Mayor
## Jean Davies Okimoto

Eva Hicks couldn't wait until Monday. Kenisha was
coming back. Eva had the news on good authority, too,
because Saturday Gramma Evelyn had seen Kenisha's
grandmother in the beauty shop. There was always a lot
of news flying around Rita's Beauty Salon. Eva's mother
said she never believed half of it, but if Gramma Evelyn
wanted to hear all that gossip, it was certainly her choice;
personally, she didn't care to go there anymore. She'd
quit Rita's years ago in favor of Gene Juarez in the downtown Nordstrom, which was called "hair design," not
"beauty salon," and was near where she worked. But Eva
was glad that Gramma Evelyn kept on at Rita's. She liked
hearing the news. And today's news was just about the
best news she'd heard in ages.

Eva Hicks and Kenisha Hayes had been close friends
up until the time Kenisha moved away, but Eva hadn't
seen or heard from her since then. And that was two

years ago. Eva had been crushed when Kenisha left. Not only did she miss her, but Eva had to go to Beacon Middle School without her, which was really terrible. But when she fussed about it, her mother just said middle school is a huge change anyway and she'd just have to toughen up and make new friends. "Steel is tempered by fire," Gramma Evelyn had echoed.

Eva didn't feel very tough, but she had made some new friends. And once she got over feeling like a midget around the eighth-graders—and learned to get out of the way when fights broke out—middle school was okay. And there had been some times that were more than just okay. A lot more. Some great times like the Halloween dance in the cafeteria, when she danced (not just jumping around with her girlfriends but actually danced) with a guy. And not just any guy. She had danced with Durell Thomas, a guy she'd liked forever. She had to admit he wasn't as cute as he used to be before he shaved his head. He always wore Chicago Bulls stuff and tried to look like Michael Jordan, but Durell had kind of a weird head and it just didn't look right. It seemed to be a little dented and not exactly round on top. Gramma Evelyn thought head shaving was nuts. "Those boys are going to be bald-headed soon enough. Life is short! Why do they want to go and rush it for?" But Durell had a great smile and it had been exciting to dance with him at the Halloween dance, even though he wore a monster mask and made odd noises instead of romantic conversation. Eva kept hoping he'd ask her again at the Valentine's or the St. Patrick's dance, but Durell stayed in a pack with his friends. Eva figured that he needed to wear his green monster mask to feel secure about dancing.

Analyzing people's behavior was something Eva had grown up with. Vivian Hicks, her mother, was a social worker and she was always giving explanations for people's behavior. Eva could hardly even say someone was a jerk without her mother trying to get her to understand why that person might be acting the way they did. And once she understood, Eva was supposed to be compassionate. Gramma Evelyn was like that too, but instead of analyzing people, she'd say things like "Do unto others," "Turn the other cheek," "He who is without sin, let him cast the first stone," and "Love thy neighbor as thyself."

The two of them didn't give Eva a lot of room to ever hate anybody. Not that she wanted to go around hating people, but she just wondered if there were other approaches to things. Her father had died of cancer when Eva was six and she sometimes wondered how he thought, if his ideas might be different from Gramma Evelyn's and her mother's, since according to them she was supposed to do one of two things: (1) turn the other cheek, which as far as Eva could tell meant you weren't supposed to fight back, or (2) understand what a miserable situation this person came from and try to help him or her.

Gramma Evelyn began telling Eva how to act toward Kenisha the minute she came home with the news. "That poor child." Her grandmother's voice was filled with concern. "Be good to her. She's going to need her friends, Eva."

That was fine with Eva. There was nothing she'd like

better than to show Kenisha around Beacon, have her over after school, maybe go downtown on Saturdays. Or roller-skating—that would be great! They could go to Skate King. And they could go shopping together and rent videos and talk on the phone all the time.

Eva didn't know a whole lot about Kenisha's family situation; Gramma Evelyn hadn't been that specific. All Eva really knew was that Kenisha and her mother went down to California so Mrs. Hayes could get a fresh start. Eva was never sure what this fresh start was all about because, from what she could tell, everything always seemed okay at Kenisha's house. She had a nice home and her mother had a job and drove a new car. And it seemed like a pretty good job since Kenisha's mother always dressed real sharp. So did Kenisha. But the fresh start must not have worked out because Mrs. Hayes sent Kenisha back up here to stay with her grandmother, and Mrs. Hayes didn't come with her.

On Monday morning, Eva couldn't wait to get to school. The minute her bus arrived at Beacon, she leaped out the door to position herself at the exact spot where Kenisha's bus would pull up. Kenisha's grandmother lived west of the school, and the bus that brought the kids from that area usually parked behind Eva's bus.

*Poor Kenisha,* Eva thought. It would probably be so hard sitting by herself on the bus, not knowing anybody, since the kids she knew before from her old neighborhood took Eva's bus. Poor Kenisha, having to start Beacon and here it was almost the end of seventh grade. What a terrible time to come to a new school!

Eva imagined Kenisha getting off the bus: her eyes

would be wide with fear; she wouldn't even know where the office was. Her heart would pound, her palms would be sweaty, but then as she fearfully came down the steps from the bus . . . there would be Eva waiting compassionately, welcoming her, smiling and making her feel as though she belonged. Then Eva would take her to the office and help her find her homeroom. (They were probably in the same homeroom, since their last names began with *H,* but she'd kindly take her to Mrs. Romero in the office just to be sure.)

When the west end bus drove up, Eva stood on her toes, practically vibrating with excitement. She tried to catch a glimpse of Kenisha through the windows, but all she could see was a bunch of bodies squished together going for the door. Some very sophisticated eighth-graders were the first to get off. Right after them came Monique White, the most popular girl in the seventh grade, who was smiling and looking over her shoulder at someone behind her. It looked like they were carrying on a fascinating conversation.

When the person behind Monique White came down the steps, Eva almost fell over. There was poor, pitiful, friendless Kenisha Hayes . . . Kenisha Hayes and Monique White acting like the best of friends! And that wasn't all. Next down the steps came Durell Thomas with his hand on Kenisha's shoulder, acting very, very friendly, as if he was trying to flirt or something.

Eva wasn't sure what to do. This was so far from what she'd expected that her mind had gone blank on her. All she could do was give a lame little wave. It even seemed to take forever to find her voice.

"Hi, Kenisha," she said finally, hoping she sounded casual.

"Hi, Eva." Kenisha waved and then got into this big, whispery conversation again with Monique, and the two of them walked toward the school.

Eva felt like a fool. She stood near the bus trying to make it seem as though she were meeting someone and waited to go in until Monique and Kenisha were through the front door and out of sight. When she got to homeroom, she was still kind of in shock but decided to save a seat for Kenisha anyway . . . just in case. Ms. Pearson, their homeroom teacher, was different from Eva's other teachers. She didn't assign seats and never cared where anyone sat.

By the time homeroom was almost over, there had been no sign of Kenisha. Eva looked at the empty seat next to her and wondered if Kenisha's last name had changed. Maybe they weren't going to be in the same homeroom after all. But then, five minutes before the bell rang, Kenisha came in, a little out of breath and holding a slip of paper, which she handed to Ms. Pearson.

"We have a new member of our homeroom," Ms. Pearson announced as she glanced at the slip. "This is Kenisha Hayes."

"Hi, everybody." Kenisha smiled at the class as though she were a television star.

How could someone seem so sure of themselves right away? Eva couldn't understand it, but she caught Kenisha's eyes and motioned to the seat next to her. Kenisha gave her a slight smile. Then, very cool, she walked slowly to the back of the room. Then, very cool, she slid into the seat next to Eva.

"Hi, Eva." Kenisha sounded a little bored as she opened her purse and took out a mirror.

"How's it goin', Kenisha?" Eva tried to be friendly, telling herself that Kenisha might not be as confident as she seemed.

"Okay." Kenisha looked at her lips in the mirror. Then she took out a lipstick and spread some on her upper lip, then smacked her lips together.

"How was California?"

"Pretty good."

"Gramma Evelyn saw your grandmother."

"Yeah, I heard." Kenisha opened her purse again and took out her schedule. "Looks like math is what I've got first period. Room 124. Mr. Lui."

"Me too!" Eva looked up at the clock; the bell was about to ring. "Hey, let me have your phone number, okay?"

"Sure." Kenisha tore a scrap of paper from her notebook, scribbled her number, and handed it to Eva.

"Mine's the same as before."

"Okay."

"Want me to call you tonight?"

"Yeah, sure."

"Want me to show you to our math class?" Eva asked as the bell rang.

"Sure, thanks. I was here at the end of last week and the counselor gave me a tour, but it'll probably take me a while to get used to this place."

In math Mr. Lui assigned Kenisha to a seat three

rows in front of Eva so they didn't get a chance to talk again. Eva was hoping that after class, Kenisha might wait for her. But when the bell rang, Kenisha bolted from the room and was halfway down the hall by the time Eva got out the door. And she wasn't walking alone, either. Poor, pitiful Kenisha was walking with Monique White and Durell Thomas.

What was it about being cool? Eva wondered. How did a person get to be that way? Everyone dressed pretty much the same. And even though Kenisha was cute, Eva could think of a lot of people who looked pretty good but who still weren't the kind of people Monique White would bother with. Kenisha had this way about her that seemed to attract people. It was hard for Eva to put her finger on it, but it seemed to be something about the way Kenisha walked and talked; this attitude she had, like she said, "I'm cool. Don't mess with me." Only she didn't have to say it. Everyone just knew. Maybe if Eva hung around Kenisha she could figure out how to be cool, too.

---

"How's Kenisha?" Gramma Evelyn asked when Eva got home that afternoon.

"Seems fine. She's friends with Monique White."

"Who's that?"

"Just the most popular girl in our class, that's all."

"Well, the poor child must be putting up a good front."

It was hard for Eva to imagine that Kenisha was really feeling miserable inside. Not only had Durell Thomas been following her around every chance he got, but so was Charles Ivory, who was in the eighth grade!

Eva wanted to call Kenisha right away that night, but she wasn't allowed to talk on the phone until her homework was done. Then she had to go over it with her mother, or Gramma Evelyn if her mother was working late. They were strict. Usually it didn't bother her, but tonight it was frustrating because she couldn't wait to call Kenisha. But by eight-thirty she finally had it done.

Eva went straight to the phone and looked at the scrap of paper where Kenisha had written her number. Then she called Kenisha. They'd probably be calling each other so much that it wouldn't be long before she knew the number by heart, Eva thought, while she waited on the line for someone to answer.

"Hello."

"Hi, Kenisha. It's me, Eva."

"Listen, I'm on the other line. My grandmother's got Call Waiting. I'll call you back."

Click.

That was it. By nine o'clock Eva hadn't heard from her. By nine-thirty there was still no call and by ten her mother told her to turn off the TV and get to bed.

At breakfast the next morning, Eva told Gramma Evelyn that Kenisha hadn't called her back.

"She probably had a lot on her mind, the poor child. She needs your kindness, Eva."

Eva wasn't so sure. But one thing was for sure, she was going to ask Kenisha about it first thing in homeroom.

"Kenisha, how come you didn't call me back?" Eva asked as Kenisha slid into the next seat.

"Huh?" Kenisha was filing her fingernails. They were long, long red ones.

"Last night. You said you were on the other line when I called."

"Oh, yeah. I was talking with Monique; then after that this guy called."

"You get to talk on the phone as long as you want?"

"Oh, sure. My grandmother's asleep in front of the TV. She doesn't know anything."

"What guy called?"

"Charles."

"Charles Ivory called? The eighth-grader?"

"I always liked older guys. He's pretty fine, don't you think?"

Eva nodded. *Poor child, Gramma Evelyn? I don't think so.*

---

Kenisha didn't have much to say to Eva until the end of the week. Then she was real friendly. She smiled at Eva as soon as she got to homeroom.

"Eva, I left my math homework at home this morning. Let me see yours, would you?"

Eva opened her notebook. They were working on fractions and decimals that week and Mr. Lui had assigned two pages of problems. It was a lot of work and it'd taken her over an hour. Eva wasn't that crazy about letting people copy off her, but she didn't want to be the kind of person who got all huffy and said no. Also she was supposed to be nice to Kenisha, so she pulled out her math homework and handed it over. "Here."

"Thanks." Kenisha grabbed the homework and copied it furiously until the bell rang. Then she gave it back to Eva and said, "Call me tonight."

"Okay." Eva smiled. Maybe it just took time with Kenisha. After all, you couldn't really expect to pick up exactly where you left off after two years. And Kenisha had changed, turning into this very cool person. But now she had asked Eva to call her! She definitely wanted her to call, no mistake about it. Maybe after they started talking on the phone, Kenisha would want to do stuff after school. Maybe they'd do stuff with Monique White and Kenisha's other new friends and she, Eva Lenore Hicks, would be hanging with the cool people. And guys, too! Maybe bald-headed Durell Thomas would start talking to her the way he did at the Halloween dance, even if it was weird noises. He was obviously a lot more mature now.

That night Eva finished her homework around eight o'clock and rushed to the phone to call Kenisha.

"Hi!"

"Eva. I'm on the other line. I'll call you back."

Click.

The rest of Eva's evening went like this:

8:30—No call from Kenisha.

8:33—Eva's mother calls from work, says she has to stay late.

9:00—No call from Kenisha.

9:25—Mrs. Robinson from First A.M.E. calls Gramma Evelyn about the rummage sale.

10:00—Gramma Evelyn is still talking to Mrs.

Robinson. Eva falls asleep by the phone in her mother's bedroom, waiting for Gramma Evelyn to quit talking to Mrs. Robinson.

———

Kenisha was so friendly to Eva in homeroom the next morning that Eva was convinced she had called while Gramma Evelyn was talking all that time to Mrs. Robinson. Eva was just sure of it.

"Gramma Evelyn was on the phone practically all night," Eva explained as the bell rang and Ms. Pearson closed the door. "And we don't have Call Waiting."

Kenisha smiled and examined her nails. "No problem. I was talking to Monique last night and we might be having a party. Maybe you could come if we do."

Eva was thrilled. She'd never been to a party, at least not the kind of party she was sure Kenisha and Monique White would have. A party with guys. Eva's other friends, Gail Dockins and Belinda Williams, talked about guys with Eva, but it was mostly that . . . a lot of talk and not much action. Parties were something you just heard about.

"Oh, Eva, could I see your math?" Kenisha smiled sweetly.

"Sure." Eva took her homework out and handed it to Kenisha just as the bell rang.

"Could I keep it and get it back to you at the beginning of math?"

"Okay."

"Thanks. See you, Eva!" Kenisha gathered up her books and Eva's homework paper and pranced out of the room.

On Friday in math, Mr. Lui made an announcement. "Class, we have six people who have had perfect homework assignments ever since we started fractions and decimals. Their papers are going on the bulletin board, and I'd like everyone to give them a hand when I call their names."

Mr. Lui, who was very big on recognition and encouragement, took the papers to the bulletin board and called the names as he put each one up. "Tyrone Benford." *Clap. Clap. Clap.* "Ashley Gallagher." *Clap. Clap. Clap.* "Kenisha Hayes." *Clap. Clap. Clap.* "Eva Hicks." *Clap. Clap. Clap.* "Susan Nguyen." *Clap. Clap. Clap.* "Tierra Wong." *Clap. Clap. Clap.*

*The nerve of that girl,* Eva thought. When Mr. Lui called Kenisha's name she held her head in the air and gave this superior smile. The kind of smile Gramma Evelyn said was like the cat that ate the canary. Then Tyrone Benford jumped out of his seat and gave her a high five!

"Next week we'll be working on ratios and percentages, and I'd like to see the number of perfect papers doubled." Mr. Lui gave them an enthusiastic smile.

Eva glared at Kenisha. She did more than glare. She put her hands on her hips and rolled her eyes, but Kenisha wouldn't even look in Eva's direction, so her evil look was wasted.

The rest of the day Eva fumed. She was furious, absolutely furious. And she was going to fix that girl. She was going to fix her good. And it didn't take her long to think of a plan, either. It came to her during social studies when they were reading newspapers for an assignment about current events.

It wasn't exactly an original plan, because Eva thought she'd seen something like it on TV. But she was sure she could carry it out because it wasn't complicated. It would take a little time, but it was simple. She'd do two sets of math homework, one for herself, where she would try her best to get the right answers as she always did, and another one where she'd deliberately mess up and put down wrong answers. That was the one she'd give to Kenisha the next time she wanted to copy Eva's homework.

The only thing that worried Eva was what Kenisha might do when she realized Eva had given her bogus homework. Sometimes people got their friends to beat someone up if they got mad enough at that person. Eva didn't think Monique White and some of Kenisha's other new friends were like that, but you could never be sure. And who knew what kind of story Kenisha might make up about her? Eva realized that when it came to knowing what Kenisha would do, she was clueless. Kenisha was so different now. There was a whole lot Eva didn't know about her. Like why she came back from California and what happened there, anyway.

When Eva got home, Gramma Evelyn was watching *Oprah.* As Eva went into the living room, the show broke for a commercial. Gramma Evelyn clicked the remote to mute.

"It sure is something, the troubles people get themselves into. Those people today, what a mess!"

"Gramma Evelyn?"

"What, sugar?"

"What was wrong with Kenisha's mother? Why'd she send Kenisha up here to stay with her grandmother?"

"Well, sugar, we've got to hate the sin but love the sinner." Then *Oprah* came back and Gramma Evelyn clicked on the sound.

What was that supposed to mean? Eva knew it wasn't right to copy other people's work, but it wasn't as bad as cheating on a test, and a lot of people did it. She knew that didn't make it right, but still it didn't seem like such a big sin, and besides, she wasn't the copier. The whole thing made her feel pretty mixed up.

She didn't know for sure if she had let Kenisha copy her work because of all that stuff Gramma Evelyn said about being nice to Kenisha or because she wanted to get in with Kenisha and be one of the cool people. Probably both reasons, she had to admit. But after the way Kenisha acted so proud in math, giving Tyrone Benford that high five, Eva felt completely ripped off. Kenisha deserved to get burned, she thought, and she decided to go ahead with her plan.

Eva had finished her math homework and was starting on the phony answers for Kenisha when she heard her mother come home. Eva went to the kitchen to help with the groceries.

"Got a good buy on this chicken," her mother said as she unpacked the last sack. "And I even forgot the coupon."

"Mom?" Eva put the milk in the refrigerator. "What does Gramma Evelyn mean when she says I should hate the sin and love the sinner?"

Eva's mother shook her head and smiled. "When did she say that?"

"It's about Kenisha. You both say I should be nice to her, but she's changed. She acts really cool and I just wanted to know the real story, that's all."

"You know I don't like telling people's business."

"I won't say anything!" Eva slammed the refrigerator door.

"Be careful!"

"Sorry." Eva leaned on the counter and drummed her nails on it. "I just don't think it's fair for everyone to tell me to be so nice to her and not tell me why."

Eva's mother put away the last of the groceries and sat at the kitchen table.

"I suppose it might be easier to be nice to her if you did know. But I'm telling you, I don't want any of this spread around school."

"Mom, I won't!"

"I mean it." She stared at Eva; her gaze was steady and direct. "You hear me, now."

"I promise."

Eva's mother got up and fixed herself a cup of tea. "Rhondelle Hayes, Kenisha's mother, was working as a bookkeeper at the Maple Street Service Center. There were rumors she was doing drugs, but they were just rumors. But what she did get in trouble for was embezzling."

"What's that?"

"It's like cooking the books, dipping into the till. She was taking money and trying to fix the books so no one would know. But she got caught."

"Did she get arrested?"

"She got caught pretty early in the game and had stolen less than five hundred dollars, so the board of directors gave her a break and didn't press charges as long as she signed a contract that she'd pay it all back. But right after that she moved down to San Francisco and I guess things weren't much better there. Drugs again. Supposedly not only using, but dealing, and Kenisha was going to be sent to a foster home. That's when her grandmother said to send her up here. I heard Rhondelle got probation and is in some treatment program now, but no one knows for sure."

"What happens if Kenisha messes up here?"

"She'll probably go to a foster home if her grandmother can't handle her." Eva's mother put her hand over Eva's. "Try and help her if you can, honey. I'm sure she's acting a lot more cool than she feels."

Eva didn't want to tell her mother about the homework because she knew what her mother would say. Vivian Hicks was very big on tough love, and she'd tell Eva to talk to the teacher about it. "You never help a person if you let them keep doing wrong," she'd always say. But it wasn't that easy. Eva couldn't stand the kind of person who told on people, and she wasn't going to be one. No way.

This was one of those times she wished her father were around because she'd like to hear another idea besides "hate the sin and love the sinner" or "tough love and tell the teacher."

Two days later in homeroom, Kenisha started talking about the party she and Monique White were going to have. "We'll let you know about it, Eva." Then she smiled. "Oh, can I see your math?"

"Kenisha, you don't have to talk all that trash about inviting me to a party. I've got my own friends."

"Didn't you used to like Durell Thomas?"

"Maybe."

"Well, we'd invite him."

"Listen, girl, I'll give you my homework, but I'd really like to help you do your own work. You know what I'm saying? All you have to do is call me tonight and we can go over it on the phone."

Kenisha pouted a minute and looked at her nails. Then she said, "Thanks. I'll give you a call." Then she grabbed Eva's homework.

———

That night Eva waited for Kenisha's call. She had her math book right by the phone, and she was sure she could explain to Kenisha how to do the ratios and the percentages. Kenisha had always been smart, and Eva knew she'd catch on if she just tried.

Gramma Evelyn was out at choir practice, and since most of her friends were in the choir, she didn't get any calls. Eva's mother sometimes didn't get home from work until after nine o'clock, which most of her friends knew, so she didn't get any calls, either. This left the line open in case anyone called for Eva, but by the end of the evening the phone hadn't rung even once. Not once. There wasn't a single call.

In homeroom the next morning, Kenisha gushed all over the place apologizing. "I just had so many calls, I couldn't get off the phone. Let me see your math, okay,

Eva? Just this once, and then I'll call you tonight so you can help me do it myself."

Eva looked at Kenisha, and all she could imagine was a horrible foster home with evil people where Kenisha wouldn't get any food. Some nasty place where the evil people would beat her and lock her in a closet. "Okay," she said quietly, and handed Eva her homework.

At the end of the week, Mr. Lui was doing his thing again about recognition and encouragement. "Congratulations, class. We have nine perfect papers! I'd like you to give these people a hand while I call their names and put their papers on the bulletin board."

Mr. Lui took the papers to the bulletin board and did his same routine, calling the names as he put up each person's paper. "Tyrone Benford." *Clap. Clap. Clap.* "Fabiola DeRosa." *Clap. Clap. Clap.* "Ashley Gallagher." *Clap. Clap. Clap.* "Eva Hicks." *Clap. Clap. Clap.* "Duong Lam." *Clap. Clap. Clap.* "Susan Nguyen." *Clap. Clap. Clap.* "Alvin Whipps." *Clap. Clap. Clap.* "Tierra Wong." *Clap. Clap. Clap.* "And we're especially lucky to have added an excellent math student to our class. This is the second perfect paper for the newest member of our class, Kenisha Hayes!"

Everyone clapped, louder than they had for anyone else. Tyrone Benford went "Wooh, wooh, wooh," as if he were at a football game, and then jumped out of his seat to give Kenisha a high five. Kenisha jumped out of her seat, slapped Tyrone's hand, and then, smiling smugly with her head in the air, she turned around and waved to the class, flashing her long red nails.

"That girl's a liar and a cheat!" Eva wanted to scream. Her hand clutched her math book, which she wanted to throw at Kenisha's head. It was all she could do to control herself. But she closed her eyes and concentrated, relaxing her grip on her math book, telling herself to stay calm and trying to remember what her mother had said about a foster home. Eva squeezed her eyes shut, imagining Kenisha in the horrible foster home, starving to death, locked in the closet, and beaten by the evil people, and so she didn't scream "She's a liar and a cheat!" or throw her book at Kenisha to bash her head in. She didn't say anything. Instead, she did everything she could to forget about it.

———

That night after Eva had finished her math homework, she started reading the newspaper for her social studies project. The assignment was to follow a current event about a person in public office and then write to the person with an opinion about it. Most of the people in the class were writing to people on the county council, trying to get them to vote for a new stadium since the Kingdome was old and the Seahawks might leave. But Eva didn't care that much since the Seahawks were such a cupcake team. She was leafing through the paper trying to find something interesting when her mother burst into her room.

"Eva, come look! Mayor Rice is going to be on TV!"

"He's always on TV. What's the big deal?"

"He's having a press conference to tell that talk-show guy on KVI to quit his hate-talk radio. It's about time someone stood up to that radio slimebag!"

Eva followed her mother into the living room and sat next to her on the couch in front of the TV.

"It'll be on right after the weather."

"What's this about, anyway?"

"There's this real nutcase who used to work for the Seattle Water Department and he got fired. Then he stood around downtown handing out flyers filled with all kinds of lies about Mayor Rice. He even sent the mayor a postcard that said, 'Your career is toast if I don't get mine back today.' Then this slimy talk radio guy broadcast the rumors all over the state." She held the remote and sat forward, turning up the sound. "Shhh, listen up now."

Mayor Rice thanked a lot of people and introduced a lot of people and Eva thought it was kind of boring, but then all of a sudden she also sat forward.

"I was raised to turn the other cheek, but there comes a time when a person has to say *'Enough.'*" The mayor paused. "*Enough* is *enough.*"

A whole lot of people cheered. Then he continued: "KVI has taken the hateful words put on paper by one disturbed former employee—even though they have admitted these words did not contain one shred of truth—and deliberately spread these lies across our state. I am here to say they are cowards. They are dangerous."

Then the mayor said this kind of talk radio was hate radio, and there was more and more cheering.

"He's right, you know, Eva," her mother said when the press conference was over. "You can't always turn the other cheek. If someone is taking advantage of you or doing something wrong, you need to have compassion for yourself, too, and stand up to them. But with tough love."

Eva decided that her project would be to write to Mayor Rice about how he had stood up to the hate radio guy. Her mother thought it was a good idea. "I'll save the paper for you, honey. So you can collect the articles."

The next morning in homeroom, Eva was looking at an article about Mayor Rice when Kenisha came in.

"Hi, Eva." Kenisha smiled as though everything were wonderful.

"Hi."

"Sorry I couldn't call you again last night about the math. Could I see your homework?"

Eva thought about poor Kenisha in the horrible foster home.

She opened her notebook.

Then she thought about Kenisha prancing in front of the class, waving to everyone when Mr. Lui had them clap especially for her.

Eva closed her notebook, and her stomach felt as if it were closing into a knot.

Then she thought about Kenisha in the horrible foster home locked in the closet.

She opened the notebook.

"Hurry up, Eva. The bell's going to ring."

Then Eva glanced at the article about Mayor Rice.

"Hurry up!"

"No." Eva shut her notebook. The knot in her stomach got tighter as she imagined Kenisha dragging her behind the school where the teachers couldn't see and pounding her into the ground.

"What did you say?"

"No. Do your own work, girl." Eva's hand shook as she clutched the article about Mayor Rice and waited for the bell.

"How come? You always gave it to me before." Kenisha seemed totally surprised.

"I got sick of helping you steal from me."

"You call that stealing?" Kenisha shouted in a huff. "It's not like I took your money!"

"It's still stealing, and I say, '*Enough.*'" Eva took a deep breath and tried to stay calm. She felt sad that Kenisha's mother was messed up, but that didn't give Kenisha the right to get away with stuff. Eva looked at the picture of Mayor Rice in the newspaper clipping and took another deep breath. Then she looked straight at Kenisha so there would be no mistake about it. *"Enough is enough."*

———

Later that week, after Eva had read all the articles about Mayor Rice, she wrote him her letter for her social studies project.

Mayor Norm Rice
12th Floor
1200 Municipal Bldg.
600 4th Ave.
Seattle, WA 98104-1873

Dear Mayor Rice,

I go to Beacon Middle School and I'm writing you for my social studies class. I just wanted to tell you that I think you did the right thing when you stood up to the guy on the radio who was spreading lies about you.

Actually, Mayor Rice, this is more than a letter for social studies because I want you to know that you really helped me. I had a little problem at school and my grandmother always tells me to turn the other cheek just like you were taught. Also, my mother says to try and help the person if you think they're doing wrong. I tried both these things and they didn't work. My father passed when I was six and even though that was a long time ago, I still wonder what he would tell me to do in certain situations. When I heard you say on television "Enough is enough," I knew that's what my dad would have said. So that's what I did. Thank you for helping me with my problem. I don't think all politicians are jerks like some people say.

Your friend,

*Eva Lenore Hicks*

Eva Lenore Hicks

P.S. I will vote for you when I am old enough.

# Jean Davies Okimoto

The character Eva Hicks in "Eva and the Mayor" was inspired by some of the students at Mercer Middle School in Seattle, where Jean Davies Okimoto has been part of a writing project sponsored by the Seattle Arts Commission. The ending of the story was based on a press conference at which Seattle's mayor, Norman B. Rice, denounced the "hate radio" that came from a local talk radio station. Students in Ms. Gretchen Coe's classes, along with Ms. Coe, provided feedback to the author as she wrote and revised the story.

Jean Davies Okimoto is the author of children's picture books and adult nonfiction, as well as middle-grade and young adult novels. Her most popular book has been *Molly by Any Other Name,* the story of an Asian girl, adopted as an infant by a white American family, who wants to find her birth mother and determine her own racial identity. Popular with middle-graders is Okimoto's recent *Take a Chance, Gramps!,* which was a Junior Library Guild selection and was placed on state reading lists in Texas, Washington, and Missouri. One of Okimoto's novels—*Jason's Women*—was named a Best Book for Young Adults by the American Library Association;

two of her books have received Readers' Choice Awards from the International Reading Association; and she has been the recipient of a *Parents' Choice* Award, the Washington Governor's Award, and the 1993 Maxwell Medallion for Best Children's Book of the Year.

Okimoto's most recent novels for teenagers are *Talent Night* and *The Eclipse of Moonbeam Dawson. Talent Night* focuses on Rodney, a biracial high-school senior whose dreams of attaining fame as the first Asian American rapper are turned upside down when Uncle Hideki, his Japanese American uncle, offers to leave his reparations money from his internment during World War II to Rodney if Rodney can prove he has retained something of his Japanese heritage. *The Eclipse of Moonbeam Dawson* describes a teenager's efforts to break away from his overly dependent single mother and find his own identity while working at a fancy resort in a remote part of British Columbia.

When something terrible happens to Little Li's family, what choice does he have except revenge?

# Little Li and the Old Soldier
## Lensey Namioka

"It worked! It worked!"

Little Li was so jubilant that he wanted to leap and twirl and dance. But he had to run as fast as he could. He had to get out of sight before the barbarian soldiers could climb out.

Behind him he could hear cries and squelching sounds. Even from a distance, the air reeked with the stink from the cesspool as the soldiers trampled each other in their attempts to struggle up from the deep pit.

As Little Li ran, tears of laughter streamed down his cheeks. Too bad none of his friends were here to see his triumph. His best friend, Ah Zhu, didn't even believe the trick would work.

"You'll be caught!" Ah Zhu had warned him. "Somebody will see you putting boards over the pit, and he'll report you to the soldiers."

Little Li wasn't caught. He was called Little Li to

193

distinguish him from his uncle, Old Li, but he was big and rawboned. He could also move fast. Quickly placing several boards over the cesspool, he had then covered the boards with straw. Not a soul had seen him.

The next step had been more dangerous. Little Li had chosen a time when the group of soldiers were lounging outside the wine shop. It was their favorite pastime after the evening meal.

By then the sun was low and visibility was poor, too poor for Little Li to be recognized. He knew that his great height would mark him out, and he had to wait until it was too dark for the soldiers to see him clearly. It would also be too dark for them to get a good look at the ground.

Little Li approached the soldiers from the back and began chanting the rudest words he could think of—"turtle's egg" and "dog's fart" were some of his best. The barbarian soldiers didn't understand much Chinese, but the dirty words were the first things they had learned.

Little Li started running away before the soldiers could turn their heads to see who it was. By the time they started the chase, he was running across the fields and heading for the cesspool. He had enough of a lead so that they didn't see him make a slight detour to avoid the boards hiding the pit.

The soldiers, of course, ran right over the boards, which immediately gave way under them. Hearing the splashing, Little Li stopped and turned back so that he could enjoy the sounds of the struggling, the choking, and the retching. The stink didn't bother him. It was wonderful!

When Little Li got home, some of his friends gathered to congratulate him. Only Ah Zhu didn't join the others in their praises. "You're too old for a prank like this, Little Li," he said. "You're seventeen already, and you should start thinking about your responsibilities."

"You're just jealous of Little Li because you didn't think of the trick first!" said Wang San. He was the youngest of the group and Little Li's greatest admirer.

"Those soldiers will have to do something to show us that we can't get away with this," warned Ah Zhu.

"It will be worth it!" declared Wang San. "After all, those barbarians have already taken our land, insulted our women, and trampled us into the ground. What more can they do?"

Several of the others echoed him. Since the north of China had been occupied by the horse-riding barbarians, the pride and spirit of the people had been crushed. Little Li's act had struck a blow for their self-respect.

True, life for peasants like Little Li and his uncle had also been hard under the Song emperors, who had ruled China since the end of the tenth century. Officials sent by the government had often been corrupt, seizing most of the harvest and leaving only enough to enable the peasants to stay alive. But at least the officials were educated people who observed the niceties of civilized behavior. They had ruled according to written laws. The new rulers were barbarians from the western deserts, who spoke an incomprehensible language and drank fermented mare's milk. It was not to be tolerated!

Old Li was proud of his nephew, but he couldn't quite hide his uneasiness. Like Ah Zhu, he expected some form of reprisal from the soldiers. At supper, he expressed his worry. "We're going to have to be very careful for a while," he warned. "Everybody should lie low and keep as quiet as possible."

"Why should we?" demanded his wife. "We've been quiet enough! That's why those barbarians think they can do anything they want! It's about time we show them we still have spirit!" She slammed her husband's bowl of noodles down on the table.

Little Li's aunt was short and square, and she had a vigorous voice. She tolerated no nonsense from either her nephew or her son, Baobao, and a scolding from her was worse than a scalding from hot water. But under her rough manner was a kind heart.

Little Li's parents had died in an epidemic, and he had come to live with Uncle's family. Auntie treated him like her own son. Knowing how much he loved garlic, she always had a dish of pickled garlic on the table for their evening meal. Little Li loved his aunt and admired her fighting spirit.

Uncle was mild and soft-spoken, unlike Auntie. He was as tall as his nephew, but thinner. He had a thoughtful, scholarly face. Little Li sometimes thought that if things had been different, Uncle might have learned to read and write and even pass a government examination to become an official.

That would never happen now, not when they had been conquered. There would be no government examinations under their new, illiterate rulers. The barbarians didn't employ scholarly officials to govern the country. They governed purely by force.

"I still think it was rash to provoke the soldiers," said Uncle. He turned to Auntie. "Maybe you should try to keep Baobao indoors as much as possible."

"*You* try," growled Auntie. "I haven't been able to keep him indoors since the day he learned to walk. Besides, why should we cower in our homes and scuttle around like cockroaches? This is *our* country, and we can do as we like!"

For a couple of days it seemed as if Little Li's aunt was right. The soldiers didn't do anything to the village, although they no longer lounged around in front of the wine shop, but kept to their barracks.

"Maybe I should think up something else," Little Li told Ah Zhu. "It's dull around here."

"If you find it dull here, why don't you come south with me?" suggested Ah Zhu.

"You're serious about going south?" asked Little Li, surprised. When Ah Zhu had mentioned that he was going south to join the remnant of a Chinese army, Little Li had thought his friend had been joking.

"Playing tricks on the barbarians doesn't accomplish anything," said Ah Zhu. "General Han was one of the best commanders in the imperial army. If I enlist under him, I might actually do something useful."

"But that's so far away!" protested Little Li.

"I hear that he and his men are somewhere down in Anhui," said Ah Zhu. "It might take me a few weeks or even months to find them, but it will be worth it."

"If you can find them at all," muttered Little Li. He felt hurt. His best friend was deserting him and fleeing south. "You're going to leave home? You're giving up and letting the barbarians take over the land your family has farmed for generations?"

"I want to go where I can do some good," insisted Ah Zhu.

Little Li was suddenly angry. "You're running away! You're abandoning your home, your village, your country, so the enemy can do whatever they want here!"

Ah Zhu grew angry as well. "So what do you expect me to do here? Play childish tricks to taunt the barbarian soldiers?" He stomped off. He didn't even turn around to say good-bye.

Little Li soon forgot about the soldiers. He even forgot about Ah Zhu. Baobao was sick with a fever and refused to eat. He was only six but was already showing signs of becoming tall like all the Li family. He was also naughty and too much of a handful for his mother to manage. Little Li was the only person in the family he listened to.

Now Baobao was tossing feverishly in bed, and Auntie was beside herself. Uncle tried to reassure her, but Little Li could see that behind his calm he was frantic with worry.

"Maybe I can go into town and get some medicine for Baobao," Little Li offered.

Auntie raised her tearful face. "Would you? I have some silver coins I saved up for an emergency—"

"This is an emergency!" said Uncle.

"I buried them in a clay pot behind the house," said Auntie. "There should be enough for the medicine."

Auntie dug up the pot, broke it apart, and took out the precious handful of coins. Little Li set off for town with the money. He would be the only person from the village to be away on that day.

Getting into the walled town was harder than he had expected. The barbarian guards at the gate looked at him suspiciously, and there was no way to communicate with them until another guard came up, a Chinese-speaking one.

If he had been less worried about Baobao, Little Li would have despised the man for being a traitor and serving the enemy. As it was, he was simply overjoyed at being able to explain his errand.

When at last he had been allowed to enter the gates and find his way to the apothecary shop, it was past noon. By the time he had purchased the medicine and headed home again, the sun was close to setting.

At least he thought the sun was setting, since there was a red glow in the sky. But the glow was coming from the east, not the west! He started to run when he realized that his village was on fire.

He could smell the burning thatch from the roofs well before he reached the first houses. He could hear crackling from pieces of burning timber. What he could not hear were human voices crying out, voices of people trying to put out the fire, of people trying to help their friends and neighbors.

The first house he reached belonged to Wang San's family. The house had already been gutted, and the fire had burned down to embers. The smell of burning thatch was mixed with the sickening stench of burning flesh.

Little Li's heart was thumping in his chest when he went up to a charred body lying across the front door. He needed all his willpower to turn the body over. It was his young friend, Wang San, and his greatest admirer. The boy had been killed by an arrow through his chest—a barbarian arrow.

Little Li's throat closed painfully, and hot tears

welled up in his eyes. But he choked back his grief and blinked away his tears. He couldn't afford to break down.

He didn't enter the Wangs' house, for the floor was still too hot. Just inside he could see the charred remains of a woman, probably Wang San's mother. He swept his eyes quickly around the one-room house and saw no sign of anyone living.

The next two houses were still burning. There were no signs of survivors here, either. Even before he reached his own home, Little Li knew with leaden certainty that there was no hope.

He saw Auntie's body first, lying facedown in front of the house. Dried blood covered the back of her battered head, crushed by a horse's hoof. She seemed to be lying on top of something. Little Li saw a small foot protruding from under Auntie's body, and he knew that she had died trying to protect Baobao.

The boy might still be alive! Little Li gently pulled Auntie's body aside and looked down at Baobao's still face. It was no longer flushed with fever, but gray white. Baobao would never need medicine again.

Where was Uncle? Maybe he had been in the fields when the barbarian fiends swooped down on the village! Maybe he and some of the men working in the fields had escaped the slaughter.

Then Little Li arrived at the village well and saw the pile of bodies. They were all men. They seemed to have been cut down in a hail of arrows while trying to get water to put out the fires.

Uncle's body was lying right by the well, and even in death his hands gripped the wooden bucket so hard that Little Li had trouble prying it loose.

Little Li hardly remembered what happened next. He walked around and around the silent village in a daze. He didn't even think about the possibility of the barbarian soldiers' returning and finding him.

Hours, perhaps days, went by. He must have buried the bodies of his relatives, for he found blisters on his hands from hard digging. Perhaps he even ate something, although he couldn't say what. He knew that time had passed because all the fires had burned out.

What finally roused him from his daze was the smell from the cesspool. It reminded him of something. Then it all came back to him. He had tricked the enemy soldiers into chasing him and falling into the cesspool. Ah Zhu had warned him that the soldiers might take reprisals for that trick.

A shaft of grief pierced his chest, and Little Li cried aloud to the heavens. *He* was responsible for the slaughter of his whole village! The barbarians had come back and killed everyone in revenge for their humiliation!

He was consumed by rage: rage against the barbarians for their hideous revenge and an even greater rage against himself for bringing destruction down on his people.

He had to do something. He would go to the barracks and kill the barbarians. He would go on killing and killing until they killed him. Only in this way would his spirit rest in peace.

He had to find a weapon. Perhaps he could use a hoe. Even a broken piece of timber was better than nothing.

As he searched the ground, he heard a soft clinking behind him. Jumping to his feet and looking wildly around, he saw that the sky was quite dark. Without his noticing it, night had fallen, and only the quarter moon provided a faint illumination.

What had made that clinking sound? Had one of the barbarians returned?

Then the faint moonlight was blotted out by a dark bulk looming in front of him. Little Li stepped back. Although he wasn't timid, he couldn't help retreating. Little Li was no dwarf, but the figure in front of him was taller than he was. It also seemed much heavier.

"Who are you?" whispered Little Li. Suddenly he shivered with cold.

There was a sigh, and with another clinking, the figure sat down on a fallen beam from the lintel of a house. "I'm an old soldier," he said in a hollow voice.

Above the smell of burning, Little Li's nose detected something different: a stale, dusty kind of smell, like the air from some box that had been kept sealed for ages.

He looked curiously at the old soldier. The man was Chinese from his speech, although his accent was strange. "Where are you from? Are you one of General Han's men?"

The soldier shook his head. "I'm from the capital. I'm one of Emperor Qin Shihuang's guards."

Little Li was confused. He had heard fabulous stories about Emperor Qin Shihuang, whose tomb was rumored to be surrounded by a river of mercury and guarded by thousands of terra-cotta soldiers. But the Qin dynasty had fallen more than a thousand years earlier!

The present dynasty was the Song. Furthermore, the barbarians had conquered the whole of the north, and the emperor had fled south to establish a new capital hundreds of miles away. Was this soldier a deserter, then? "Are you on leave?" Little Li asked tactfully.

"No, I'm still on duty," said the soldier, laughing. Even his laugh had a hollow sound. "I'll be on guard duty forever and ever."

Little Li wondered if his companion was mad. Not only did he talk of serving an emperor dead for a thousand years, he used phrases that were quaint and unfamiliar. Perhaps that was how members of the Imperial guard talked.

The armor of this guard was also different from what Little Li had seen worn by other Chinese soldiers. It had a long tunic made of linked pieces of some material that produced the odd clinking sound. In the moonlight the man looked curiously monotone. His skin, hair, uniform, and boots all seemed to be of the same sandy color.

However strange the man was, he looked immensely strong. Would he be willing to strike a blow against the barbarians?

"What are your plans?" Little Li asked the soldier.

The man looked at him quizzically. "I've told you already: I'm forever on guard duty. What are *your* plans?"

Little Li had nothing to lose by telling the truth. "I plan to go down to the barracks of those barbarians and kill as many of them as I can—even if I die in the attempt."

The other man sighed. "And what do you hope to accomplish by that?"

"They killed my family!" cried Little Li. "They massacred the whole village! How can I live under the same sky with these monsters?"

The soldier didn't answer immediately. Finally he

sighed again. "What will happen then? After you kill a few of the barbarians, and you're killed in turn, what will happen next?"

"What happens next doesn't concern me," muttered Little Li. "I won't be around to see it."

"I'll tell you what will happen next," said the soldier. "The barbarians will have to show the local people that they can't get away with the killing. So they will go to the next village—probably the one where your mother or your aunt comes from—and massacre all the people there, too."

"Are you telling me that I should do nothing?" demanded Little Li. He was shocked. The man had impressed him as a strong, confident, and courageous warrior. He didn't look like someone who would choose a cowardly way out.

"Let me tell you what I've seen," said the soldier. "I'm old—very, very old. And over many centuries I've seen our country conquered by various barbarian tribes."

The soldier had said he was very old, but that he had seen many centuries pass was simply too incredible to believe. Something else he had said made Little Li very curious, however. "Why did all those barbarians succeed in conquering our country?" he asked. "We've had plenty of good soldiers, and good generals, too."

The old soldier gave his hollow laugh again. "Sometimes our defeats were the result of court intrigues and corruption. Sometimes the barbarians used new weapons that were too powerful for us."

Little Li began to understand. "These barbarians are wonderful archers! Our soldiers are no match for them."

"That's been the case during more than one

conquest," said the old soldier. "The tribes from the far western interior are particularly skilled in horsemanship, and they can shoot with deadly accuracy while riding their horses at full gallop. Some of our emperors tried to hire the horsemen for the Chinese army, but the plan usually backfired."

A wave of hopelessness swept over Little Li. "Do we have to submit tamely to the conqueror, then? I'd rather die!"

"Don't despair," said the soldier. His voice was becoming fainter. "We've always won out in the end."

"So you think I should go fight the barbarian soldiers after all?" asked Little Li.

"We don't always win by force. We win because we're civilized and we rule by law." There was another laugh, even fainter. "The barbarians always adopt our ways in the end."

To Little Li's astonishment, the old soldier seemed to be fading in front of his eyes. "Don't go!" he begged. "Tell me more about how we win in the end!"

He reached out and tried to grab the tunic of the soldier. His hand closed on something hard, but in the next instant the man was gone.

Little Li fell on his knees, and as he bumped the ground, he opened his eyes.

It was no longer dark. A faint glow low in the sky showed that the sun would be rising soon.

There was no soldier in armor, no imperial guard. Little Li had fallen asleep while sitting on the charred beam in front of his gutted house. That conversation about conquests and being more civilized and winning in the end, that was all a dream.

He was alone. There was nothing left for him except to go and kill the barbarian soldiers and be killed in turn.

Then the words of the old soldier came back to him. What did he hope to accomplish by killing and being killed? Yet the alternative was to stay in his village and scratch out a living under the yoke of the conquerors.

Would the conquerors eventually become civilized and rule by law? What did that old soldier mean?

Then Little Li laughed at himself. He was expecting answers from someone he himself had dreamed!

Suddenly he made his decision. He would go south and try to find his friend, Ah Zhu. Together they would join the remnants of General Han's army and find some way to resist the conquerors. It meant giving up the land of his ancestors to the barbarians—barbarians who might someday become civilized.

As Little Li pushed himself up from the beam, he found that he was holding something in his hand. It looked like a squarish piece of pottery of some sort—a piece of terra-cotta.

# Lensey Namioka

Lensey Namioka enjoys writing stories that are based on ancient tales she heard as a child growing up in China. Although the idea behind "Little Li and the Old Soldier" was prompted by the reprisals and counterreprisals in today's Bosnia, Northern Ireland, and the Middle East, the old soldier in the story is a reference to the warriors who protected Emperor Qin, who unified China twenty-two hundred years ago; terra-cotta replicas of hundreds of those warriors have guarded Qin's tomb ever since.

Born in Beijing, Namioka emigrated to America with her family when she was nine years old. After marrying and traveling all over the world with her Japanese-born husband, Isaac, she settled with him in Seattle.

A number of her novels for young people—like *White Serpent Castle, The Samurai and the Long-Nosed Devils,* and *Island of Ogres*—are set in feudal Japan and feature two young samurai warriors, Matsuzo and Zenta. Both *Village of the Vampire Cat* and *Island of Ogres* were American Library Association Best Books for Young Adults, and *Village of the Vampire Cat* was nominated for an Edgar Award. The most recent two books about Matsuzo and Zenta are *The Coming of the Bear* and *Den of the White Fox.*

Namioka has also published several novels about contemporary Chinese American young people, including the autobiographical *Who's Hu?* and the humorous *Yang the Youngest and His Terrible Ear* and *Yang the Third and Her Impossible Family,* which was a 1995 *Parents' Choice* Award winner. For older teenage readers there is *April and the Dragon Lady,* a story about the generational conflict that exists in a Chinese American family, especially between the contemporary high-school girl and her old-world grandmother. That novel, like *White Serpent Castle* before it, won the Washington State Governor's Award.

Sometimes we don't like the face that looks
back at us in the mirror. Cassie, though, is
horrified by what she sees.

# Stranger
## Walter Dean Myers

You couldn't put much past Cassie Holliday. Girl got straight Bs in school in District 5. You didn't get no straight Bs in District 5 unless you had some smarts. Everybody said Cassie was smart and was going to make something of herself.

Things didn't go the way she thought they was supposed to, though. What she thought was, she was going to finish school and get her a good job and get on with it. That's what she thought, but everything was harder than it was supposed to be and nobody seemed to care. Maybe it was the not caring that made it hurt so much. Or maybe it was when her mother said she couldn't cope no more and Cassie had to make it on her own without even a piece of clue as how to do it. Anyway, she took a little something to ease things. Not much at first and not all the time. But then it took more just to stop the hurt. And then it took more and more, and finally it was taking

209

too much. It was taking pieces of her clear away and Cassie knew it.

She was tired when she first saw the stranger, but she knew what she seen. That morning she had gone downtown to the employment agency to look for a job. She hadn't been sitting around all the time before, doing nothing, either. What she had been doing was looking for a job when she could, when her knee wasn't feeling so bad. She hadn't got anything but it wasn't because she wasn't looking.

What made Cassie decide to go downtown and look for a job is that she wanted to get herself a new beginning. She had done that before, look for a new beginning, and it hadn't worked, but she still was trying. But on the night before she went downtown she had stopped over to the Africa House to see if they had any applications for the G.E.D. See, Cassie was getting herself together. Dropping out of high school wasn't a big thing, or at least it wasn't a big thing at the time she did it. But when she applied for a job and people kept asking her about high school, it got to be a drag. Cassie wasn't going to let no little thing like that stop her.

She got the application and was sitting on a bench in that little park across from the Africa House when this guy come up to her and ask her if she in the life.

"What life you talking about?" Cassie asked. This guy looked like a bum. His clothes is so dirty they got a shine on them. He wearing skips on his feet and his breath stunk.

"Sweet as you look I thought you might be looking for some extra cash," the man said. "How old are you?"

He pull some one-dollar bills out his pocket, which was as dirty as he was, and started counting them out.

"I'm eighteen and I don't know what you talking about!" Cassie said, putting her age up a year and loud talking the guy. "And you better get your *funky* self out my face!"

Cassie jumped up from the bench and started footing down the street. Here she was getting herself together and had to deal with this lowlife. She started on uptown, getting madder and madder as she went. Malcolm X Boulevard was just crawling with people because it was too hot to be in no house without some serious AC. People was sitting on folding chairs or boxes or just standing around having them a beer or maybe a soft-shell crab sandwich, whatever they was selling on the street or you could bring out your house.

That was what made her sick. She was walking too fast in too much heat in too many smells and sounds coming out boom boxes and people fighting and laughing and being themselves on the hot streets. Cassie was feeling terrible and knew she needed something to get herself together.

The thing was that sometimes things went good and sometimes things went wrong and sometimes you just needed you something to get you through the night. Cassie was needing something bad.

She needed something but that was all right, she told herself, because she was getting herself together. That's why she was going for her G.E.D. She walked a little faster, walking past some kids jumping rope and some other little long-headed black boys playing basketball and who should have had their tails in bed a long time ago no matter how hot it was.

She stopped and got a little something. It made her tired to deal with the brother she bought the stuff from, or maybe it didn't make her tired but just made her sicker for the minute. Cassie thought that since she knew she was going to feel better she wasn't fighting the sick feeling. That's all there was to it. She was going to feel better and then she was going to go home and cop some dream time and then get it together in the morning. Anyway, when she got home she was feeling all right in a way and bad in another way. She was telling herself that she shouldn't have made herself feel better, she should have gone on and been sick and laid up in the room and puked and moaned and whatever else she was going to do and start off in the morning like it was a new day.

It didn't matter. That's what she figured out. It didn't matter because when the sun came beaming up over the warehouse which faced her apartment it was a new day and a new beginning. That's what it was.

Cassie walked up the three flights to her apartment and declared that one thing she was going to do, as God was her Secret Judge, was to move out the rat hole she was living in and stop paying rent to the mealymouth yellow Negro who was probably just a front anyway.

She walked into the house, put both locks and the chain on the door, and started toward her bedroom. That's when she passed the mirror and saw the stranger.

It shocked her at first, made her insides kind of jump and shake, and she couldn't settle down. She went into the bedroom, turned on the radio as loud as it would go on, and laid down across the bed.

If it was burglars, Cassie thought, they would know she was home. She had left her bag out on the table and they could take that if they wanted. But it didn't have to be burglars, Cassie knew. The girl in the mirror looked something like her, had her hair combed back from her face the way Cassie combed her hair back. But that's where it ended. Cassie had calm eyes and looked good. The girl she had seen was thin and desperate-looking. Cassie wondered if she was on crack. She changed the radio station, switching it from station to station so they would know she was in the house.

She went over and closed the bedroom door to give them a chance to leave, whoever they was.

What she wanted to do, what she really wanted to do, was to move out right then and there. Pack a bag and get into the wind.

She jumped up and ran to the bedroom door and flung it open.

"Get out of here! Get out of here!" she screamed.

This time she slammed the door shut and went back to the bed. That was a bad move. She should have thought it through. Now they knew she was in there and didn't have no man with her to kick their butts. They could come in and mess with her. But a girl wouldn't want to mess with her. Maybe a man would but a girl wouldn't want to mess with her.

She sat on the edge of the bed, her head forward over her brown knees, her breath coming in shallow gasps. She listened, turning her head slightly. Did she hear the front door close? She edged toward the bed-room door and listened. Nothing. She cracked the door and looked down the hallway. It was empty. She closed the door and sat back down again. It was hard to live alone.

Cassie thought about her mother, wondering what she was doing. When she thought about her mother she thought about the woman laughing. Her mother had the kind of laugh that was sweet and pure and tinkly. Her laugh would start low and fly up and end with a note that seemed to go back inside her, as if the laugh was done and she was withdrawing the joy of it. When Cassie was a little girl and they lived in Brooklyn, she used to try to play her mother's laugh on the old upright piano some-body had painted green with gold trim.

"Mama, laugh," she would say. And then, even before her mother could laugh, Cassie would laugh her-self. But still she would try to get those notes, try to play them on the piano, and her mother would shake her head and say, "Girl, you some kind of crazy!"

That was so long ago. Or maybe it was just so long ago that her mother had laughed, hadn't looked at her and wondered aloud why Jesus was letting Cassie go through the trials she was going through.

Now her mother always had something to say, always had to fix her mouth about something that Cassie knew she could take care of if she just had enough time. She didn't know why her mother just didn't understand. God knows she had explained it to her enough times.

Her stomach growled and cramped. She knew she

was going to get sick again. They had messed up her feeling all right. They had just messed that up.

She didn't have any more money. No, she had a few dollars. She needed that to get downtown and look for a job. But that was tomorrow. She was sick now.

She opened the bedroom door and walked out quiet as she could. She couldn't hardly breathe she was so scared when she passed the mirror. She looked over to her left where the girl had to be standing to get her reflection in the mirror. Nothing. They had gone.

In the hallway she ran to the stairs and down them as fast as possible. When she got out to the street her whole body was shaking. If whoever was in her apartment was still in there, they would have to leave because they didn't know if she was coming back with the cops or what she was going to do.

On the street she looked in her handkerchief and saw that she had twenty dollars. She was feeling real bad now and needed something.

That's how her life was going. Her being sick and needing to get well. She wasn't the kind that stayed sick, like with Big C or AIDS or nothing like that. It was always a little sickness, something she had to get over for a few minutes, or for a few hours, sometimes the whole day. That's the way it was.

Her mouth was dry by the time Cassie got something to take the edge off her sickness. She bought a bottle of soda to get her stomach calm before she went upstairs. She wasn't looking for no trouble but she wasn't going to just fold up and die, either. That wasn't the way she was. She went on up the stairs like she owned them.

Like she owned them and didn't care about nothing or nobody. That's what you have to do sometime.

She stomped into the bedroom and a little fear came into her but she went right to the bed and laid down. She didn't have a dream, not a real dream, but some pictures that came into her mind as she lay in the darkness that made her feel good.

The first picture was of her standing on the stage at Bethel Church of God in Christ. Her mother had taken the picture and she had the image of it mingled with the feeling of it. Cassie's face had been round then and there was a sweet smile on her face, which sometimes she tried to put on, but it never worked. Smiling didn't feel the same way it used to. Cassie thought that was because she wasn't a girl anymore. She was a woman now.

The next picture was of her standing with Coley, her first boyfriend. Coley was jive but he was sweet. He had lost a tooth playing basketball and always kept his mouth shut when he smiled. He looked funny. He was jive, but sweet.

When she woke up in the morning, she knew it was the new beginning she had been waiting for. She checked out what money she had and then looked in the refrigerator to see what she had to eat.

There were two eggs, an onion, and four slices of cheese wrapped in plastic. It didn't do nothing for her so she skipped breakfast and got herself ready to go for a job.

She was in a hurry, looking around the house grabbing what she could to put on, even putting on her lip gloss without looking into the mirror. She grabbed some toilet paper, took off the excess gloss, and started off. She had put on her dark skirt, the one that didn't look too bold in case she came across an office job.

At the door she didn't know what to do. Should she lock the door and leave that girl in there or leave it open? She didn't see a guy but that didn't make a difference. There could have been one.

Cassie went down the stairs and into the lobby. The mailman had the boxes open and Mrs. Lucas, who lived on the top floor, was standing there waiting for him to finish distributing the mail.

"Good morning, Mrs. Lucas," Cassie said.

Mrs. Lucas didn't say nothing, just looked at her. Cassie didn't know what was wrong with her. Cassie had run errands for Mrs. Lucas plenty of times and now she wasn't even speaking. Maybe she was getting senile or something.

"Good morning, Mrs. Lucas," Cassie said, raising her voice. "How you doing?"

Mrs. Lucas straightened up and squinted right at her. "Girl, you sure have gone down," the older woman said. "You got to do something with yourself."

"I know what you mean," Cassie said. "I think I got a touch of the flu."

"You know you're from a good family," Mrs. Lucas went on.

"You sure right about that," Cassie said as she went out the door.

It's not even me she's talking about, Cassie thought. It's that girl up there in my apartment. She favor me some and Mrs. Lucas probably saw her on my floor.

Cassie wondered if the strange girl was homeless. As

she walked down the street past Unity Funeral Home she was shaking her head. She had heard what some homeless girls had to do to get money. An old man sat near the curb on a folding chair reading his Bible. Cassie nodded to him and he nodded back.

The job place was on Fourteenth Street and Cassie got to it at ten-thirty.

"We don't have anything right now." The man behind the desk wore rimless glasses. "You get down here the first thing in the morning I'll see if I can find you something."

Disgusted. That's what Cassie felt. It was the nineteenth and her rent was already a month past due. She walked over and got the number 3 train uptown and she was beginning to feel sick. She needed to get home and lie down for a while and decided to do just that. Coming uptown, between 96th Street and 116th Street she had made a decision. What she was going to do was just to ignore the girl if she saw her again.

Jeannie Tate was standing at the bus stop and Cassie stopped to say hello.

"How you doing, girlfriend?" Jeannie was wearing dark brown slacks and a soft beige sweater.

"I'm getting by," Cassie said.

"You still going to school?"

"Yeah, you know how that is," Cassie said. She didn't know why she was lying to Jeannie, because Jeannie wasn't all that much.

"Well, that's good," Jeannie said. "I'm thinking about going to community college next fall."

"Get on with your bad self!" Cassie said. The crosstown bus stopped and Jeannie stepped aside to let people off.

"You take care of yourself," Jeannie said over her shoulder as she got on the bus.

Cassie was anxious to get home but she thought she'd stop and tell Barry that she had seen Jeannie. Barry had a cast eye so when one eye was looking dead at you the other one was a little off. He was good-looking, though. If he wasn't so old, almost thirty or so, she would have given him a play herself. But Barry had always been sweet on Jeannie, even when they were little and going to grade school.

Barry hung in Terry's, a shoeshine parlor that sold newspapers, gum, candy, and other little stuff.

"Barry, guess who I just saw?"

"What's happening?" Barry was sitting up on the shine stand like it was his throne. "And who you seen?"

"Jeannie Tate," Cassie said. "She was looking good, too."

Barry smiled. He had a tooth that was outlined in gold. "You know she getting married?"

"Get out of here!"

"Some dude from Brooklyn," Barry said. "Where you see her?"

"At the bus stop," Cassie said. "She was probably just visiting her mother. I thought she had come to see you."

"No, she didn't come to see me," Barry said. "I ain't got time for married ladies."

"Yeah, you stay busy," Cassie said.

"You needing something?"

"I shouldn't . . . I had to fight that number three train in all this heat," Cassie shook her head. "You don't know how aggravated I am."

"Then you need a pick-me-up," Barry said. "I got a little something in the back room."

What Cassie thought was that if she stayed out of the apartment until she was really tired it would be easier for her to get to sleep. She wanted to tease Barry about Jeannie some more because she knew he was still sweet on her, even though he was trying to nonchalant the whole deal. That's the way Barry was, always trying to nonchalant things.

Cassie got tired like she knew she would if she hung out all day and was just about falling asleep when she got to her apartment. She checked the door and it was open.

She went in and crossed right to the refrigerator to see if the girl had eaten her food. She hadn't and Cassie made herself an omelette. It was the kind her mother used to make before she had to move out and get her own place. Her mother was okay but she kept getting into Cassie's business, accusing her of things like she didn't have any sense.

Cassie washed the pan and the dish, making sure she made a lot of noise so if the girl was still there she would know Cassie wasn't afraid. Once she thought she heard her, but when she listened close she didn't hear anything more. She thought about Barry. She really didn't like him. He was the kind of guy that used girls. That's what he really wanted that back room for, so he could mess around with girls. Some people said he free-based back there, but Cassie hadn't seen anything he could freebase with.

She put the dish and pan away and the feeling of tiredness came down over her like somebody was pouring water over her head and let it run down on her shoulders. She started for the bedroom and stopped in the hallway mirror.

There she was! Cassie whirled around but she was gone. In her heart she knew what was going to go down next. The girl was messing with her! When she turned around again she was going to show up again, standing behind her so Cassie could see her in the mirror.

Ignore her. Cassie took a breath. She took it in slow and deep and released the tension from her clenched fists. Then she turned back to the mirror. She was right. There she was leaning back against the wall. Cassie pretended she was looking at the reflection of the crucifix on the wall, but kept taking glances toward the stranger. She was trying to conceal herself, pressing against the door-jamb, her face half in shadow. A thin hand ran itself through her uncombed hair. The blouse was buttoned wrong, making her look like something thrown away. Cassie was relieved she didn't look violent as she turned and walked deliberately to the bedroom. She fell across the bed and pulled the top of the spread over her head. She wanted to cut out the girl's image and the thought of her.

Cassie lay on the bed for a long time, wishing and hoping for sleep, trying to will herself through the night. Outside it was raining and the hiss of tires sounded like brushes on cymbals in the heavy darkness. The blind moved gently against the window, its rhythm clashing with the blare of the radio down the street. Cassie was almost there, almost past the day's tiredness, almost past the day's unbearable weight, when she heard the sound.

She tensed, pulling her mind back to the present, back to awareness. She listened to see if she could hear it again. There. There it was. Cassie listened. There were the soft sounds of muffled sobbing. The girl was crying.

Cassie pulled the cover from the foot of the bed and balled it up in front of her mouth. If she could make it through the night she would face it in the morning. For the time being it was just too much.

# Walter Dean Myers

Walter Dean Myers has published more than thirty novels for young adults, along with several nonfiction books and a handful of picture books, including *Brown Angels*. The list of awards these books have received is longer than the space available here. Among the most important awards Myers's books have received are the following. Seven books, including *It Ain't All for Nothin'*, *The Legend of Tarik*, and *The Glory Field*, have been named Best Books for Young Adults by the American Library Association, and *Scorpions* was one of the ALA's 100 Best of the Best Books for Young Adults published between 1967 and 1992. *Scorpions* was also a Newbery Honor Book, as was *Somewhere in the Darkness*. That book, along with *Malcolm X: By Any Means Necessary*, was a Coretta Scott King Honor Book, as well as a *Boston Globe–Horn Book* Honor Book. Three of Myers's novels—*Won't Know Till I Get There*, *The Outside Shot*, and *Fallen Angels*—have been *Parents' Choice* Award winners. And *Fallen Angels*, along with *The Young Landlords*, *Motown and Didi*, and *Now Is Your Time*, received the Coretta Scott King Award.

In addition to those specific awards, Myers has been the recipient of the prestigious Margaret A. Edwards

Award for his lifetime writing achievements, as well as the ALAN Award for his outstanding contributions to young adult literature.

*Fallen Angels,* an action-packed story of two young African American soldiers fighting in Vietnam, and *Somewhere in the Darkness,* a poignant story about the relationship between a teenage boy and his convict father on a journey to understanding, are two of Walter Dean Myers's most popular novels, along with *Scorpions,* an intimate examination of the life of a young man caught up in the violence of a Harlem neighborhood gang. In his most recent novel, *Slam!,* Myers examines the life of an inner-city high-school basketball player who is trying to make something of his life.

# How Do I Get Myself Out of This?

Knowing right from wrong doesn't mean you will always do the right thing—especially if you're a guy who's determined to become part of a group that will accept and protect you.

# X-15s
## Jack Gantos

When I was fourteen, I kept pestering a gang until they invited me join them. We were called the X-15s after the black pointy-toed shoes I was told to buy. I also had to buy a pair of beige Levi's and a black V-neck T-shirt. Every time I locked my bedroom door and put that outfit on, I felt great. I'd look into the mirror and know other guys were doing the same thing. And like me, they were thinking no matter what shit hit the fan they had someone to back them up. They had me, and I had them. We were friends. Or we were going to be friends. I still had to pass the initiation.

The clubhouse was an abandoned half-built house in a housing development that had run out of money. There were about twenty houses laid out in a field, all of them in various stages of completion. Most had the walls up. Some had the trusses set and covered with sheets of plywood.

On my first night there I wore my new clothes. The leader, Robby, announced that each of us new members was to go hunting and return to the headquarters with a dead pet. "Cat, dog, or monkey," he said. He cleaned his fingernails with the toothpick he removed from his mouth. "No turtles or goldfish," he warned us, as though someone before had made that mistake. He had combed his hair down to his eyebrows and over his ears so that it looked like a German helmet.

I didn't want to spoil my initiation and so listened carefully as the more experienced members stood to one side and talked among themselves. I looked around and spotted a few of the new guys standing alone in the shadows. They looked as anxious as I felt. But after the initiation I'd be standing with the old members. I'd be one more among them.

"The last one back has to eat a dead whatever," Robby said, and twisted his dark lips into a purplish sneer. He was bigger than the rest of us. He was the only one who had enough patience to lift weights. "And don't make me wait around all night," he added, poking himself in the chest. "I got something to do later on." He had been spending time with Bonnie Three Fingers. She was beautiful except for her mangled hand.

"Now beat it," Robby ordered as we broke up. I jumped on my bicycle and headed toward home. The other new guys scattered in all directions. I rode as quickly as I could. I was afraid of Robby's threat and didn't want to be the one to chew on a maggoty dead animal. I pedaled so fast I began to sweat across my upper lip. My teeth ached, but I felt good about myself because I seldom sweat, not even when I work hard in the sun. I figured I must be getting stronger.

It didn't take long to reach my house. I pedaled up the driveway, then struggled to keep the bike moving as I steered across the grass toward the backyard. When I reached the screened-in porch, I stopped and carefully eased the bike down. I stood by the back door and listened. Across the canal the parents of the Down syndrome girl argued. "It's your turn to help," the wife insisted. "I've been trapped in this house for weeks." There was no response. A door slammed.

When I was certain my parents were in bed, I opened the back door. I walked through the kitchen and went into the Florida room, where the cat, Simon, slept in an open wicker suitcase.

He was asleep. I petted him a few times. "Goodbye, Simon," I whispered. "I'll try to make this painless." Then I swiftly closed the case. He struggled to get out, scratched against the wicker, and cried, but by then I was going out the door. I felt I had used up too much time already. That gang was a fast group, and I expected them to steal pets from old people who walked their animals on a leash. They'd probably snatch the leash away as they sped by on their bicycles and drag the animal along the asphalt until it was skinned down like a potato.

I ran to the edge of the canal behind our house and got down on my stomach. With my right arm, which was my stronger, I swung the basket over my head and into the water. I felt Simon struggling, but he didn't make any sounds. I didn't know how long to hold him down for, so I began to count. "One thousand one, one thousand two."

I turned my head to look up at the sky. "I'm sorry," I whispered toward the stars. "If I don't do this, it might be done to me."

I knew that wasn't true. I knew better than to hang around with people who were cruel. I thought that just *knowing better* made me different from the other guys in the gang. But maybe it didn't. Maybe I was just like them. Maybe that's what made people bad—*knowing better* but just not giving a shit. But the thought of all those guys standing shoulder to shoulder, always there for each other, pulled me into their circle of friendship and drew me further away from myself.

The couple across the canal continued to argue. During the day they fastened a leash onto their daughter's leather harness and let her run around the backyard. She ran screaming with her arms up in the air, as if chasing after a runaway kite. She could imitate the tinny carnival sound of noisemakers on New Year's Eve. When she ran out of rope, she snapped back like a fish being pulled out of water. I couldn't bear to look at her, especially her mouth, which was always red and swollen. Maybe they beat her. Maybe she ran into things. I didn't know. It scared me to think that no matter how hard anyone tried she couldn't be fixed. That's how I felt about myself. But I couldn't say what was wrong with me. I just knew I was mixed up about everything. Maybe I'm as bad on the inside as she is on the outside, I thought. Maybe I can't be fixed either. Maybe that's why I need to be around guys who are as messed up as I am. If nothing else, I won't seem as screwed up.

Once, Kenny Knob, the kid from next door, hid

behind a palm tree and threw rocks at the girl. She didn't even notice, but her mother did. She came out of the house with a large soup spoon in her hand.

"Don't you dare throw rocks at my daughter," she hollered. She waved the spoon in the air and with her other hand drew the girl toward her waist. "This is my child and I love her," she said loudly. The houses were close together, and I knew the neighbors were watching.

"Sorry," Kenny said reluctantly.

"Next time I'll tell your mother," she said.

"So tell her," he shot back. "At least my mom's kids are normal."

I knew I wasn't like Kenny. I could never have done or said what he did. I was smart enough to be sneaky about the mean things I did. I knew how to be good. I had good manners. I had a nice smile. I could be helpful when needed. I could be upset when hearing about cruelty and thrilled when hearing about happy family news. I could be anything as long as I could fit in. I looked up at the stars again. They were shiny but cold.

I was thinking about myself and lost count of how long Simon was under. When I pulled him up, he wasn't moving. I felt as though I had taken too much time, and I wondered if I should go back at all. I didn't want to be last.

I balanced the wicker suitcase on the handlebars of my bike and pedaled as hard as I could. There were no cars out, and I liked riding freely down the center of the street. But when I looked up at the sky, the stars still troubled me. They looked like pieces of broken mirror. I didn't know how to make shapes out of them, and I didn't have time to make some up. To my right, another new kid pulled up on his bicycle.

"What'd you get?" he asked. We were both breathing hard. He had a sack in his rear basket.

"A cat," I said. "You?"

"A duck."

I didn't think a duck qualified as a pet. I felt better just thinking that he might be the loser because of this mistake in judgment. Anybody could kill a duck in Fort Lauderdale. They were everywhere, like pigeons. I watched him pedal his bicycle. He was wearing the same kind of beige Levi's and black sleeveless shirt. I could see that my arms were slightly bigger than his.

"Where did you get the cat?" he asked.

"Neighbors."

"Which one?"

"It doesn't matter," I said. Just then Simon began to move around. He sneezed, then began to cry and claw at the wicker.

"Hold it," I said to the new kid. "This thing's not dead yet." I stopped as quickly as I could without going over the handlebars.

"See you later," he shouted, and pumped up and down even harder. "I'm not going to be the last one."

Simon was hysterical, and I was afraid to open the case. He would claw me, then run off. I was desperate. I looked around by the side of the road. I couldn't find anything to beat him with. What I needed was a sharp stick, something I could drive through both the wicker suitcase and him.

Time was passing. The other new kid would be at

the club by now. If the gang wanted a victim, it would probably be me. I had no reputation. I was only let into the group because Kenny said I was okay. But he wasn't the type to stick up for me, especially if something went wrong.

I pedaled up the driveway of a stranger's house. Their car was parked in the carport. I set the cat case down by the road and my bike farther off to one side. All their lights were off. I opened the car door and put the gearshift into neutral, then began to push hard against the fender to get it rolling down the slope. When it started to drift, I got into the driver's seat and held the door open with my head sticking out so that I could guide the wheels. The back wheel passed over the wicker. Simon cried sharply, but then before the front wheel hit the case, he clawed through the crushed side and ran across the street and into the bushes. The car rolled out into the road and came to a stop. I jumped out, grabbed the cat case, and fled on my bicycle. "Damn," I said. "What do I do next?"

When I reached the clubhouse, I quietly walked my bike up to one of the back windows. Robby had a fire going on the concrete slab floor. I counted the new members. There were ten. I made eleven. Someone was missing. Just then I noticed another guy to my right, behind a bush, looking through a window. He was counting out loud. "One, two, three . . ."

I dropped the cat case through the window and jumped into the house behind it. "I got a cat," I yelled. I held the case up for everyone to see. The wicker was crushed down and splintered. The cat pillow was bunched up and wet. In the dark I hoped my bluff would pass as the real thing.

Before anyone got nosey, the other kid jumped in through the window. "Mine's better," he yelled, and held up a miniature poodle.

"I'm afraid it's a tie," Robby said. "You'll have to fight it out."

That was a lucky break for me. The attention shifted away from my fake cat to the fight. I wasn't going to let anyone beat me. In one motion I flung the cat case into a dark corner, then turned and punched the other kid in the face. He dropped the poodle and fell backward, tripped over a drainpipe, and landed on his back. When his head hit the concrete, it sounded the same as when my uncle let me kill a hog with a sledgehammer.

The poodle kid remained on the concrete. He rocked his head back and forth from side to side like he was saying "No. No. No."

Robby stepped out of what was to be the front door and returned with a dead German shepherd. Its back was broken, and I recognized the dog as one that I'd seen flattened alongside the highway on my way to school. He must have found the dog first, then thought of the initiation. Cheater, I thought, but I wasn't going to say so. I was lucky that it wasn't me flat on my back. I had gotten away with my cat trick, and I felt Robby's acceptance for knocking out the other kid. I had what I wanted.

Robby held the dog by its hind legs and dragged it over the kid's face.

"Lick it," he said impatiently. "It's late and I want to get outta here."

Because the dog was over his face, we couldn't tell if he licked it or not.

"Bite it," hollered Robby. The kid bit the tail. It crunched like someone walking on gravel, and we all turned away and made faces. "Enough," Robby said, then strolled over to the window and tossed the dog out. He jerked an aluminum comb out of his back pocket and combed his helmet of hair. The kid stood up, spit, and rubbed the top of his head. I kept my fist balled up in case he tried something.

"Now everyone take your animals back to where you found them," Robby said.

We all raced off on our bicycles. On my way home I threw the cat case hard at a house. It hit the striped awning over a window and made a sound like a car hood slamming.

When I returned home, Simon was at the front door. I walked toward him. "I'm sorry," I whispered. "Sorry." I bent down and held out my hand to rub his head. He hissed and ran off into a boxwood hedge.

"Well, I wouldn't trust me either," I said under my breath. I pulled my T-shirt up over my head and sat on the front steps. I dropped my head down onto my knees. I don't need them, I said to myself. I need something, but not this shit.

I could hear the words begging me to listen. They were my words. They were ringing in my ears. And I was trying my best to wrap my life around them.

# Jack Gantos

Although Jack Gantos has been publishing novels for young adults only since 1994, he has been writing books for children for the past twenty years. He is best known to younger readers for his award-winning Rotten Ralph picture books, many of which have been singled out by the American Library Association as Best Books for Young Readers. Four Rotten Ralph television specials have been produced for the Disney Channel.

In 1994 Gantos published the first of his books for middle-school readers. In *Heads or Tails: Stories from the Sixth Grade,* Gantos based the story of Jack Henry on his own feelings and wacky experiences as a sixth-grader trying to grow up in Florida. *Book Links* named that book one of "A Few Good Books" published that year, and both *School Library Journal* and *Publishers Weekly* gave it starred reviews. Jack's autobiographical adventures continue in *Jack's New Power,* in which he describes his family's move to the Caribbean, where they have hilarious adventures. *School Library Journal* and *The Bulletin of the Center for Children's Books* both named that a Best Book of the Year. Jack's most recent adventures, in seventh and eighth grades, can be found in *Jack's Black Book,* which describes how it feels to be labeled stupid after scoring low on a test.

Gantos's most recent novel is his most serious. *Desire Lines* explores what happens to two young women when someone exposes the secret of their relationship.

Besides writing, Jack Gantos has been a professor of literature and children's book writing for nearly twenty years, first at Emerson College in Boston and currently in the Vermont College M.F.A. Writing Program. His short story about the X-15s gang is a reflection of his own experiences as a teenager in Florida, where, he says, "there were a lot of local gangs, most of them centered around one strong individual. I didn't join any of these gangs, but floated through them."

As a son, Duke has always been a disappointment to his father. Harry wants only what's best for his son. Are they ever going to see eye to eye?

# Cradle Hold
## David Klass

When Duke was five years old, Harry began to worry that his son was exhibiting too many feminine tendencies. Duke was small for his age, and he preferred dolls to guns and reading picture books to playing outdoors. Harry bought him a long plastic sword, which Duke tossed into the bottom of his play chest, and a two-headed ax, which Duke traded to the boy three houses down for a large stuffed pink elephant. When Harry saw the elephant, he decided that things had gone too far and that he'd better take matters into his own hands.

He took Duke to a football game, and the boy spent the entire time crawling around collecting bits of tinfoil that fans discarded on the bleachers as they finished their hot dogs. He brought home John Wayne movies on video and said, "See, that's who you're named after," but when he played them, Duke curled up into a little ball on the couch and promptly went to sleep. Finally, Harry decided that he'd take Duke bass fishing.

They went down to the lake on a cold morning in October and rented a boat and two rods. Harry purchased a dozen night crawlers, and Duke couldn't keep his eyes off the little white cardboard box that they loaded the worms into. It looked like the box the bakery packed cookies in.

"Now," Harry said when they were out on the lake, "I'm gonna show you how to bait a hook. Watch carefully." He took a night crawler out of the white box and skewered it once and then twice with the barbed hook. Duke began to cry when he saw what his father was doing, but Harry didn't pay him any attention. "If worms were our size, and we were their size, they'd be doing the same thing to us, or worse," he muttered. "Now, there, they're all baited up. Let's drop line and see what's biting."

A half an hour later, Harry hooked a largemouth bass. When he netted it in the water and pulled it on board, Duke began pleading for its life. "Don't kill it, Dad. Please don't. Please."

"Be proud of your place on top of the food chain," Harry said, raising the length of tree branch he had brought along for this purpose.

"No, please—"

*Thump,* and the fish stopped wriggling in Harry's hand.

Duke began to cry again and then to weep and then he began to wail with such volume that Harry worried other fishermen might hear. "Pipe down," he said. "You'll forget all about how that fish died when you taste it tonight with some butter and lemon."

Duke refused to eat dinner, and he had bad dreams for nearly a month. When his mother asked Harry what he had done to the boy, Harry merely shrugged. "We just went bass fishing. He'll get over it."

Duke grew into a friendly but shy adolescent who kept pretty much to himself. He was particularly shy with girls. By the time Duke reached junior high school, Harry began noticing out loud that Duke spent every weekend studying and never went out on any dates. "You're only young once, you should be enjoying yourself," Harry told him. "Hell, if I had it to do over again . . ." Harry saw the look his wife threw him and stopped himself just in time. "I mean, you're a red-blooded American boy, and I want you to enjoy your salad days."

Harry began buying *Playboy* magazines and leaving them around the house, hoping his son would pick them up and page through them. Duke did occasionally leaf through them, but more often than not he read the articles and the interviews and ignored the pictorials.

When Duke was fourteen, they went on a family trip to Oceanside at the Jersey shore. It was a hot day in August, and the beach was packed. Harry suggested to Duke that they take a walk together. Harry had a tiny paunch, but his bright red-and-white Hawaiian bathing suit and the way he walked vigorously through the cold Atlantic surf gave him a carefree, youthful quality. Duke, on the other hand, wore conservative brown swim trunks and scampered out of the way of high-breaking waves. At fourteen and forty, Duke and Harry were almost exactly the same height, and except for the wrinkles around Harry's eyes and his almost completely bald pate, they might have been brothers.

As soon as they got out of earshot of his wife, Harry began making comments about the women they were passing. "Lookit those legs! Don't they get your motor goin'? Hey, getta load of that masterpiece." Finally, he stopped dead in his tracks. "Wow," he said, pointing. "We must have found heaven."

Four blond girls played a fast game of volleyball twenty yards away. All four of the girls were lovely-looking, and all of them wore tiny bikinis. "Whatta ya think of that?" Harry asked Duke. "How's that for a free show?"

"Can we go back now?" Duke mumbled.

"Go back? If I were you, I'd walk right up there and get in that game and meet those girls."

"Why don't you?"

"Don't be a smart-ass. I don't because I'm not you. But you're you. So what are you waiting for?"

"They have two teams. They don't need me."

"For Christ's sake," Harry said, "is something wrong with you?"

"No. Is something wrong with you?"

For a long moment father and son studied each other. Then Duke turned around and headed back toward his mother. Harry watched the blond girls play volleyball for a few more minutes, shook his head, and then headed back.

About a year after the trip to Oceanside, Duke got his first girlfriend. She was a quiet girl named Hillary, with a pretty smile and a talent for baking. For the first three months that they dated, Duke ate several meals a month with Hillary and her family, but he steadfastly refused to bring her home to meet his parents.

"Why? Is something wrong with them?" Hillary finally asked.

"Not really."

"So it's me?"

He kissed her. He had just learned that a kiss could be an acceptable answer to many of the difficult questions that crop up in a relationship. "Okay," he whispered, "if that's really what you want. But give me a week to get ready."

All that next week, at every opportunity, Duke warned Harry about what he would do if Harry didn't behave himself for Hillary's visit.

"What do you mean, behave myself? What the hell is that supposed to mean?"

"You know what it means."

"No, I don't."

"It means don't do anything weird. Don't say anything weird."

"What am I, some kind of creep?"

"Just don't."

"I won't. Whatever it is you mean."

Hillary showed up for dinner in a pretty blue dress that made her look adorable. Her hair was cut in neat bangs, she wore a pearl choker, and she brought a tin of pecan fudge brownies that she had baked herself.

Harry's face lit up when he first saw her. "Hey," he said, "welcome. More than welcome. I'm Harry. Duke's old man. You look great. . . ."

Harry's wife immediately led Hillary away into the

kitchen before Harry had a chance to say anything else to her. Harry was left in the living room, looking at Duke.

"Don't," Duke said. "Please."

"I don't know what you're talking about."

"I'll leave. And I won't come back."

Harry straightened up at the threat and looked carefully across the living room at his son. "Okay, but you can't stop me from thinking how proud I am of you."

"You can think whatever you want," Duke told him. "But if you say one thing to her, I'm out the door."

Harry was a perfect gentleman all evening. He treated Hillary with polite, restrained hospitality, carried on his share of the dinner table conversation amiably, and did not insist that Duke eat his roast beef blood rare.

Duke and his mother's only scary moment came during dessert, when Harry pulled a small, flat box out of his shirt pocket. "Hillary," he said, "my wife and I want you to know how welcome you are under our roof, so we decided to present you with a small token of our esteem." It was the first that Harry's wife had heard about such a plan, and she stared at her husband in surprise. "I guarantee you, you've never seen one of these before," Harry told Hillary as she carefully peeled off the wrapping paper and gold string. As Duke watched her open the box, thoughts of different odd and uncouth presents that his father might have bought flashed through his imagination. He almost reached out and snatched the box from her, but resisted the urge at the last second.

Hillary's face brightened as she reached into the box

and drew out a pretty wooden bracelet. "It's lovely," she whispered. "I've never seen one like it."

"It's Navajo," Harry said. "Handmade. I picked it out myself in a store in New York."

"Thank you so much. I don't know what to say."

"Please come and join us for dinner anytime," Harry told her. "We want you to feel like one of the family."

That night, as Duke walked Hillary home, she commented over and over about how nice his parents were. "I like your mother very much. And your father is *so nice.* I couldn't believe they bought me that bracelet. He's *so nice.*"

"Yeah, well," Duke mumbled, looking down at the Navajo bracelet on Hillary's wrist. "Once you get to know him, you'll realize that he's got his problems, like we all do."

"I think he's great," she said. "The way you didn't want to invite me over for so long, I thought maybe there was some problem or something that you didn't want me to see. But they're so nice and modest and gentle. I loved them."

The next day in the post office, Harry let loose. "You should see my boy's babe," he told Frank Wells when they were sorting the local mail.

Frank Wells was a short black man with a neat mustache. He was the only man in the post office who put up with Harry, because Harry occasionally gave him horseracing tips that paid off. "Nice?"

"They didn't make girls like that when we were young."

"Lucky kid."

"I don't know about lucky, but he landed a beauty queen. Like a tall glass of lemonade on a hot day." Harry licked his lips. "Know what I mean?"

Frank shrugged. "You're screwing up those letters."

"To hell with the letters. I'm telling you, that kid has got his little piece of heaven. What do you think, Franky? Kinda hurts to grow old when you see something like that sitting down across from you at your dinner table."

"Hey, watch what you're saying," Frank told him, moving a half step away. "That's your son's girlfriend."

"Yeah," Harry said proudly. "I know." And in a different, sadder voice, he repeated, "I know."

For a few weeks after the dinner with Hillary, Duke watched his father suspiciously. He couldn't exactly explain why, but the more Duke thought about Harry's perfect manners and restrained behavior, the more he felt as if he had been betrayed. Every time Hillary mentioned what a nice father he had, Duke clamped his teeth together until his jaws hurt.

Later that year, Duke surprised and delighted his father by going out for the high-school wrestling team. He was still a thin and gawky kid—more elbows than shoulders—and it looked for a long time as though he was going to be cut, but he went to all the practices and called Coach Waterman "sir," and ended up making the junior varsity as a substitute at 135 pounds.

Harry didn't miss a single wrestling match all season. Some of the junior varsity matches were held in tiny gyms in junior high schools and even elementary schools, and the team's bus driver often got lost trying to find his way to the right little school, but when the bus finally did pull to a stop, Harry's lime green Mercury Comet was always sitting in the parking lot.

Duke's teammates teased him a bit about how his father showed up at all the matches, even though Duke only wrestled occasionally and spent most of the time sitting on the bench. One of Duke's teammates, Al Gordon, the heavyweight, took a different view. "My father's never come to see me wrestle," he told Duke. "Not once. I think it's kinda neat the way your father takes the time to show up in Totowa, Moonachie, Elmwood Park, Bogota, wherever. Hell, I'd take a father like that in a minute."

"Take him," Duke said.

"I would if I could, but you got him. How does he know where we're going to be wrestling? Sometimes even the bus driver doesn't know."

"He calls the school the morning of each match. He's got a dozen different local maps in his glove compartment, and he knows where all the high schools and junior high schools are in the whole county."

"Remarkable," Al said with a whistle.

"Yeah," Duke repeated bitterly, "remarkable."

Duke began slowly as a high-school wrestler, but in his sophomore year he started on the junior varsity, and between his sophomore and junior seasons he suddenly blossomed into a powerhouse. Other kids on the team worked out during the off-season and merely stayed in shape—each time Duke worked out, new muscles seemed to sprout on his calves, arms, shoulders, and back. Coach Waterman took one look at Duke's definition on the first day of preseason of his junior year and put him with the varsity team. "I think you've got a good chance of challenging for a starting spot," he told Duke. "Let's work your butt off in preseason and see what happens."

What happened was that Duke won a starting place on the varsity squad and finished out the season with a twelve-and-four record. Harry came to every single match and shouted himself hoarse. Sometimes Harry sat next to Hillary, and as he screamed and punched the air, she twisted a little white handkerchief in her hands. When Duke won and the referee held his arm up in victory, Harry's face lit up brighter and brighter till it seemed ready to explode, like a star going supernova. On the rare occasions when Duke lost, Harry retreated into sullen depressions and refused to say a word for days on end.

Duke got a lot of publicity before his senior season. Several local newspapers tapped him as the second-best wrestler at his weight in the entire county, behind only Bankman of Hackensack. Recruiters from more than two dozen colleges, including three Ivy League schools, came calling with information packets and invitations to come see their colleges. Duke answered all their questions about his academics and health history politely enough, but when it came to choosing a school he said, "I'll see about that when the season's over."

Harry spent many afternoons paging through the college packets, studying the different campuses over and over again. He tried to call Duke's attention to different details and knew the pictures in the packets by heart. "At least look at the one from Princeton," he'd beg. "All that ivy—such class. Here's a photo of a Nobel Prize—winning chemist who teaches there. His suit's a little small for him, and his pants are too short, but you can just see how intelligent he is by the lines in his face."

"I'm not interested in chemistry."

"Okay, check this one out. From Lafayette. What a babe! Whoever put her picture in the brochure knew a thing or two. I agree with you—to hell with chemistry. Take a gander at this little piece of academia. . . ."

Harry held the brochure in front of Duke's face, and Duke ripped it out of his father's hands and threw it to the floor. For a second, Duke's shoulders and arms tensed and the muscles stood out from his wrists to his neck. Harry drew back. Duke let out a long breath, turned his back on his father, and walked down into the basement, where he had installed a chin-up bar. He did fifty chin-ups in rapid fire, never breaking rhythm. When he stopped at fifty, he was not even breathing hard.

Duke's senior season lived up to expectations. His speed was such that at the beginning of a match he could shoot in for a single- or even a double-leg takedown, and even when his opponents knew he was coming, they couldn't do much to stop him. As soon as he had a controlling position, he'd slap on a cross-face or hook a leg and work right for the pin. Many of his matches ended in the first period, and the *Bergen Record* made him "Athlete of the Week" in February.

The county high-school wrestling championships were held in the large Edgewood High School gym. The winners of the county championship at each weight class would go on to the state tournament, so there was a lot at stake. A cable TV station broadcast all the matches, and more than a dozen sports reporters hung around the tournament following the progress of the favorites.

Duke was seeded second in the county, behind Bankman of Hackensack, who had won the title the previous year. On the first three days of the tournament, Duke and Bankman waltzed through their preliminary and quarterfinal and semifinal matches, and neither of them was even pushed. Harry took the days off from work and always sat in the center of the second row of bleachers, screaming for Duke during his matches and studying Bankman carefully when the Hackensack grappler was on the mats.

The night before the county final, during dinner, Harry tried to advise Duke. "It's the damn cradle that makes him so dangerous. He's got more ways of working someone into that cradle than a dog has fleas. Once he gets it, or even a half cradle, or even a cross-face, it's goodbye, Charlie. Take my advice, and—"

Duke put down his fork. "What do you know about wrestling?" he asked, cutting his father off. "Have you ever wrestled?"

Harry's wife, who was eating peas with a spoon, paused between scoops to wait for her husband's answer. Her face seemed to be blank, yet Harry read a tiny, sarcastic smile in the turn of her lips. Harry frowned at her and then looked back at Duke. "No, I've never wrestled, but I've seen enough to have picked up a few things."

"Just don't talk about tomorrow," Duke said. "Whatever happens is gonna happen, and I don't want to think about it."

"You're gonna win. You're gonna pin that clown."

Duke stood up from the table. "I said don't talk about it."

"I just wanted to tell you to be aware of that cradle hold. I won't say any more—"

The fury in Duke's voice surprised everyone at the table as he half shouted, "You have no idea. None at all. Do you know what it's like out there on the mat when the ref blows the whistle and it's just you and some other guy, trying to pin each other, and hundreds of people watching? Do you know what it's like to be tied up and pinned, to be put on your back and held there? A cradle's the worst—you can't straighten out, your own strength is useless, it's a nightmare . . . you have no idea."

"I was just trying to make a suggestion," Harry mumbled.

"Well, don't."

Harry's mumble sank down to a whisper. "I just want to see you win tomorrow."

The anger stayed in Duke's voice, but his eyes softened the tiniest bit as he growled, "I know you do."

The state final match at 135 pounds was the only county final that pitted two undefeated wrestlers against each other. As Duke and Bankman walked onto the mat, the crowd rewarded them for their outstanding seasons with a burst of applause. The two young wrestlers eyed each other. Bankman was two inches shorter than Duke, with black hair that he wore in a military-style crew cut and a long scar that stretched from his nose to his left ear. As soon as he graduated from high school he planned to join the U.S. Marines.

Harry sat in his usual spot in the second row. On

this final day of the tournament, his wife sat next to him, and as he watched his son and Bankman, he made dozens of excited observations to her. "See the way Bankman walks—his feet never lift, they just slide. See, even just standing still, he keeps his hands in close to his body. Duke's got better technique, but that cradle scares the hell outta me. Up, there they go. . . . *C'mon, Duke!*"

The first period seesawed back and forth for several minutes. Bankman started off in the control position, but Duke wrestled carefully and soon engineered a neat escape. They circled in the center of the mat, and then Duke shot in for a leg and took Bankman down hard. Harry jumped to his feet and punched the air with both fists. *"C'mon, Duke, pin that clown. Pin him."*

For more than a minute, Duke stayed in control, trying to set up a pinning combination. Near the end of the first period he got a bit overeager and careless, and Bankman pulled off a stunning reversal. Suddenly Duke was on the bottom and Bankman was on top, and the wrestler from Hackensack brought his arms around in a flash and clamped on a cradle hold.

The large crowd roared as Bankman went for the pin. The ref got down on his knees, watching Duke's shoulders as Duke rocked back and forth and strained and tried to bridge with his head and neck.

Harry was standing and punching the air with both fists when he suddenly realized that Bankman had pulled a masterful reversal. Harry's fists slowly unclenched, but he never fully lowered his arms. He watched Duke's desperate efforts to resist the pin, saw that there was still more than a minute left in the period and Duke would never make it, and then he started moving forward.

Harry's wife grabbed for his arm but missed. As soon as Harry was down on the floor of the gym, he raced straight for the mats. The roar of the crowd swelled in his ears, and his eyes were fixed on his son's shoulders, which were being forced down slowly but inexorably.

When Harry reached the two wrestlers, he hooked his right arm under Bankman's jaw and his left hand under his stomach and tried to yank the Hackensack wrestler off. Bankman resisted and then yielded, more out of confusion than necessity. He thought that it had to be the referee trying to pull him off and that his opponent must have given up or lost consciousness.

As soon as Bankman let go of Duke, Harry released him. The referee, Harry, and Bankman stood looking at each other as Duke got up on one knee and recognized his father.

"What are you, crazy?" the referee asked Harry.

Harry couldn't think of anything to say. He looked down at his son, who was glaring back up at him with more anger than it seemed possible for a human face to contain. Without a word, Harry turned and hurried toward the rear exit. The crowd had grown quiet, and nobody made a move to stop Harry as he disappeared out the back door of the gym.

"Do you know that guy? Is he with your team? Should we get the police after him?" the ref asked Duke in rapid fire.

Duke stood up. "Don't get the police."

"I'm gonna have to talk to the judges, but I think he should win on a forfeit," the ref said to Duke.

"Absolutely." Duke held out his right hand to Bankman. "Congratulations."

"Thanks," Bankman said, still very confused. "Who the hell was that idiot?"

Duke shrugged, turned, and walked off the mats. He didn't go home till late that night. When he walked through the door, his mother, looking nervous, got up from the living room armchair. "Thank God you're home," she said.

"Why?" Duke said.

"I've been worried about your father."

At the mention of his father, Duke felt his body tense with fury from his jaw to the bottoms of his feet. "Where is he?"

She pointed out the front door.

"I didn't see him when I came in."

"He's walking around the block."

"What do you mean, he's walking around the block? What's he doing?"

"Just walking," she said.

"How long has he been out there?"

"Since the wrestling meet. I tried to talk to him, but he just kept walking."

Without another word, Duke walked out of the living room, through the hall, and out the front door. He waited halfway up the walk, and sure enough, within five minutes he made out his father's figure walking quickly through the gloom. When his father saw him, he slowed momentarily and then resumed his pace.

Duke walked the rest of the way out to the sidewalk. Harry reached him and hurried right by him without saying a word. "Hey," Duke said. *"Hey."* He ran after Harry and fell into step alongside him. "Is this a stunt or what? Are you trying for sympathy? Do you want us all to think you're completely crazy? Is that the game now?"

"I'm just walking," Harry said.

"Do you realize what you did today? Do you know how hard I worked for that chance at the county title? Of course you do."

"I owe you an apology," Harry said. "I'm sorry."

"An apology? What good is an apology?" They rounded the corner onto Chestnut Street, never slackening pace for a moment. "Everyone on the team thinks you're insane. Mom thinks so too. Coach Waterman wanted to try to have you arrested."

"I don't know what to say," Harry said.

"Why don't you start by saying something true," Duke told him, "and we'll take it from there. Say one true thing about what happened today and what's going on."

Harry stopped walking. He was breathing a bit hard. "I love you," he said. "You're my boy and I love you."

Duke ground his knuckles together in fury. "Why did you do that?"

"I couldn't let him pin you. I just couldn't."

"Well, I just can't take it anymore."

"You're leaving?"

"For a while," Duke said. "I'm gonna stay with a guy on the team. Al Gordon. His parents have a big house with a spare room. They said it would be okay."

"They're nice folks, to put you up like that," Harry

said. He began walking again, more slowly this time. Duke walked with him.

"I wish I could understand you. I wish you'd at least try. I think you owe me that."

"Do you know what I do all day?" Harry asked. "I sort mail into bins."

"Don't try to turn your career into a sob story. It's a good job."

"Maybe it is, but you asked and I'm trying to answer. I sort mail into big gray metal bins. And I think about you." Harry paused and inhaled the cold, clear air of the suburban New Jersey night. "You never knew this, but before you were born, we decided we were going to call you Herbert. But when I saw you for the first time, I thought of John Wayne and I changed it in a flash to Duke. . . ." His voice dropped off. "You don't know what it's like to sort mail. And you don't know . . ." Harry was silent for a long minute. "You don't know what it's like not to be eighteen years old."

"That's an explanation?"

"Who says there has to be a good explanation for everything? That's the most I can say."

"It's nonsense," Duke said.

"Maybe it is."

They turned onto Grove Street and headed for home. Their footsteps rang together, sounding with almost perfect symmetry. "At least he didn't pin you," Harry finally said with the thinnest of smiles.

"That's true. He didn't pin me."

"Walk with me one more time around the block?" Harry asked. "We don't have to talk. Just walk with me. Even if you hate me."

They reached their house, and Duke slowed down and hesitated. Then he sped up again and rejoined Harry. They passed the Greenfields' flagstone driveway and the Murdochs' overgrown front yard, which was the disgrace of the block, and Mr. Beeman waved to them from the rocker on his winterized front porch. They passed the bus stop on the corner, and the mail box where Duke had cut his forehead when he was ten, and the stoplight.

"I don't hate you," Duke muttered from between tight lips.

Harry glanced sideways at his son. "Nice night."

"Getting cold."

"Ring around the moon. Rain tomorrow."

"More likely snow."

"You looked good out there today," Harry told him. "Bankman's tough, but you were beating him. Breaks didn't go your way."

"That cradle hold's one of the toughest to break," Duke muttered, glancing at his father. The mixed emotions in his voice almost choked him. "Once it's clamped on there's no real way out."

Harry nodded. "What can I say? For me too. You'll do better with your kid. Anyway, you looked good."

"Thanks. We're almost at the house. I should go now."

"To Al Gordon's?"

"Yes. His parents are probably waiting up for me. You should go in to Mom. She's worried."

"I will," Harry promised. "I think I'm gonna just take one more turn around the block and then I'll go in. Join me?"

"It's too cold. My nose is getting numb. Goodbye. I'll call you or something."

They both stopped walking and stood facing each other. Suddenly Harry stepped forward and reached out with both arms, and before Duke could react, he was wrapped up in the first embrace he had ever received from his father. He didn't know what to do. He didn't try to break away. He also didn't hug Harry back. Instead, Duke stood there stiffly in the cold night, feeling his father's hands clasping together around the small of his back, and waited for his father to release him.

# David Klass

Like the story "Cradle Hold," most of David Klass's novels for teenagers focus on student athletes. Klass is the author of *Breakaway Run, A Different Season, The Atami Dragons,* and *Wrestling with Honor,* which the American Library Association lists as one of the 100 Best of the Best Books for Young Adults published between 1967 and 1992. *California Blue,* a novel that combines the world of high-school track with ecological concerns and parental conflict, received numerous awards; it was a *School Library Journal* Best Book of 1994, a National Council of Social Studies Notable Trade Book in the Field of Social Studies, and an ALA Best Book for Reluctant Young Adult Readers, and won a Young Adult Book Award for 1996 from the Keystone State Reading Association. *Danger Zone* follows a group of high-school basketball stars in an international tournament disrupted by racial bigotry. Klass's newest novel, featuring his first female lead character, is titled *Screen Test.*

Born in New Jersey and graduated from Yale University, David Klass recently moved from Los Angeles to New York City, where he concentrates on writing screenplays for action movies. Among his film-writing credits are *Kiss the Girls,* based on the novel by James Patterson and starring Morgan Freeman, and *Desperate Measures,* an original story by Klass starring Michael Keaton and Andy Garcia.

Belinda knows how it got there. But now she's
terribly confused over what to do about it.

# Wishing It Away
## Rita Williams-Garcia

Belinda Tobias had always been a big girl. No one
noticed or said anything when her breasts swelled, her
moon face glowed, her eyes hollowed—she had dull eyes
to begin with—and her stomach rose to a mound. Even
when Belinda's belly jumped or did the electric boogaloo
under her baggy plaid shirt, no one saw it. Or said anything. It was simply amazing. Her mother, who wore
either tight skirts or stretch pants, said, "You kids and
your big clothes! So unladylike! Sloppy!" This made her
sister's eyes roll from Belinda's growing form, then up to
the heavens.

Her glowing face screamed the obvious, though her
mouth, a licorice strip ideal for keeping secrets, kept this
one. Or wouldn't tell what was not asked. Anyhow,
Belinda cast an intimidating figure. Not that she actually
knew or tested the ferocity of her will, but people
assumed she could not be told what to do. In actuality

she was a blob with eyes either vacant or hooded since she looked down a lot. Lately.

She cut school to be with Teddy every other day yet never bothered to intercept the truancy notices that flooded her mailbox; nor did her mother offer a serious reprisal other than "Belinda! What am I going to do with you?" Belinda, a beached whale of a girl, just sighed. Heavily. Her mother knew where she was. Either up in her room with Teddy or on Fulton Street shopping. Looking. Sometimes slipping trinkets into her big pockets. No one said anything, even if they caught her. Although, once a little girl out with her nana pointed her finger and sang, "Shame, shame, I know your name." Belinda smiled at the girl, then dropped the glitter nail polish back into the bin. Glitter. She would have never worn it anyway.

In the beginning, Belinda got sucked up into the Teddy-Belinda thing, back when there was planning. The night before their first date, Belinda set two bottles of pink lemonade on her windowsill and stashed a bag of corn chips and a pack of Ring-Dings in her top drawer. When he called, they discussed what period to duck out of. Which exit was the least guarded. What time her mother got back from being "out." What to say if someone saw them.

Then the planning stopped or became unnecessary since no one said anything. Every other sunny day, Teddy and Belinda left school and casually strolled past the school officials, truancy officers, and neighbors and went to her house.

She would turn on the soaps, move Raffey, her stuffed giraffe, aside, and lie down while the room pulsed around her as *The Young and the Restless* jumped from bedroom to bedroom. The only sounds she heard were those of Teddy cursing and grunting in her ear, the bed squeaking, her mother's heels click-clacking below them. And even though she moaned "Oh baby, my baby" over and over, the thought of an actual baby did not occur to her. Truly.

When the subject of birth control came up—once— the first time, he said he'd pull out. But with Teddy cursing and grunting and stroking her hair, she didn't dare ask him to pull out. Sometimes he did on his own, but not always.

On their second date she took a condom from her mother's drawer. He whined, "It won't feel the same," like a baby. That sound, that whining, made her want to spit. She almost told him to get out, but *The Young and the Restless* was on, the room was pulsing, and she could hear her mother's heels click-clacking downstairs awaiting the start of their dance.

Once, during gym, she happened to squat close enough to hear a classmate tell how her grandma came home from Atlantic City and caught the classmate and her boyfriend doing it. So Grandma went down into the kitchen, boiled water as though she were fixing tea, then came upstairs and scalded the boyfriend on the butt, and man, he jumped! Then Grandma grabbed the girl by the ear and gave her what for, and Grandma has been on the case ever since.

*Oh man,* Belinda thought. *I wish my mother tried that!*

The closest her mother came was yelling, "I know what you're doing up there!", then calling her a name other than Belinda. But she didn't say *stop*. At this point it wouldn't have mattered, because Teddy and Belinda kept doing it to the rhythm of her mother's heels click-clacking across the floor. And they'd laugh like jackals when they matched her rhythm down to the *clack-a-lack.*

One morning, Tuesday, Belinda had awakened with mercury on her tongue. She had never tasted mercury but was sure this was it. Plus, she was heavy. Unh. Her every step required effort. Unh. And she was losing control of her body. Unh.

Belinda then thought, *Wishing will make it go away. If the third car that passes by is blue, it will go away. If the phone rings four times before my sister picks it up, it will go away. If the numbers 16 (my age), 22 (my lucky number), and 46 (a good age to die) are played for Lotto it will go away.*

Be that as she wished, for nine weeks she rose with mercury on her tongue, so she sought advice from well-informed sources.

*Eat okra.* She ate okra. She got diarrhea.

*Eat Ajax.* She swallowed a teaspoon. Her throat and stomach burned, her nose bled, and she thought she would die from the burning in her stomach. And when she awoke the next morning, the taste of mercury and Ajax was on her tongue.

*Stand on your head.* Although she was endowed with a flat head, the rest of her was not inclined to cooperate. Besides, she wanted it to go away; she didn't want to break her neck.

*Do a million sit-ups.* Twenty-three was all she could squeeze out of her blob of a body.

*Reach up there and take it out.* YOU CRAZY?

She went back to wishing it away. It seemed to work. Or no one said anything.

When Teddy was no longer invited to cut class and have sex in her bedroom, he took the hint and figured she had someone else. Even with Belinda's face swollen, her breasts full, her clothing extra baggy, he asked no questions. If she didn't say anything, why should he?

Half a year passed and no one said a word. Or asked.

It was on a Monday night as they watched *90210* reruns. Belinda's sister could not help but notice how the TV screen reflected its green light onto Belinda's face only. This caused her sister to inch away in silent horror, thinking Belinda's face could erupt any minute.

Belinda grimaced, then relaxed. Repeatedly. This had been going on all day. Being squeezed from all sides. Then the squeezes ended in stabs, each one becoming progressively sharper. Lasting longer. Now it was unbearable. She made fists and kicked the sofa.

"What's the matter with you, girl?" her mother demanded.

Her sister's eyes went from Belinda's greenish face up to the heavens.

Belinda then hoisted herself up. Unh. Went into the kitchen. Unh. Scooped out a dish of ice cream. Ice cream usually made it, the baby, settle down. Unfortunately, ice cream did not work this time, so she reverted to wishing it away and that worked, for a while.

She made it up to her room, sat on her bed, and rocked back and forth. Then she lay on her side. Went to the bathroom. Nothing. Lay down again. Checked the clock. After two-thirty. Had more pains. Took off her pants. Bit into her pillow. Threw Raffey, the stuffed giraffe, at the window. Tore out every page of this week's *TV Guide* with her teeth. Squatted against the wall. Bit her lip until the skin broke. Said nothing. Pulled out its head. Said nothing. The shoulders. Gave not a cry. And pulled out everything else, with her own hands. Then breathed . . . huh . . . huh . . . for two, maybe three minutes. Then she stared at it. The stuff that came out of her. So much of it. Her stuff. She was amazed.

The licorice strip on her moon face tightened. More so. She put on her baggy pants. Took it, the baby, and wrapped it in her gym T-shirt, put that under her flannel shirt, snatched a GLAD Bag from the kitchen, and went outside. She hobbled to the corner of Marcy and DeKalb, his block, and found a Dumpster. Then she put it, the baby, inside the GLAD bag, lifted the heavy Dumpster lid, and put it, the baby, on top of the garbage heap, breathed . . . huh . . . huh . . . , turned around and went home. She took off her pants, which were bloodied, and slept on the side of the bed that was not.

———

*"We're here for Belinda Tobias,"* said a huge policewoman flanked by two diminutive policemen.

"She was here all night. She didn't do nothing," Belinda's mother said.

By now a crowd of neighbors had gathered. Their murmurs grew loud with speculation, louder with accusation.

"Did Belinda Tobias abandon a baby?"

"Baby? What baby? Belinda was not even pregnant. She's just a big, sloppy girl."

Belinda's sister's eyes flew to the heavens.

*News One* was on her block. On her stoop. From her window she saw the white-and-blue van, the cameraman. The lady with the big microphone. Did they want to talk to her too?

Still moonfaced, but nonetheless dull, Belinda trod downstairs in her big sloppy clothes.

"Belinda Tobias, are you the mother of the baby girl found in the Dumpster on Marcy and DeKalb?"

The licorice strip opened. Finally. "Girl?"

"Belinda Tobias, did you put the baby girl in the Dumpster?"

*News One,* in her face.

"Say nothing," her mother ordered.

Then he, Teddy, jumped out of the bouquet of murmuring mouths.

"She's the one! She threw my baby girl in the Dumpster!"

This passion in his face. Amazing! More passionate than when he grunted and cursed and pulled her hair.

"Monster!" came from the bouquet. And worse.

"Belinda Tobias, did you put the baby in the Dumpster?"

The noise! The talking!

Half of what she said was eaten up in her mother's squawking, the crowd yelling, the ponytailed police-woman demanding, Teddy crying. The other half, the "I took it out," was only heard by her sister. Then they heard from Belinda the one word they needed to hear. Clearly: "Yes."

"Belinda Tobias, you are under arrest for attempted infanticide, abandonment, and endangering the welfare of Baby Jane Doe."

The big woman placed her hand on the flat of Belinda's head and pushed her down into the squad car while the crowd cheered. Action was being taken. At last.

"I didn't even know she was pregnant."

"You knew. We all knew."

"I can't believe she did that to my baby girl. *My* baby girl."

"The monster." And worse.

From inside the squad car, Belinda tried to imagine what they were saying. The neighbors. Teddy. Her sister. Her mother. *News One.* About her. What she had done. Her eyes were too dull, too vacant, to lip-read their faces—some cheering, some angry . . . which? So she counted every third blue car, recalled her lucky numbers, and reverted to wishing. Wishing it away.

# Rita Williams-Garcia

Before she started writing for teenagers, Rita Williams-Garcia pursued a career as a dancer. That experience provided her with the background for her first novel, *Blue Tights,* the story of a teenage girl who joins an African dance group, meets a Muslim drummer, and becomes more aware of her African American heritage. The search for identity is a strong theme also in *Fast Talk on a Slow Track,* the story of a slick, competitive, high-achieving young man who encounters failure for the first time. That novel won a *Parents' Choice* Award and was named a Best Book for Young Adults by the American Library Association.

Williams-Garcia's third novel was also an ALA Best Book for Young Adults, as well as a Coretta Scott King Honor Book. *Like Sisters on the Homefront* describes the experiences of a smart-mouthed black teenage mother sent to live with strict relatives in rural Georgia, where she meets the dying matriarch of the family, who is also the keeper of the family's oral history.

Unlike Belinda in "Wishing It Away," whose story is all too familiar in many poor neighborhoods, Rita Williams-Garcia grew up in a traditional African

American family, where, she says, "my parents laid down the law, and my sister, brother, and I adhered to it. Back in the sixties, morality was a lot simpler."

Williams-Garcia, who grew up in Seaside, California, and then moved with her family to Jamaica, New York, recently completed a master's degree at Queens College in creative writing while working as the manager of software distribution for a marketing services firm and continuing to write for young people. Her efforts have earned her a PEN/Norma Klein Special Citation. She is hoping to produce the film version of *Like Sisters on the Homefront* while she continues to work on her next book, *Everytime a Rainbow Dies.*

# I'm Sorry

Both Ken and Rollin understand enough
about computers to know that if you want
to get rid of something you've written, you
put it into the Trash and press Empty
Trash. It's gone forever, then. Right?

# Trashback
## Alden R. Carter

". . . and the other nerd says, 'Hey, if you can guess
how many chickens I've got in this bag, you can
have *both* of 'em.'" I waited for the laughter. There
wasn't much.

Mrs. Carruthers gave a tired sigh. "Exactly why, Kenneth, have you interrupted class with yet another of your
tasteless nerd jokes?"

"Well, it's a grammar joke, Mrs. C. Kind of appro-
priate for English, I thought."

"You thought wrong. Sarah, would you pick from the
jar this time?"

Sarah shrugged and got up to select a slip of paper
from the tall jar on the window ledge. I started to protest
but swallowed it, as my beloved classmates—who I'd
worked so hard to entertain—started hooting and laughing. Up at the front, Rolf Egglehart, the nerd's nerd,
turned to give me what I suppose he thought was a sneer.

It made him look more than ever like he needed to wipe his nose. I smiled evilly at him and made a gesture like I was wringing the neck of a chicken. He flushed and turned away.

Sarah took the top slip in the jar and read: " 'You're the elf in charge of answering Santa's mail. Write a letter that will get you fired, drive Santa to drink, and cause a police investigation of Santa's workshop.' "

"I can't do that one!" I yelped. "I mean, that's one I made up."

Almost everyone laughed. Sarah rolled her blue eyes up to gaze at the ceiling. Mrs. Carruthers, who I could tell wanted to give a hoot or two of her own, said, "Settle down, class. It is ironic, Kenneth, that Sarah happened to select your suggestion. But hoist upon your own petard or not, that is your assignment. Five hundred words should do it. By Monday, please."

Sarah looked at me and shook her head. I could interpret: "Don't even ask me; I will not bail you out of this one."

---

As always, I rendezvoused at the cafeteria doors with my best buddy, Rollin Acres. (His real name, I swear.) Three or four freshmen gave way to our size and genuine Argyle High football jerseys. "Heard you got in trouble with that chicken joke," Rollin said, slopping a second ladle of gravy on his mashed potatoes. "I thought that was a pretty good joke."

"You were supposed to like it," I said. "You're my straight man."

"I'm sick of being your straight man. Maybe I ought to tell the jokes for a while."

I shook my head. "Never work. Trust me on this one, Rollin. Anybody with parents dumb enough to name him Rollin Acres is a natural straight man."

He nodded sadly. "I suppose you're right. Do you think there's some kid around whose parents were dumb enough to name him Rollin Stone?"

"Not a chance," I said.

"Too bad. That'd be kinda cool. So, what'd you get from the ol' penalty jar?"

"I got nailed. Remember when Sarah told us about the drama club's skit for the kiddies in the grade schools?"

"Oh, yeah. *Santa's Workshop*. And you got silly and wrote a slip about Santa's chief elf getting—"

"Right. That's the one I got. Serves me right."

He grimaced. "Ain't an easy one. What're you going to do?"

"Get Sarah to help me. What else?"

"One of these days, she's going to tell you to buzz off."

"Na. I've known her since kindergarten. She always comes through. There she is. Come on."

Sarah looked up from the book she had open beside her tray. "Don't even start, Kenny! I do not want to hear about it. No whining, no pitiful looks. Write your own essay this time."

I sat down across from her and grinned. "Not to worry. Rollin and me got it all figured out. Just a matter of writing it up. We're going to do it next hour in the computer lab."

"Well, keep the talk down. I'm the student supervisor next hour."

"Sure. But, hey, Sarah. If you've got any suggestions, we'd be happy to listen."

She glared at me. "No! You work this out yourself."

I shrugged. "Sure. Not a problem." I dug into my lunch.

"Hmmmp," she said, and went back to reading her book.

Rollin got involved in a conversation with some kids at the other end of the table. "So," I said, "want to go out Friday? Go to a movie or something?"

Sarah put her finger on her place in the book, gave a tired sigh that Mrs. Carruthers would have envied, and stared at me. "Kenny, if you ever bothered to act your age, I might just say yes. But you don't, so it's still no, thanks."

"Hey," I said, "I'll start right now."

She scoffed. "Right. Think about your essay. I gotta go study." She got up with her tray and book.

———

Rollin and I gazed at the blank computer screen. "Well," Rollin said, "let 'er rip."

"I'm a stand-up," I said. "Funny stuff doesn't come to me sitting down."

"Stand up then."

"Can't write standing up."

"Then we've got a problem."

"Uh-huh," I said. I felt the back of my neck crawl and turned to catch Rolf watching us. I glared, and he ducked back behind his computer. I let the front legs of my chair drop to the floor. "Well, here goes," I said. I typed:

```
Dear Mary,
     I am Fritz, one of Santa's elves. Santa asked
me to write to you. I am sorry, but we are not
delivering any presents this year because the
workshop elves are on strike.
```

"Boring," Rollin said. "Besides, why's he gonna get fired for writing that?"

"You're right," I said.

We stared for another couple of minutes at the screen. I began again:

```
Dear Mary,
     I'm Fritz, Santa's selfish elf. I'm supposed
to tell you that all your presents are coming.
But none of them are. Because I'm keeping them
all. Ha, ha, ha.
```

"Still boring," Rollin said. "Maybe even worse."

I sighed, leaned back, and thought. "Okay, he's got to get fired."

"Right."

"Which means he's got to do something wrong."

"You're on the right track, Einstein."

"It's got to be something so bad that Santa starts drinking."

"Uh-huh."

"And the police come to investigate."

"Tall order," Rollin said.

"Yeah," I said, and started typing a third time:

```
Hey, Mary,
     I'm Fritz, Santa's perverted elf. I collect
little girls' panties. What color are yours? I'd
like  to  peek  up  your  dress  to  see.  Maybe
Christmas Eve, when I ride with Santa, I'll ask
if . . .
```

Rollin was laughing and my fingers were moving about as fast as my so-so skills on the keyboard would take them. I kept on for a page or so like that. Nothing real, real bad. Just a lot of dumb stuff, but it was funny.

"Okay, what are you two morons up to?" Sarah leaned over my shoulder to read the screen. After a few seconds, she slapped me on the back of the head.

"Ouch," I said, still giggling.

"Kenny, you are such a jerk sometimes. And you too, Rollin. You shouldn't encourage him."

"Oh, come on," I said. "We're just having a little fun. I'm not stupid enough to hand it in."

"You shouldn't even write it. You shouldn't even *think* it. Now erase that junk. Everything."

"I want a printout," Rollin said.

"Not on your life," she said. "Kenny, you dump that stuff right now."

"Okay, okay," I said, dumped the file in the trash, and punched the Erase command. "It's gone."

She fumed, glanced at the clock, sighed, and sat down at the computer beside me. "Rollin, go find something to do. I gotta straighten this kid out." She opened a new document. "Okay, quick outline." Her long fingers started moving on the keys. "Santa's broken some kind of environmental rule. Let's see." She brushed blond hair back from her cheek and chewed her lip for a moment. "Okay, he's using lead paint on the Christmas toys. Our elf hero blows the whistle. That may get him fired, but he thinks Santa isn't really responsible these days. Nipping the schnapps too much. So, our elf hero is willing to risk his job to protect the kiddies and get Santa some professional help . . . ."

She took the outline to the end, and it was a pretty good story. "Okay, you write it out, and we'll go over it tomorrow."

"Okay," I said, "but maybe it'd be simpler if you just—"

"No! I am not going to waste my evening doing your work."

"Just a suggestion," I said, though I was talking to her back. But it was a nice back.

That evening I used the PC at home to write the letter from Albert, the whistle-blowing nerd elf, to Mary, brave daughter of the chief of Canada's environmental protection agency (a little detail I added). It was pretty funny, if I must say so myself. Not as funny as Fritz the perverted elf, but funny.

––––––––

Sarah looked over my efforts the next afternoon. I sat close so I could smell her perfume until she slid her chair away a foot. She grumped, "How can you spell so many things wrong when you've got a spell-checker?"

"Oops," I said. "Guess I forgot to run it."

She shook her head. "Did you bring the disk?"

"Sure thing." I grinned, knowing that she'd clean up more than just the spelling once she got started.

"You know," she said, as we waited for my disk to boot, "now that football's over, you might actually try to do something useful with all your comic energy."

"Like what?"

"Like join the drama club. We could use you in the Santa's workshop skit we're doing in the grade schools."

"Hey, I'm a stand-up. I don't want to be an elf."

She shook her head. "Kenny, you are not funny. You never were funny. All you do is get in trouble trying to be funny. And that makes me sad."

I was taken aback. Not because she didn't think I was funny. I mean, hey, there's no accounting for taste. But that she felt sad when I got in trouble? I mean, maybe a little embarrassed, but *sad*? "Okay," I said. "I'll be an elf."

"And will you stop with the jokes, particularly in English?"

I grimaced. "Well, I'll try. But did you hear about the nerd who—"

"No, and I don't want to!"

---

Anyway, that's how I became an elf. I tried to talk Rollin into becoming one too. "Nothing much to it," I told him. "We go into a grade school, grab a few kids out of the audience to play parts, and then put on the skit."

"No way," he said. "Remember, I've got three little

brothers. I *know* what little kids are like. And believe me, football's as rough a game as I want to play."

"Suit yourself. But I kinda like little kids; they're an easy audience. Besides, we get out of a lot of classes during the two or three weeks before Christmas."

"Come to think of it," Rollin said, "maybe it would be kind of fun to be an elf."

The next evening, we were issued elf costumes—which were just a little tight in the crotch, thank you—and started learning our parts.

Besides having the female lead, Sarah was Mr. McDunn's associate producer, which meant she'd be in charge anytime we went out to one of the grade schools while he was teaching. McDunn pointed to me. "Which elf are you, Bauer?"

"Fritz," I said without thinking. Sarah gave me a warning look.

"There is no Fritz in the script. There's a Franz."

"That's what I meant."

---

We had our first performance two weeks later. It went pretty well, and we got better after that. Sarah (Mrs. Claus) and Bill Kappus (Santa) would select four kids from the audience and turn them over to Rollin and me. We'd rush them into the hall and jam them into costumes, while Santa, Mrs. Claus, and the reindeer (two sophomores and two semi-nerd freshmen) sang a couple of Christmas songs with the remaining kids.

Because little kids come in a remarkable number of different sizes and shapes, getting them into their costumes took a lot of stuffing, tucking, and buckling. But the kids went along with it fine, liking my jokes and giggling when I tickled them. Then, bam, back onstage. Let the play begin.

I was having fun and doing a pretty darn good job. And not only with the play. My grades were up, and I hadn't gotten in trouble with a nerd joke in weeks. That's why I didn't expect anything bad when I was called to the principal's office ten minutes before afternoon homeroom the week before school let out for Christmas vacation.

"Hey, Mrs. G.," I said to the secretary. "What's up?"

She gave me a peculiar look. "Mr. Wenzel wants to see you in his office."

"Why?"

"You'll have to ask him. This way, please."

Not only Mr. Wenzel, but Mr. Mathias, the assistant principal, and Mr. McDunn, the drama coach, were all waiting for me. Mr. Wenzel straightened in his chair. "Hello, Ken. Sit down, please."

"Uh, sure. What's going on?"

He studied me for a long moment. "We've received a copy of a rather disturbing letter. It's been alleged that you wrote it."

*Alleged.* What the heck was going on here? "Well, maybe," I said, "but I don't remember writing any letters recently. And certainly nothing disturbing. Unless, you mean, because I don't spell so good—"

He turned over a sheet on his desk and pushed it toward me. "Did you write this?"

I read:

```
Hey, Mary,
    I'm Fritz, Santa's perverted elf. I collect
little girls' panties. What color are . . .
```

"Hey," I blurted. "Where'd you get this?"

"Did you write it?"

"Yes . . . I mean, not exactly. Kind of. But I never . . ." I took a deep breath. "Yes, I wrote it. But it was just me and a friend messing around in the computer lab before we got down to work. I didn't send it to anybody."

Mr. Mathias spoke. "Who is this Mary you were writing to?"

"No one! It was just a name we picked out. I picked out. Look, let me explain . . . ." I told them about telling the nerd joke in Mrs. Carruthers's class and then getting the extra writing assignment for wasting the class's time.

"So," Mr. Wenzel said, "you fancy yourself quite the class comedian."

"Well, a little, I guess. But not so much anymore. I've really enjoyed being in the drama club recently. It's been a lot of fun performing out there in the grade schools, and—"

"And it's just that involvement with youngsters that concerns us," Mr. Wenzel said. "Mr. McDunn tells us you are in physical contact with children before every performance."

I stared at him. "Hey, wait a second! I never touched one of those kids. I mean, yeah, I touched. I have to get them in their costumes. But I never touched one of them, you know, the wrong way. Who says I did?"

"No one. Or at least not yet. But it does concern us that you wrote—"

"Mr. Wenzel, that letter is just dumb stuff. I was just trying to be funny. It doesn't have anything to do with how I feel about kids."

No one said anything for a minute. "So, who saw the letter?" Mr. Wenzel asked.

"Just me, my friend, and I guess one other friend. She told us we were jerks and that I ought to erase it. And I did. I don't know how anybody found it after I dumped the electronic trash, but it was gone when I finished at the computer."

"Who was the friend who helped you write it?"

I hesitated. "I'd rather not say."

"Why not?"

"I don't want to get him in trouble. He didn't really help write it. He just read it and laughed."

"Who was the girl who told you to erase it?"

I suddenly felt very cold. These guys were really trying to get me. Me and my friends. I leaned back. "I guess I'm not going to tell you that, either."

"Very well." He looked past me. "Mr. McDunn, I think you should plan on doing the rest of your performances without young Mr. Bauer's participation. Mr. Mathias, please get in contact with the grade schools. Don't upset anyone, but find out if there have been any reports of inappropriate behavior." He stared at me. "And, son, I don't think I'd have any contact with children until we get this cleared up."

---

I leaned against my locker, too dazed to move amid the tumult of kids shouting, laughing, and generally enjoying the heck out of Friday afternoon. How had this happened? I'd trashed that letter. Closed the document, dragged the icon to the trash, and then dumped the trash, erasing it from the hard drive. Or maybe I hadn't. Had I been stupid enough to drag it to the trash and then not dump it? It seemed the only possibility. Unless . . .

I looked across the hall to where Rollin was tossing his books into his locker. He slammed the door and headed my way. "Hey, Ken. How goes it?"

"Rollin, were you dumb enough to retype that letter I wrote?"

He looked confused. "What letter?"

"Fritz's letter. You know, Santa's perverted elf."

He grinned. "Oh, yeah. I'd forgotten about him. I wish you'd kept that letter. It was pretty funny."

"Not very. Did you retype it after I dumped it in the trash?"

"No. What's going on?"

"I'll tell you in a minute. Did you see me drag it to the trash?"

"Sure. Right after Sarah called you a jerk."

"Did I dump the trash?"

"Yeah, I think so. Come on, what's up?"

I told him. His face got very serious. "You kept me out of it?"

"Yeah, I kept you out of it."

He thought for a long minute. "Who's trying to get you?"

"I don't know. I wish to heck I did."

"Sarah was the only other person to read that letter. And she wouldn't. I mean, why would she be that mad at you?"

"I don't know. But I guess I'd better ask her."

———

"Norton Utilities," Sarah said.

"Huh?" I said.

She closed the wardrobe closet and sat down at the makeup table. We were backstage, the silence echoing around us. "You can use it to find files accidentally trashed," she said. "When you dump the trash, its contents aren't really erased. All that's erased are the icons and names in the directory window. The documents still exist on the hard drive until they're overwritten. So, somebody could have gone into the hard drive and found your stupid letter with Norton Utilities."

"But who?" I asked.

She shrugged. "Anyone who knows jack about computers. Which you obviously don't."

I thought. And then I had it. "You mean *any* nerd! Rolf Egglehart was in the lab that period. I remember staring him down."

"You're right!" Rollin yelped. "And I saw him down there just a few minutes ago."

"Let's go," I said. "I am going to strangle that kid."

"Now, take it easy, Kenny," Sarah said. She paused to lock the stage door before hurrying after us.

———

Rolf glanced up from his computer screen and then looked at the oversized watch on his skinny wrist.

"Thirty-six minutes. Not bad. But then Sarah probably helped you figure it out."

"You nerd!" I snarled. "I'm going—"

"Careful," he said. "I wouldn't make any threats if I were you. Not until you've seen this."

He swiveled the terminal so we could see:

```
FRITZ THE PERVERTED ELF
BROUGHT TO YOU BY
THAT STAR OF ARGYLE FOOTBALL
KENNETH "THE JERK" BAUER


Hey, Mary,
    I'm Fritz, Santa's perverted elf. I collect
little girls'. . .
```

Rolf punched a command on the keyboard and leaned back. "In five minutes, that's going to hit the network. Every computer's going to have it by e-mail, and every fax machine and printer in every school building in the system is going to spit out a copy. And none of you, not even Sarah, knows enough to stop it."

My insides went hollow. I stared at him. "What do you want from me?"

"Not a thing. I got what I want. Payback. Big-time."

"For what? For a few—"

He was out of his chair, anger suddenly making him look hard, almost vicious. "No, for *a lot* of stupid jokes! For a lot of . . ." He made a gesture like he was wringing the neck of a chicken. "For all the years, for all the gym classes, for every time somebody put me down just because I don't happen to have the genes to be a jock or six feet tall or handsome enough to get dates with girls like her." He gestured at Sarah. "For all that. Well, this time, *I* win."

I stared at him, openmouthed. "Hey, I never gave you that much trouble. I never—"

He made the neck-wringing gesture again. "It only took once." He sat down and folded his arms.

I slumped in a chair by a laser printer. "Hey, Rolf," Rollin said. "A lot of that was just teasing. It's not like—"

"Wrong approach," Rolf snapped. "Besides, nobody respects a straight man. Ask Ed McMahon." He glanced over his shoulder at the counter ticking away in the corner of the computer screen. "Two minutes, twenty seconds left. Do you want to give it a shot, Sarah?"

She compressed her lips. "Look, Rolf. I never liked the nerd jokes. They were tasteless, they weren't funny, and I'm sorry you took them so personally. But I don't think they're a big enough reason to destroy Kenny's life. And that's what's going to happen, you know. It's bad enough that McDunn, Mathias, and Wenzel saw that letter, but if everyone sees it . . . Well, it's just going to be awful, Rolf." And to my astonishment, she choked back a sob.

"I'm touched," Rolf said. "But, hey, he wrote the letter. And maybe everybody should know what kind of thoughts he can—"

I slammed my fist on the table. "I'm not a pervert! I wrote something stupid, but I never hurt a kid. Call me anything else you want, but I am no pervert."

Rolf smiled crookedly. "Well, that certainly opens up some interesting possibilities for name-calling. But I'll give you that. I think you're a jerk, but I don't think you'd sexually abuse a kid." He turned to the keyboard. "Well, this isn't getting us anywhere. Let's speed things up."

He hit a couple of keys, the counter went to zero, and I think for a second my heart actually stopped. Beside me, the laser printer hummed to life and a sheet slid out. With leaden fingers, I turned it over.

```
Dear Mr. Wenzel:
    I am the one who sent you Fritz the perverted
elf's letter. I recovered it from the hard drive
of the computer Ken Bauer was using in the lab. I
did not find it by accident but by intentionally
using the recovery procedure available with Nor-
ton Utilities. I sent it to you not out of a
sense of civic duty but to do as much damage to
Ken's reputation as I could. I do not regret
that. Nor do I apologize for inconveniencing you.
I've seen you at every sporting event I've ever
attended in Argyle, but not once at a Quiz Bowl
or a forensics contest. So, you can figure out
exactly what I think your time is worth.
    I do not, by the way, think Ken Bauer is a
pervert. A jerk and a lot of other things, but I
don't think he harms little kids. That, for what
it's worth, is my opinion.
    The game's over now. I have permanently
erased Fritz the perverted elf's letter from
the lab computer, which means you have the only
remaining copy. Do with it what you like and
with this letter also. I could care less.
    Sincerely,


    Rolf Egglehart
```

Rolf took the letter from my fingers and scrawled his signature on it. "The Fritz letter didn't go out on the network?" I asked.

"Nope. It's erased, as I said."

"How do I know you don't have a copy somewhere?"

"You don't." He handed the letter back to me.

"What am I supposed to do with this?"

"You can chew it up and choke on it for all I care. But if I were you, I'd give it to Wenzel."

"But he's going to punish you for—"

He laughed, for the first time actually sounding amused. "Well, now, I really am touched that you should care. But what can he do to a nerd? Take my athletic eligibility? Ban me from the computer lab? Suspend me for a few days? I'd like that. I've got a computer at home that can torch anything here. I'd love a few days to work on it."

"How about your folks?" Sarah asked.

He shrugged. "It's just Dad and me. And he's kind of a nerd too. He'll understand."

"You win," I said.

"Darn right I do," he said, and walked, his head high, out of the room.

I stared at the letter. "You gonna give it to Wenzel?" Rollin asked.

I nodded. "That's what Rolf wants. He wants to stick it to everybody. And some of us just may deserve it."

———

Rolf's letter didn't solve everything, of course. I'd still written the Fritz letter, and Wenzel, Mathias, and

McDunn still thought that was pretty weird. But Rollin and Sarah stood up for me, telling them I was dumb but not dangerous. And I told Mrs. Carruthers everything, because I knew I could count on her to tell them the same thing but make it stick better.

Rolf came out of his interview with Wenzel looking neither shaken nor contrite. The only thing he didn't get was the three days he wanted at home. I guess Wenzel figured it was time that everybody just shut up about the whole thing.

I never got to do *Santa's Workshop* again that year. If they do it again next year, I might try to convince everyone that I'm okay. Or maybe I'll just let it pass.

I said hi to Rolf in the halls a few times in the weeks after Christmas vacation, but he ignored me. I let it be for a while, but then I got stubborn and started again. Finally, one day, he stopped. "All right! Hello, Ken. Now, what do you want?"

I hesitated. "To be friends, I guess."

"Now, that is asking a lot. A heck of a lot."

"I kind of think that's what you ask of friends."

He shook his head in frustration. "Why would you want to be friends?"

I shrugged. "I don't know, Rolf. I really don't. It's just that we've been through something together. I had a fight with Rollin in grade school one time. It was only after that we really got to be friends. We'd been through something together."

"And you think this is an analogous situation?"

"Well, it's sort of the same, anyway."

He sighed. "That's what *analogous* means. Well, I'm

gonna have to think about this." He turned and started down the hall.

"Uh, I'll see you next week," I called after him.

He waved a hand without turning.

————

"So, no more nerd jokes?" Sarah asked.

"Haven't told one in a couple of months. I thought you'd noticed," I said.

"I did, but with you there's always the chance of a relapse."

"No, I'm off nerd jokes for good. Some of the guys I used to call nerds really scare me now, and I don't take chances anymore. But, hey, did you hear about the blonde who—"

"Kenny," she said, "shut up."

And since we spend a lot of time together these days, doing the boyfriend-girlfriend thing, I said, "Yes, ma'am," grinned at her, and leaned in to see if there might just be a quick kiss in it for me. There was.

# Alden R. Carter

Alden R. Carter has published eight highly regarded novels for young adults, as well as twenty nonfiction books covering subjects as varied as the Spanish-American War, Shoshoni Indians, Chinese history, and the development of radio. He also teamed up with his eight-year-old daughter, Siri, on *I'm Tougher Than Asthma,* a picture book for children.

Most of his novels, including *Sheila's Dying, Between a Rock and a Hard Place,* and *Wart, Son of Toad,* were named Best Books for Young Adults by the American Library Association, and *Up Country,* the story of a troubled city boy who is sent to live with relatives on a Wisconsin farm, was named by the ALA one of the 100 Best of the Best Books for Young Adults published between 1967 and 1992. *Dancing on Dark Water* (originally titled *Robodad*), which recounts the experiences of a family after a ruptured aneurysm diminishes the father's emotional reactions, was named the Best Children's Fiction Book of 1990 by the Society of Midland Authors. And *Dogwolf,* a tensely told story about a teenage boy's struggle with a vicious dog-wolf and with his own ethnic identity in a summer of drought and forest fires, was an *American Bookseller* Pick of the Lists.

In *Between a Rock and a Hard Place,* Carter tells the story of two teenage boys who face death during a trek across the rugged outback of northern Minnesota. And in his most recent novel, *Bull Catcher,* based on a story Carter published in *Scholastic Scope,* Neil "The Bull" Larsen describes how a group of high-school friends mature as they pursue a championship through four seasons of baseball.

Alden Carter sympathizes with the character of Ken in "Trashback" because, Carter says, his own sense of humor has gotten him into trouble "more times than I care to remember. Personally, I think I'm hysterically funny, but others have rarely agreed."

Everybody knows Randy's a retard. The rest of
the guys just want to have some fun with him.

# The Doi Store Monkey
## Graham Salisbury

"Rossman, listen . . . I . . . I'm sorry about the monkey,
okay? . . . Rossman?"

Johnny Smythe slapped the back of his neck, once,
twice. Then his arm. "I know you're hiding in there, so
come out, okay? It's creepy out here, Rossman. And these
mosquitoes are"—*slap!*—"eating me alive."

Stupid mosquitoes.

"Rossman, listen. It's past *midnight,* already. What do
you want me to do? Beg? Okay, I'm *begging* you to come
out of there and go back to the dorm with me."

But nothing came from the black jungle that edged
the school. No rustle of leaves, no skittering insects, not
even a ghostly whisper. Nothing. The only thing on earth
Smythe could hear was the mosquitoes. And the nagging
voice in his head. *Worm, maggot, scorpion. Heartless
scumbag. Yeah, that's you, Smythe.*

Tsk.

"Could be black widows in there, Rossman. Or maybe the loloman. Yeah, what if the loloman's in that jungle with you?"

*Hmmmff.* That would make him think.

Smythe shuddered and looked around for moving shadows, remembering the crazy man. He didn't live far from here. They'd found him by accident—*they* being himself, Riggins, Pang, and McCarty. Riggins thought the loloman was probably only about thirty years old, but he looked a hundred because his teeth were gone; at least from a distance it looked like they were.

This crazy wacko loloman, as they called him, lived in a broken-down one-room shed in the jungle. Riggins discovered him one afternoon during the second week of school when they were farting around out behind the dorm. They'd all crawled up on their hands and knees and peeked through the bushes. Smythe remembered how his hands had trembled with fear and excitement as he watched this wild-haired man standing in his doorway scraping a fork on the doorjamb to clean it. When the man had gone back inside, they'd all raced back to see if they could find Rossman and talk him into sneaking up and peeking into the crazy guy's house. Rossman would do stuff like that. He'd do it because he wanted friends. Any friends.

Stupid Rossman, Smythe thought.

But anyway, they'd found him and brought him back and sent him into the clearing by the loloman's shack with that big, fat, stupid, lopsided grin of his plastered all over his face. He just stumbled up and looked in the door.

Oh, man, did that lolo guy go nuts. From inside his shack he *screamed* at Rossman in some strange language none of them understood. Smythe remembered how Rossman had staggered back, looking more stunned than scared. Confused, disoriented. And that's all Smythe had seen, because he and the rest of the guys took off out of there, terrified that maybe the crazy man had a gun and would come out shooting.

Rossman was mad as a hornet when he got back to the dorm, and to avoid Riggins and the rest of them, he hid out in the jungle for three hours, hid right there where Smythe was now, slapping mosquitoes.

But Rossman got over it and soon came slinking back to the dorm, where he joined in and laughed about it with everyone else, just like every other time Riggins and the rest of them faked him out or got him to do something stupid like that.

But this monkey thing . . .

"Rossman! Come *out* of there," Smythe said, scowling in the dark. "This is getting old."

*Worm.*

Still no sound came from the shadows.

"Rossman?"

Smythe took a step closer to the jungle, but it was thick and dense and dark and way too spooky at night to go inside, and he sure as spit wasn't going in there to drag Rossman out. So he sat down just outside the bushes in the tall, cool grass, smooth and silvery in the moonlight. "You know what your problem is, Rossman? You try too hard, that's what. It makes you look stupid."

Was that it? Smythe thought. Was that really it? Or

was that just an excuse? A smokescreen for a maggot? Smythe frowned and bunched up his lips.

He looked up at the moon, bright as a fresh pearl. But clouds kept passing over it, making the night blacker. Smythe picked at the long pasture grass, tearing blades out of the ground and ripping them apart. When his thoughts drifted back to the monkey, he ripped a whole hank of grass up and threw it and punched his hand. "Rossman! Come *out of there!*"

*Jeez,* Rossman drove him crazy.

Or was it guilt that did that?

"Come on, Rossman," Smythe said, now more gently, as if he were talking to a true friend or some scared kid. "Just come back to the dorm. I'm sorry, okay? We're all sorry."

So Riggins was a worm. I guess we all were, Smythe admitted. If you thought about it. Yes. Definitely scumbags. Okay, maybe Pang wasn't, because he tried to do the right thing by staying out of it. But the rest of us were worms for sure.

Prep school. What it does to you. Turns you into morons.

But it's weird, Smythe thought. Ever since he'd been there, he'd had more fun than ever before in his life. All the guys. All the cussing and insulting and joking around and being cool and stealing each other's love letters and cookie stashes and hanging out in the dorm with no parents to crab all over them. He couldn't believe that he even liked the Saturday-morning white-glove locker inspections. And flag ceremony. And even Sunday chapel, for cripes sake. Not the kind of life he was used to, but he liked it. Algebra, geography, French.

Oh, and private lessons from people like Riggins on how to be a first-rate genuine-article blue-bellied zit-faced screaming-eagle scumbag.

"Hey, Rossman. Remember when Pang opened that reeking jar of kimchi in Mr. Chapman's class? Man, was that funny. Remember that?"

A slight rustle.

Or something. Maybe a black widow, rubbing its hands together.

Shet.

Smythe mashed down the grass and made himself comfortable, looked up at the moon. Wait him out, he thought. For a while, anyway. There was a limit to this guilt. He hoped. *Why don't you guys just leave him alone,* Pang had said. *He's just like that monkey, except at least the monkey can get out of his cage once in a while.* Smythe remembered wondering what the spit Pang was talking about, at least the monkey could get out of his cage. What kind of mumbo jumbo was that?

The clouds moved away from the bright, glowing moon, leaving it alone in the sky. Smythe covered his eyes with the crook of his arm. Why couldn't he just forget about the stupid monkey?

And Rossman.

Who'd showed up at school a couple of days late. Classes had already started, and everyone was pretty much settled into dorm life. Being late like that would have made it hard for anyone. That's for sure, Smythe thought. I mean, you'd get the worst bunk and the worst locker and you wouldn't know anyone and you'd have a pile of homework to catch up on, and at that school they dished up homework like saltpetered mashed potatoes.

But for Rossman, being late was only a small problem. Very small.

You see, Rossman had some kind of disease, or something. Smythe didn't know what it was, but they called him a spastic.

His body didn't work. His mouth was lopsided and he drooled. He slurred his words when he talked, and he was hard to understand. His arms and legs went every which way when he walked. But he didn't use a wheelchair or a cane. He just stumbled ahead on his own.

Smythe still found it hard to believe that someone had actually sent him there to live with a bunch of idiot ninth-graders whose parents had kicked them out of the house because they were too busy to raise them or they didn't like them or they wanted them to get into some hoity-toity Ivy League college and turn into lawyers and doctors and investment bankers. Jeez. So funny. Could you even imagine someone like Riggins as a banker? Embezzler maybe, would be more like it.

Anyway, Smythe thought, what were they thinking when they dumped this Rossman kid into the midst of us scorpions? Who did they think was going to help him? Who was going to understand him? Who was going to stop people from making fun of him? Criminy, it was like dropping a fly into a jar of toads.

At first, Smythe felt embarrassed for him. He looked like a goof, and everyone laughed at him. Smythe laughed at him. Rossman even laughed at himself. That's the kind of guy Rossman was, now that Smythe thought about it. Someone who could laugh at himself. Smythe figured it took a pretty big person to laugh at himself.

Jeez, Rossman. You should have ignored us from day one. *Beat it, assholes,* you should have said, and maybe we would have left you alone.

Anyway, the school was new, only about seven years old. But the buildings they all lived in were dusty old military barracks. It was started by some bishop, but people called the students cadets, thinking it was a military school. Altogether, there were about a hundred and twenty boys, all sent away to boarding school, to *prep* school. To another planet, is what it was. At least that's what it felt like to Smythe.

The campus—Smythe half laughed when he thought of that place as a *campus*—was a square yard, maybe four or five acres, way up in the mountains on the Big Island of Hawaii. A row of barracks edged around it in a U shape. There was a chapel surrounded by a grassy lawn in the middle. An American flag flapped high on a silver flagpole, with metal halyard clips that clanged in the breeze. Tall swaying trees crowded in and leaned over everything on three sides. And then there was the thick jungle behind the trees, where Rossman was now, hiding like a rat.

Anyway, the ninth- and tenth-grade dorm, which was in the bottom corner of the U shape, right by the flagpole, had two open rooms, each filled with bunks and long lockers that nobody locked, except McCarty, who always had cookies from home that he hoarded for himself. Ninth-graders were in one room, tenth- in the other. The shower and bathroom were in between. The floor was wood planked, and old, and dusty. Steam radiators stood in back, like exposed plumbing under windows that looked out into the jungle.

Right next door to their dorm, a square green building called the mess hall squatted under the towering trees, looking like an old toad. Smythe thought that was pretty cool—*mess hall*, like in the army. It was there, on the day Rossman had arrived, that Smythe had gotten his first close look at him.

Smythe remembered being called to dinner by the bell. The bunch of them filed out of their dorm and into the mess hall. They'd all been assigned positions at long tables, each headed by a faculty member. Smythe and all the boys in school had been told they would each take turns waiting on tables and cleaning up. And they'd sit when they were told they could sit, and they'd eat when they were told they could eat. They would say grace, say please pass this and please pass that, and most important, they would learn to tip their soup bowls away from them and eat like civilized human beings.

Smythe had been assigned to a table in back, near the kitchen, and there Rossman stood crookedly across from him, waiting along with everyone else for permission to sit. Smythe figured Rossman must have been kind of nervous, coming into school late like that, a thought that now made Smythe's guilt grow even greater as he lay under the moon remembering all of this. *He* sure would have been nervous, if it had been him.

Anyway, Rossman's hair was blond and cut in a close buzz, and his clothes were new. Smythe remembered the way Rossman had gaped across the table at him, with his lopsided mouth slightly open. Not smiling, not glaring, just looking in this tilted way, as if he were sinking on one side. Smythe watched him a minute, then looked down at his hands, fingers laced together in front of him. Rossman looked goofy. Smythe didn't know what to do, how to act. He peeked around at the other guys at the table and wondered if he was the only one who felt that way.

The headmaster came in and told the boys they could sit. Chairs scraped over the floor and silverware rattled as all hundred and twenty of them settled down. Dinner began, large stainless-steel bowls of food passing silently from one hand to the next.

Smythe noticed that Rossman drooled as he ate and kept wiping his chin on the back of his wrist. No one spoke to him, or even asked him to pass anything. But by the end of the first week of school he was the great oddity of the ninth grade, if not the entire school. Everyone talked about him.

"The guy walks funny."

"Can you understand him when he talks?"

"Man, has he got mega b.o."

"God, how can you even sit next to him? He drools. Sick."

"How come he's here, anyway? He shouldn't be here."

Rossman often just stood in one spot and stared at things, at people, at clouds, at spiders in sticky white webs. He held himself up by his own strange kind of balance, leaning at an unlikely angle with his arms hanging down like an ape. And at night in the dorm he snored louder than a flushing toilet.

It would have been easy to ignore him or at least avoid him. That would have been the easy thing to do.

He was different. He wasn't at all like everyone else. We could've just left him alone, Smythe thought. And maybe we would have.

Except that Rossman wouldn't allow it.

Because, they soon discovered, Rossman had a personality. He was a *person*. There was a *boy* inside that crooked body. A boy who wanted to be just like everyone else. He wanted to make friends, he wanted to talk to you, and if you listened and tried to understand him, you could even have a conversation with him. It took some work, but it could be done. The thing with Rossman was that he tried harder than anyone in school to get to know the other guys.

A wispy cloud crossed over the moon, and Smythe humphed, thinking that Rossman tried *too* hard, actually. Anyway, how do you really get to know somebody you can barely understand?

Smythe worked hard at trying to convince himself that they had tried. They'd let him listen to their jokes, hadn't they? And Rossman laughed at them just like they did. And they'd let him hang around, right? Wasn't that trying?

Right.

Smythe tore up another hank of grass and tossed it, remembering back to that Saturday afternoon after their first full week of school. He and Riggins and a bunch of guys were standing around talking and joking and spitting off the porch at certain targets, like spiders in webs, leaves, or long-distance targets out in the quad. After a while Rossman came out of the dorm and lurched over to see what they were up to. They stopped spitting, a little uncertain if they should go on, since . . . well, since Rossman drooled and spit all the time . . . because he couldn't help it. So anyway they all decided, in some unspoken way, that they'd continue spitting. So what if it made Rossman feel bad?

After a while they got tired of those targets and started spitting at each other, laughing their heads off when somebody actually got hit. Pang got splattered first. Riggins lobbed a lugie that hit his neck and headed down his shirt collar. Pang wiped it away as if it were death itself, putting on a great show of disgust, which was easy to do if you got spit on you. Everyone, including Rossman, thought it was hilarious.

"You're gonna pay for that, asshole," Pang said, and went after Riggins, and since Riggins was laughing so hard, Pang caught him easily, and the two of them wrestled in the dirt. It was pretty funny, you had to admit. Even now, lying in the dark grass by a creepy jungle, Smythe smiled at the memory.

So anyway, soon Rossman wanted to get in on the action.

That was great news because Rossman was the *king* of spit.

Immediately everybody ran for it, not wanting to be washed by any of Rossman's abundant slobber. Rossman, being Rossman, thought that was great. Such power. Such friends. Such good guys. He stumbled after Riggins, then Pang, then Smythe and McCarty, lobbing lugie after lugie at whoever was closest. They all wailed with delight, dancing around him like puppies, moving in, moving out, giving him a clear target, then racing back before he could react, none of which were great acts of courage because Rossman was slower than mud, and his spit flew harmlessly to the ground. Still, he laughed and wiped his chin with the back of his arm after each shot.

Poor slob, Smythe thought. Wasn't even a contest.

Then Riggins spit back, and hit Rossman.

Rossman stopped a moment, as if to consider it. For a second all the guys fell silent. Then, with even greater determination, Rossman grinned and stumbled off after Riggins, who ran for his life.

Then McCarty spit, hitting Rossman on the shoulder of his shirt.

This time Rossman scowled. He was clearly at a loss in this game, clearly outclassed. He was a joke, not a contender. He tried to get McCarty but ended up getting more spit on himself, again and again.

Finally Rossman snapped. Sudden anger roared out of him in one long slurred warning to get the hell away from him. Everyone gaped at him a moment, then walked off in a pack, calling him a spazmo and mumbling what a dork he was and why did he even come to this school and why wasn't he in some other kind of school, like a hospital for weirdos, or something.

Smythe scowled in the dark as he remembered glancing back at Rossman and getting a full-on view of Rossman's middle finger.

———

That first Sunday Smythe discovered that they would all be going to church. *Every* Sunday. He'd never gone to church in his life and didn't have a clue about what went on there. He was told he'd have to wear a tie and a white shirt and a coat with brass buttons. So *that's* why his mother packed those things. He found that he had one white shirt and a clip-on bow tie and a clip-on regular tie. So at least he was ready for it. Whatever *it* was.

Along with everyone else in the dorm, Smythe filed over to St. James Chapel with his neck squeezed into a choking starched collar. But he was okay with that. It felt kind of cool to puff around in the brass-buttoned coat. Like he was important, or something. Rossman scowled along behind them. He looked like a drunk, Smythe thought, the way he walked. And his ill-fitting coat and wrinkled tie made him look like he'd just been tossed out of a bar.

In the chapel, Smythe settled into a long wooden pew with Pang, Riggins, and McCarty flanking him. They were pretty far back in the chapel, back behind the upperclassmen. In the pew just behind him, Smythe could hear Rossman blowing his nose. Riggins leaned forward to put more distance between himself and the gross nose honking going on behind him.

A tenth-grader named Cunningham, who was an ace keyboard player, blew hymns out of a pint-sized organ while everyone else sat there waiting for something to happen.

After a while, a priestlike guy entered the room wearing a long black robe. Everyone rose when he walked in, and watched him float to the pulpit. When he got there, he stood looking out over his congregation. "Let us sing," he finally said, as if what he'd seen before him was so discouraging he needed a song to wash the sight from his brain. A black felt signboard with white letters hanging on the wall behind him told the page numbers and order of the songs for the service. Smythe flipped the pages, and didn't find "Rock of Ages" until after everyone had already started singing. Rossman, singing in the pew behind him, slurred the words off-key.

When the song ended, the service started.

Smythe followed the crowd, kneeling on a padded bench when everyone else did, then standing, and listening, and reading out loud from a prayer book, and kneeling again, and sitting, and staring out the windows, dreaming of the beach and the hot sun and cool, wet ocean that waited for them that afternoon. Time passed. Clouds flew across the blue sky. The cows on the distant hillside paddock didn't seem to move at all, frozen reddish dots. Smythe sang, and prayed, and dreamed, and sat waiting for the unfathomable sermon to get over, his knee bouncing up and down with pent-up energy.

"Boys, boys, boys," the reverend was saying. "If I could only impress upon you one simple truth, it would be this . . . the smallest act of kindness is worth more than a thousand good intentions. Think about that awhile."

At that moment, Rossman sneezed, and Smythe felt a light spray of moisture hit the back of his neck. He flicked up the collar on his brass-buttoned coat and leaned forward, as Riggins had. Riggins started laughing, not out loud, but silently giggling at Smythe's show of absolute disgust, his head in his hands, down below the back of the pew in front of him. His shoulders shook, it was so funny to him. Smythe elbowed him, which only set Riggins off more.

"Let us read from the Bible," the reverend said. "Psalm nineteen, verse fourteen."

Smythe flicked his collar back down and fumbled for one of the blue, hard-covered Bibles in the book rack in front of him.

*Honk, honnnnk.* Rossman blew again. *"Sick,"* Riggins whispered, but Smythe ignored him, not wanting to get in trouble and miss going to the beach.

Pages ruffled and swished, and in a dull, murmuring rumble the mass of them read: " 'Let the words of my mouth, and the meditation of my heart, be acceptable in Thy sight, O Lord, my strength, and my redeemer. Amen.' "

After the service ended, the reverend walked down the aisle to the back of the chapel and waited to greet the boys as they filed out slowly, in order, from the front of the chapel to the back. Somebody cut one, and Smythe covered his nose with his coat. Riggins started laughing, so it was easy to see who'd caused the problem. But Riggins covered his own nose and whispered, "Jeez, Rossman, couldn't you wait until we got outside?"

Rossman ignored him.

The reverend was shaking every boy's hand as they passed on out the door, taking his time with each of them, smiling and wishing them well.

Which drove Riggins nuts.

———

After lunch, Smythe left his coat and tie and white shirt crumpled on the floor of his locker and tore out to climb aboard the brand-new school bus. He sat with Riggins,

Pang, McCarty, and some other guys about halfway back. Rossman, white as a peeled banana in his swim shorts, sat up front, behind the driver, who was Mr. Marshall, who Smythe thought was a pretty decent guy. From somewhere on the mainland, like all their instructors. East Coast, mostly.

The bus pulled out onto the road and lumbered away, grinding down to sea level, an elevation drop of almost three thousand feet. Down near Kawaihae, they turned left onto a crushed-coral road that raised so much dust they had to close the windows and sweat it out until they reached the beach. Just about every kid on the bus made a big show of gasping and choking and generally dying in the heat. But Rossman, Smythe noticed, just sat bouncing in his seat down the bumpy road.

Why did he keep thinking about Rossman, anyway?

———

What happened at the beach wasn't important. But afterward. Because that's when they discovered the monkey.

They'd all dragged themselves back onto the bus and headed back down the dusty road to Kawaihae, a scorchingly hot, dry, and desolate deep-water port that Smythe had never seen before. The place looked so dusty and foreign that he felt as if he were in some movie like *Lawrence of Arabia*. He actually looked around for camels as the bus pulled over and sat in its own dust.

He followed everyone off the bus.

Smythe kind of liked the place. Thick, monster heat. Light green harbor, still as a tidal pool. And quiet. Except for the sound of an occasional truck that rumbled past to the giant harbor storage sheds, the place was dead silent.

There was a store there. Just one.

It sat on a rise right off the road. Doi Store, the sign read. Smythe and the guys followed the rest of the boys up the steep driveway to go get Cokes and cracked seed and Popsicles and whatever else they could find to satisfy their raging hunger before heading back up the mountain to school.

Smythe had just enough money for two ice-cold Cokes and a bag of peanuts. He bought them and went back outside. It was almost eerie how there wasn't a breath of breeze to ease the stifling heat. Not even the faintest whisper. Weird. The place was like science fiction.

He stood with Riggins and McCarty in a sliver of shade, munching and drinking and checking the place out. Smythe spotted Rossman making his way back down to the bus, moving pretty slowly so he wouldn't trip. Rossman had stayed in the sun too long, Smythe thought. His face was as red as an apple. Smythe shook his head as he watched Rossman inch down the hill kind of sideways, a strawberry soda in one hand and his towel in the other. Jeez. Dorkman didn't even have the brains to leave his stupid towel on the bus.

"Hey, look what I found," someone said, and Smythe turned to see Pang standing over by something that looked like a cage. "There's a monkey in here."

The bunch of them slouched over to the large outdoor chicken-wire cage. Inside was a water bowl and a naked, well-worn tree branch. But no monkey, that Smythe could see, anyway. "Where is it?"

Pang spit out a peanut shell and pointed to the back of the cage.

The monkey was back in the far corner in a shadowy spot, still as an old shoe. "What kind of monkey is that?" Smythe said. "Just sits there."

It was one of those skinny ones, and it had a bare, red butt. The naked branch was worn so smooth Smythe figured the monkey must have been in that cage a long time.

"Rhesus, or something," Pang said.

Riggins said, "Somebody make it do some tricks."

Pang threw a peanut into the cage. It landed on the concrete floor, but the monkey didn't move.

The four of them hooked their fingers onto the wire mesh. "Stupid monkey looks half dead," McCarty said.

In that second—*Wham! Bam!*—that half-dead monkey *leaped* at them, slamming into the mesh, screeching like it had just been shot with a BB gun. Scared the spit out of Smythe, who flew back. The monkey shook the wire mesh, shook it and rattled it, trying to get at them. Smythe's heart pumped like a piston.

The owner of the store came running out. "What'-choo kids doing? Get away from there! What'choo doing?"

"Nothing," Riggins said. "The monkey's crazy."

"Get out of here. Go somewheres else."

So they left, mumbling on the bus on the way back up to school about the godawful lulu weirdo psycho monkey. After they got tired of complaining and reliving the experience, Riggins called toward the front of the bus. "Hey, Rossman, we met your brother today."

Rossman didn't move, but half the guys in the bus laughed. The other half, the upperclass guys in back, ignored the remark.

"I could tell he was your brother because his butt looks like your face."

Rossman raised his hand, still facing the front of the bus, and flipped Riggins off, which made everyone roar.

―――――

One week later Smythe, Riggins, McCarty, and Pang were back at Doi Store, checking out the monkey.

Riggins was eating a fast-melting Fudgsicle. "Hey." *Slurp.* "Psycho primate." *Slurp.* He was about to say more when―*pthooth*―the monkey blew out a bullet spitwad that hit the mesh and splintered into a shotgun blast of slimy, disgusting spray that splattered all over Riggins's hand and Fudgsicle, which was now poisoned.

Smythe, Pang, and McCarty nearly fell over laughing.

Riggins dropped the Fudgsicle. Almost instantly, it melted into a gooey brown puddle. He wasn't even halfway through it. *"Shet!"* he said, so mad he hawked up a wad of his own and spit back. It missed, but the monkey went ballistic, banging and screeching and running around in circles, calling to the guy in the store to come get these creeps out of there.

They all took off.

On the way back to school Riggins brooded about it. Just sat in his seat in a silent stupor. Pang slept, but Smythe and McCarty talked about how totally insane that monkey was and how it needed to be castrated to calm it down. Riggins rubbed his skin and mumbled that he was going to die if that stupid bus didn't hurry and get him back to school so he could take a hot shower and boil the poisonous, cancerous spit off his arms and hands and T-shirt, which he said he might throw away.

All week long Riggins stewed about the monkey and waited for Sunday, when the bus would take him back down to the beach. He didn't know what, but he was going to do something to get that monkey. He couldn't think of anything, until one night he dreamed of giving it a jalapeño pepper.

"Someone gave me one of those once," Pang said. "Man, was it nasty."

"Good," Riggins said. "The nastier the better."

That week, Smythe followed Riggins around to every store in town looking for jalapeños. But nobody had any. In fact, some people didn't even know what they were. So Riggins called his mother in Honolulu and asked her to mail him a couple. When she asked what in the world for, he said it was for a science experiment.

"Look what I got," Riggins said when they arrived in the mail, special delivery. He held up a jar of pre-served jalapeño peppers. "One of these will make him sorry."

"I don't think monkeys eat peppers," Pang said.

"Maybe they do, maybe they don't."

"Ask his brother," McCarty said, snickering.

Riggins grinned and walked over to Rossman's bunk. Rossman was lying there reading his geography book. "Hey, Dorkman," Riggins said. "Your red-butt brother eat these?"

"Grow up," Rossman said, and rolled away from us.

"Stupid retard," Riggins said back.

Smythe laughed. But didn't know why. It wasn't funny.

---

Pang was right.

When Riggins threw a jalapeño in the cage, the monkey picked it up, smelled it, and threw it back out. Dumb idea.

Pang, McCarty, and Smythe, munching peanuts and M&M's, waited to see what Riggins would do next.

"Smythe," Riggins finally said. "Gimme some of those peanuts?"

Smythe gave him a few.

Riggins peeled a pepper open with his thumb and stuffed the peanuts inside. "It's the little seeds that make it hot, right?" he said. "Well, maybe he'll go for the peanuts and get those hot little things all over his fingers." He looked up and flicked his eyebrows.

"Hey, psycho," Riggins whispered. "You're the absolute ugliest, stupidest, stinkingest, sorriest monkey I've ever seen in my life."

McCarty snickered. The monkey stared at Riggins from the far corner.

"Hey," Riggins went on. "I'm talking to you. I got something better." He dangled the pepper from his fingers, then eased it into the cage, gently, so the peanuts wouldn't fall out. Then he threw a peanut next to it as bait.

The monkey blinked.

A moment later he scrambled over, picked up the peanut, and ate it on the spot. Then he picked up the pepper and ran back to his corner. He looked at it and smelled it. But this time he saw the peanuts and started picking them out.

Smythe glanced back toward the store, praying the owner wouldn't come out. Then he turned back and watched the monkey eat one of the peanuts. And another. And . . .

The monkey froze. Looked up. Dropped his jaw.

And went *berserk,* screaming, screaming, screaming, bouncing around the cage like a pinball, charging the mesh, slamming into it and shaking it, shrieking at Riggins, who, along with Smythe, McCarty, and Pang, ran for their lives, laughing themselves to tears.

"I going call the *police!*" somebody yelled.

———

Back at school, when Rossman heard the jalapeño story, he went looking for Riggins, and when he found him, he told Riggins in front of Smythe and Pang and McCarty that he was the saddest case of a human being he'd ever seen.

"Fuck you, Dorkman," Riggins said. "You can't even control your own goddam drool, fucking spazmo."

Smythe winced.

Pang found something he needed to do elsewhere.

But McCarty laughed and walked off with Riggins.

———

"I got another idea," Riggins said to Smythe and Pang a few days later. He grinned and leaned closer, as if he didn't want anyone else to hear. "Spit," he said.

"What?"

"Spit. We get the monkey to spit at Dorkman."

"Why?" Smythe said.

"What do you mean, why? Rossman's an asshole, that's why."

"He . . . he's not so bad."

"You're such a loser, Smythe," Riggins said. "'You heard what that idiot called me."

"Well, yeah."

"You bet your sweet ass you did, and if you think I'm letting it pass, you're as crazy as that stupid monkey. Come on, Smythe, don't be such a fucking coward. God, it'll be funny. Listen, you got to get Rossman to come see the monkey, okay? He won't do jack for me."

"I don't know . . . ."

Riggins gave Smythe a sour, disgusted look and said, "Fricken pansy."

"Okay, okay," Smythe said.

"There you go," Riggins said, slapping Smythe on the back. "Hey, sorry about calling you a pansy. I was just mad, okay?"

"Sure."

That's when Pang told Riggins he should just leave Rossman alone, that Rossman was just like the monkey, only the monkey could at least get out of his cage.

"I had it wrong, Smythe," Riggins said. "Pang's the pansy."

Pang shook his head, and Riggins walked off with his arm draped over Smythe's shoulder.

---

Well, I sure got suckered into that, didn't I, Smythe thought, lying there in the dark, waiting for Rossman to come to his senses and come out of the jungle.

And he *had*. Fallen into it like a slug of lead. Riggins got Smythe to sweet-talk Rossman back into the group, telling him they were all sorry about everything. And

Rossman bought it. Smythe closed his eyes and shook his head, remembering that Sunday.

After the beach, Rossman, Smythe, Riggins, McCarty, and a handful of other guys who'd heard what was going down all bought Cokes and candy and ice cream from Doi Store as usual, then gathered around the monkey's cage. Rossman, standing crooked, grinned and seemed to Smythe to be genuinely happy about being one of the guys again.

Riggins nodded to Smythe, and Smythe put his hand on Rossman's back. "Have you seen this monkey yet?"

Rossman, still grinning, said he hadn't and moved closer to the cage. Smythe pointed the monkey out, and Rossman smiled and studied the monkey. And the monkey studied him back.

Riggins mouthed to Smythe, *Make him go closer.*

Smythe frowned, feeling kind of weird, but said to Rossman, "Take a closer look. Here, throw him a couple peanuts." He gave Rossman a handful.

No one moved, just munched and slurped and ate like they were all at the movies. But Smythe knew they were all biting their lips to keep from laughing. Everyone knew what was coming.

Rossman said, "Here mongey, mongey, mongey," and dropped a peanut through the mesh.

*Boom! Bam! Wham!*

The monkey flew at the mesh.

Rossman jerked back and almost fell over, and Smythe saw the look on his face and it burned into his brain, and even to this night remembering it all in the dark he couldn't get that face, that look out of his

318

head. Everyone whooped with laughter, having known the monkey would do that, whooped and laughed and staggered around bent over with exaggerated laughing pains.

The monkey spit a wad at Rossman and hit him in the chest. Rossman looked down at it. Smythe watched him wipe the spit away, smearing it with the palm of his hand.

"*Ahh,* he *touched* it," McCarty said. "Sick!"

They all backed off, maybe hoping Rossman would chase them.

But Rossman just stood there, mouth half open, looking back at the monkey, the terror fading, the sudden fright.

The monkey screeched one last screech, then ambled back over to its corner.

Still Rossman didn't move.

And Smythe kept watching him. What now grew in Rossman's eyes? Rage? Sorrow? Smythe couldn't stop looking.

"God, Rossman," Riggins said. "You just going to *stand* there? Spit back."

The guy from the store came running out and everyone backed off, everyone but Rossman. The man waved his hands at him. "You go home! Go!"

Rossman looked at the man, then blinked, then slowly listed away.

He didn't say a word on the bus. Didn't turn around once. Didn't smile, laugh, or joke with anyone. Didn't even flip Riggins off when Riggins yelled something about if his hand was rotting off yet.

Again, Smythe laughed but didn't know why.

———

That was yesterday.

What a sucker, Smythe thought, lying in the grass. What a heartless sucker.

Now Rossman had disappeared. No one had seen him all day. Smythe remembered again the headmaster's scowl at dinner, his accusing, face-searching silence after announcing that Rossman was missing and did anyone in the room have any knowledge of where he had gone. And why. When nobody answered—not even with a cough—he'd walked out of the mess hall with the place so quiet you could hear the floorboards creaking under his feet.

It wasn't until after lights out that Smythe remembered Rossman's jungle place.

———

"Rossman," he whispered, now squinting into the black undergrowth.

Thick, mucky silence.

He has to be here, Smythe thought. In there with the toads and mosquitoes and worms. Where else would he go? Where else *could* he go?

Smythe looked up, watched the clouds cover the moon, heavier clouds now. Clouds that stayed there. A faint light spot marked where the moon was.

"Rossman . . . I'm . . . I'm really sorry. *Please* . . . come back to the dorm, okay? Don't hide out here. Don't."

Smythe realized that he was begging. Really. As if he were down on his knees pleading with Rossman to forgive him, to release him from his . . . his . . . guilt.

"Rossm . . . um . . . Randy . . . listen, things will be different now. You have my word on that, okay? Really, I promise. Really."

No breath of wind fluttered the leaves. No crickets, no toads, no stirring animals. The blackened sky swelled and came down and enveloped Smythe in its eerie silence. Even the mosquitoes had vanished.

"Rossman?"

But Rossman never came out.

Because he wasn't there.

Never had been.

———

The next day they heard that Rossman had somehow made it all the way down to Hilo, fifty miles, about, and, finding nowhere to go, had checked into the police station, where he was now, waiting for his parents to fly over from Honolulu to get him. And take him home, where it was safe.

Not one of them would ever see Rossman again.

Except Smythe.

Who'd see him every night, in the cage of his mind.

# Graham Salisbury

Although he has published only two books for young people, with a third—*Shark Bait*—about to be published, Graham Salisbury already has received some of the book world's most respected awards, including the 1992 PEN/Norma Klein Award for an emerging voice among American writers of fiction for children and young adults.

His first book, *Blue Skin of the Sea,* is presented as a series of short stories tracing the life of a boy in Kailua-Kona, Hawaii, where Salisbury grew up. Through his relationships with friends and family members, the boy learns to respect the sea and understand his fisherman father's way of life. This book was named an American Library Association Best Book for Young Adults, a *School Library Journal* Best Book of the Year, and a Notable Trade Book in the Language Arts by the National Council of Teachers of English. It also received the 1992 Bank Street College Child Study Book Award, the *Parents' Choice* Book Award, the 1993 Oregon Book Award for Young Readers, and the Judy Lopez Memorial Award for Children's Literature.

Salisbury's second book, *Under the Blood-Red Sun,* also set in Hawaii, examines prejudice, friendships, and

# About the Editor

The recipient of the 1992 ALAN Award for outstanding contributions to the field of adolescent literature, Donald R. Gallo is the editor of a number of award-winning books for young people as well as for their teachers. He has compiled and edited six previous collections of short stories for Bantam Doubleday Dell, including *Short Circuits, Join In,* and *Ultimate Sports.* His first collection, *Sixteen: Short Stories by Outstanding Writers for Young Adults,* was named by the American Library Association one of the 100 Best of the Best Books for Young Adults published between 1967 and 1992. His most recent book for teachers, coauthored with Sarah K. Herz, is *From Hinton to* Hamlet*: Building Bridges Between Young Adult Literature and the Classics.*